THE ADVENTURES OF
SLIM & HOWDY

THE ADVENTURES OF
SLIM & HOWDY

A NOVEL

KIX
BROOKS
&
RONNIE
DUNN

WITH BILL FITZHUGH

CENTER
STREET ®

New York   Boston   Nashville

Center Street
Hachette Book Group USA
237 Park Avenue
New York, NY 10017

Visit our Web site at www.centerstreet.com

Center Street is a division of Hachette Book Group USA, Inc.
The Center Street name and logo are trademarks of Hachette Book Group USA, Inc.

Printed in the United States of America
First Edition: May 2008
10 9 8 7 6 5 4 3 2 1

Book design by Ralph Fowler / rlf design

Library of Congress Cataloging-in-Publication Data

Brooks, Kix.
 The Adventures of Slim & Howdy : a novel / Kix Brooks and Ronnie Dunn, with Bill Fitzhugh. — 1st ed.
     p. cm.
 ISBN-13: 978-1-931722-82-7
 ISBN-10: 1-931722-82-X
 1. Country musicians—Fiction.   I. Dunn, Ronnie.   II. Fitzhugh, Bill.   III. Title.
IV. Title: Adventures of Slim & Howdy.

PS3602.R64435A65 2008
 813'.6—dc22

2007031642

Destiny is a hard one to get your hands around—just when you think you're leading the horse, he'll take a step to the right and keep you from getting snake bit. This book is a fine example.

We started writing *The Adventures of Slim & Howdy* in our CD covers to give the listeners something to stare at while they listened to the music. That's what we liked to do when we bought a new album, so we gave it a try. A story here and there is one thing, but a whole book is a special talent we're not really trained for. A book seemed like a fun idea, but it never would have happened without the talent of Bill Fitzhugh, a guy who sees the world a lot like we do, and understood the personalities of these two...mmmm...not sure what you call 'em, but truth is they're a lot like us. It's a good yarn, and don't plan on reading just a little bit—you'll want to turn the page for sure.

This book is dedicated to all the talented people who have helped us on this journey—thanks for the ticket; we've certainly enjoyed the ride.

Kix and Ronnie

PREFACE

WHEN THEY MET, IT WAS LIKE A HEAD-ON COLLISION, THOUGH with a lot less blood and glass and hissing radiator steam. They didn't need an ambulance or a tow truck, and nobody called the cops, though this one fella thought about it. Like a rung bell, it couldn't be undone, things got dented, and it changed them both. It wasn't the sort of thing one could insure against either, probably wasn't the sort of thing you'd want to. Like trying to keep life from happening to you. Somewhere between impossible and a bad idea to begin with.

So call it what you will. Fate, the hand of God, kismet. Or just two paths crossing. Naming it wouldn't make it any different from what it was.

And what it was, was the Adventures of Slim & Howdy.

THE ADVENTURES OF

SLIM & HOWDY

1

A SUN-FADED BLUE CHEVY PICKUP WAS ROLLING DOWN A RED
dirt road. No, faded sounds too nice, like a pair of jeans you've been
waiting to get just right. Besides, it wasn't just that the deep admiral
blue had oxidized into a pale imitation of itself. Point was, this truck
was a beater. It had rust holes in the wheel wells, bullet holes in the
side, a hole where the antenna used to be, and a wrecked quarter
panel that looked like a sheet of crumpled construction paper.

The front bumper hung at the angle of a crooked smile, there were
two busted spotlights mounted on the cab, and the passenger door
had come from a different truck altogether, which explained why it
was pale orange.

In other words, the truck was a survivor from a time when pickups
were things used for work on the ranch or the farm, not for tooling
around Boston or Miami, or for towing a fifth wheel, a pleasure boat,
two Jet Skis, and an ATV. It was built at a time when trucks didn't
come in feminine taffy colors with extended cabs, heated seats, and
DVD players. They were made of real metal, not alloy, and they had
bumpers like steel I-beams that would bust a hole in a cinder block
wall if you hit it right or gave it a couple of shots.

If you were towing anything it was cattle to market or a horse
trailer or maybe a bass boat. It had a bench seat, a busted AM-FM
radio, and brackets where an eight-track tape player was once proudly
mounted. It was a relic from a different age, held together with duct
tape, bailing wire, Bondo, and the occasional prayer.

Somewhat like the dark haired guy at the wheel. Howdy looked like the kind who might've spent some time on the back of a tractor or a cutting horse or maybe both at one point or another in his day. He wore a black Resistol, a Cowboy Classic with a three-piece silver-tone buckle clasp that gave the impression of a guy familiar with working outdoors and, at the same time, one who wasn't unfamiliar with the inside of a honky-tonk.

As he steered that beater down the road, Howdy couldn't believe he was still thinking about her. Marilyn Justine, the kind of girl who makes you shake your head later in life. There'd been a time when, if you'd asked him, and if he knew you well enough, he would have said the thing he loved about that girl was her unpredictability. And he'd have stuck to that story right up until she disappeared without any warning or explanation, let alone any reason he could think of. Would've been nice if she'd left a note, he thought, maybe some hints on self-improvement, if that was the problem, or that margarita recipe he liked so. But she was long gone, last seen in a crowded coffee shop south of San Jose, according to those who had caught a glimpse.

Howdy looked in the rearview at the cloud of dust he was leaving like a smoke signal to the state of Louisiana that said he'd be back someday, but first he had some things to do.

With Lake Charles over one shoulder and Sulphur over the other, he was heading for Beaumont, Texas, where he heard he might get a better price for his truck, maybe enough to get a good horse to put under the saddle that was bouncing around in the bed behind him. Be nice to put a little folding money in his pocket and get work someplace where all you need is a horse and a stake, like it was for a cowboy in the old days. This was the sort of idealized notion that appealed to Howdy. Truth was, he'd always been a bit of a romantic, it was one of the things that Marilyn Justine had liked about him.

Howdy rested his arm on the beat-up guitar case propped up in the passenger seat like an old friend sleeping one off. He looked down the road and wondered if he was heading toward something or if he was just leaving something behind. Either way, he figured he might get a good song out of all this. He'd be sure to keep his eyes and ears open for the lyrics.

2

SLIM HAD WORKED HIS WAY FROM WEST TEXAS TO EAST FOR no particular reason other than it was easier to steer straight than it was to turn around. At least that's how it had started, before that business at Diablo's Cantina back in Del Rio. After that, with help from some friends who were keeping their ears to the ground for him, he headed east because that's where he needed to go. That's where the thing had ended up. East Texas.

Started out on old Highway 90, heading for Hondo, doing all he could to stay off the interstates, not because his old car—a tattered and worn '69 Chevy Nova SS, metal flake blue with a black vinyl interior, four on the floor with a Hurst stick, and 396 horses—couldn't handle the high speeds anymore, but because he preferred the scenery offered by the older roads, the Blue Highways as somebody called them a long time ago. He took the long way around San Antonio, past the Verna-Anacacho oil field and down to Jourdanton where he saw the fine old Atascosa County Courthouse.

You can talk all you want about how big Texas is, Slim thought, but until you go across the thing side to side, you have no idea. He just hoped the old Chevy would get him where he was going, which, according to his friends, was somewhere near the Louisiana line.

He'd had the Chevy as long as he could remember, a used gift from his grandmother on his eighteenth birthday. He'd wrecked it good one time, but somehow put it back together. The odometer had retired years ago with two hundred one thousand and change on it. In fact the only gauge that still worked was the temp, always leaning toward overheating. The old engine gave him a scare outside Corpus Christi, a bad case of blue smoke trailing out the pipe for a minute before he hit a pothole and, honest to goodness, it seemed to fix whatever was wrong. He gave the dashboard a pat and kept on driving, though with slightly more clench to his cheeks. He skirted around the sprawl called Houston, gave Galveston a passing thought and Glen Campbell came to mind.

He took the ferry over to Port Bolivar then drove old 87 with the Gulf of Mexico keeping him company on the right. Straight ahead was Port Arthur, and just like that he thought of Janis Joplin singing about how she wished the Lord would buy her a Mercedes-Benz, a color TV, and a night on the town. Yeah, Slim thought, me too. Except he'd skip on the Benz and take a new truck, one of those fancy Silverados maybe, long as the Lord was buying.

He skirted north to Bridge City, where a friend told him he needed to head over to Beaumont. That's where he'd find the thing he was looking for. He crossed the Beaumont city limits, saw a sign that read, "Texas with a little something extra." *Extra what,* he wondered. *Maybe it was the spirit of George Jones.* And then he started singing in his head, "B double E double R you in?" Always liked that one.

The blue smoke started up again about a mile later. Slim looked for another pothole but things were paved pretty smooth on that particular edge of Beaumont. That ain't to say it was the glamorous side of town, at least Slim hoped it wasn't, just bars, cheap motels, and used-car lots. And it looked like Slim was going to have to do a bit of business on this stretch of road before he went on to take care of that other thing.

3

RED'S USED CARS WASN'T A BIG OPERATION. JUST AN OLD trailer with Red inside and a couple dozen cars and trucks sitting under a few tired strings of red-white-and-blue pennants outside. The lot itself couldn't have been more than a half acre, all cracked asphalt, cigarette butts, and Styrofoam burger boxes lodged against the cyclone fence like modern-day tumbleweeds. Red boasted a fine selection of pre-owned vehicles, if by pre-owned you meant something with more than ninety-five thousand miles on. Red was always quick to throw in a clean cardboard box to put underneath to catch the drips.

Slim got there first. Climbed out of the Nova, unfolded his six feet plus, and got a long overdue stretch. Then he just leaned against the side of his car waiting for someone to come out of the trailer and make him an offer, like he was Jeff Gordon sitting on the hood of his number twenty-four DuPont Chevrolet.

Howdy pulled up a few minutes later and saw the tall, thin stranger in the black jeans and T-shirt and dark glasses. The guy wore a short brown leather jacket and boots that had seen better days. No hat, but plenty of hair, on top of his head and all around his mouth in the form of a thick goatee, and of a rusty color that made sense, given the sign over the used-car lot.

Howdy got out of the truck and approached the guy. Nobody else around, so he said, "You Red?"

Slim shook his head. "Thought you might be."

"Nope." Howdy extended his hand and said, "Howdy."

"Howdy," Slim said back, shaking the hand.

"No, that's my name. Howdy. What about you?"

"Oh. Call me Slim," he said.

"And you can both call me Red." They turned to see a bullfrog of a man hopping down the steps from the trailer. "What can I do you for?"

Turned out both men wanted to sell. Neither was looking to trade up or down. Slim just wanted to get enough money to get cab fare so he could go take care of his business. He'd worry about transportation later.

Howdy just wanted to get enough cash to buy a horse or a bus ticket, or hell, he'd even take a job selling used cars if there was some money in it. But Red wasn't hiring. What Red was doing was trying to play Slim against Howdy and vice versa.

Red talked pretty fast, trying to get both of them down on the price they'd be willing to take for their vehicles. "Fellas, it's a simple matter of supply and demand," he said. "Right now I got a bad case of the former and none of the latter." Without so much as a cursory look at either vehicle, Red started talking about the obvious transmission problems, and the cracked heads, and the valve jobs, and the twisted differential, and so forth, lowering his offer with each imaginary problem, and before long it started to sound like an auction going in reverse.

Howdy gave Slim a look that cast a dark shadow on Red's character. He nodded to his left and said, "Can I talk to you a minute?"

"Y'all go on," Red said. "I'll be in the trailer."

Howdy waited until the man was out of earshot. "Tell you the truth," he said. "I don't think we're gonna get fair market value from Red here. In fact, I think if we stay here much longer we're gonna end up paying him."

"You might be right," Slim said.

"And then where we gonna be?"

"Up that creek."

They sized each other up as they talked. Slim took as a good sign the fact that Howdy had a guitar and a nice saddle that looked like it had been taken care of. That he reminded Slim of Frank Zappa with a cowboy hat was interesting but neither here nor there.

The thing Howdy liked about Slim was his easygoing confidence. He seemed like a no-nonsense kind of guy. Serious without being prickly. Accountable. Couldn't understand why he didn't wear a hat, but, as he knew, people were funny.

Slim rapped his knuckles on the roof of the old Nova and said, "This has been a good ride, but I don't think I'd trust it to get as far as Sabine Lake. How's yours?"

"Runs better than she looks," Howdy said. "Probably got another hundred thousand in her, long as she gets her oil."

They talked for a few minutes before they agreed they'd be better off working together than working at odds. And they'd sure be better off if they had at least one vehicle between them. So they decided to ride together for a while, partner up, as it were.

They sold the Nova SS, split the money, and agreed to put both their names on the title to Howdy's truck. "Fair enough," Slim said.

And off they went.

4

AS THEY EASED OUT OF RED'S USED CARS, HOWDY SAID, "Where to?"

Slim pulled a slip of paper from his pocket and pointed up the road. "I gotta see a guy about something."

"Okay," Howdy said, putting the truck in gear. "But I was thinking more about the long term. You know, hopes, dreams, aspirations, destinations. That sort of thing."

"Oh," Slim said. "That'll have to wait till after."

"Fine by me."

Slim gave Howdy directions that led to the Settler's Cove Apartments, a few miles farther on. When they got there, Howdy pulled to the curb. He leaned out the window, looking at the thirty-six units of modest floor plans, thin walls, and a place to hang your satellite dish. "Not exactly my cup of tea," Howdy said. "I don't like living so close to people that I know their TV and bathroom habits."

As Slim got out of the truck he said, "Nobody's asking you to move here."

"Good point."

It was late afternoon. A young Mexican guy wearing a two-tone straw cowboy hat was cutting the grass around the complex.

As they headed down the sidewalk, Howdy kept up a steady stream of small talk, trying to pry a few words from his new pal. He nodded at the guy pushing the mower. "Ever do yard work for a living?"

"Yep."

"Me too," Howdy said. "Longest summer of my life. Tough way

to make the rent." He paused to see if Slim had anything to add on the subject. He didn't. Then Howdy said, "So, who're we visiting?"

"A guy I know."

Slim tended to keep his answers short, as if instructed by his attorney not to give more information than absolutely necessary. He sometimes answered Howdy's question with one of his own.

Like when Howdy said, "What kind of work you do?"

And Slim gave a shrug. "What kind you got?"

Like that.

As they passed by the landscaper's truck, Slim casually grabbed a pair of hedge clippers, never breaking his step. He snapped them a couple of times and seemed satisfied they'd do.

"Whatcha gone do with those?" Howdy's tone indicated he didn't see any trouble coming, which meant he needed either his eyes or his head examined.

"Trim this guy's shrubs," Slim said.

As they climbed the stairs to the second floor, Howdy couldn't help but say, "Must be some tall ones."

They walked down past two, three, four apartments before Slim stopped in front of number 206. He leaned toward the door and listened for a second, heard the television. Sounded like Dr. Phil. Howdy turned to look down at a couple of pretty girls sitting by the pool. He tipped his hat when one of them looked up his way and gave a friendly wave.

Slim reached back, put his hand on the rail behind him, then, much to Howdy's surprise, he kicked the door wide open and charged inside. The girls down at the pool seemed surprised too. They jumped up and moved, not to get away from any trouble so much as to get a better view of it. Girls like that.

Howdy wasn't sure what the next best thing to do was, so he tipped his hat again and followed Slim inside, where he found a steely-eyed man with both hands raised, a TV remote in one, a beer in the other.

A quick look told Howdy this guy was bad luck and trouble. Third-degree burn scars all around his mouth gave him a painful, waxy sneer. His nose, bent and humped, looked like it had been broken more times than a politician's promise. He was a mad dog disciple of violence and retribution with one droopy eye and the overall countenance of a man who drank to get the crawl off his skin. Seemed half biker, half roughneck, and all crazy.

Slim had him backed against a wall with the hedge trimmers aimed low. He gave a smirk and said, "Brushfire Boone, how you doin'?"

"The name's Boone Tate," the waxy sneer said. "And I knew I shoulda killed you back in Del Rio."

"As I recall, you hadn't drunk enough courage that night," Slim said.

It was fair to say none of this was on the list of things Howdy had been expecting. He said, "Whoa, whoa, whoa! What's going on?"

"Taking care of some business," Slim said, without turning around. "Doesn't involve you."

"Well, now, to the extent anybody saw me come in here with you, I think it does. I mean, I'm not a lawyer, don't really like 'em much, but I've seen some Court TV and, well, why don't we all just take a minute and calm down?" Howdy looked at the man with the droopy eye, aimed a thumb at the kitchen, and said, "Hey, champ, you got a couple more cold ones in there?"

Boone nodded once. His eyes never left the dirty hedge clippers.

Howdy, standing at the open fridge, called out, "Slim, he's got regular and lite, you care one way or another? You don't look like you need the lite, but maybe that's why you're kinda thin in the first place."

When Slim turned to tell Howdy to shut the hell up, Brushfire Boone jammed that TV remote in between the blades of the hedge trimmers and produced a knife of bowie proportions. It was long and sharp enough to lead directly to a Mexican standoff, each man taking jabs and swipes at the other, but unable to gain an advantage.

Howdy calmly watched the action while sipping on his beer and shaking his head at the turn of events. Finally he set the beer down and told this Brushfire Boone to "Drop it!"

When Slim and Brushfire turned, they were both surprised to see Howdy with a pistol trained in their general direction. "I said drop it."

The bowie knife fell to the floor. There was a tone of incredulity in Slim's voice when he said, "You have a gun?"

"Well, it ain't a weed whacker," was Howdy's response.

"Is it loaded?"

Howdy aimed it at the fridge, pulled the trigger. *Bang!* Like a clap of thunder, a .32 slug right through the door. "Oh, man, I'm sorry," Howdy said, and it sounded like he meant it. "I think I just put a hole in your crisper." He opened the door, looked. "Awww, got your mustard too."

Slim said, "Why didn't you tell me you had a gun?"

"First of all, you didn't ask," Howdy said. "Second, you didn't tell me you were going to kick in this man's door and threaten to make him a soprano with a pair of dirty hedge clippers."

"He stole my guitar." Slim pointed at the instrument leaning in the corner of the apartment. It was an old Martin D-28 with the dark Brazilian rosewood.

"That's a beauty." Howdy seemed pleasantly surprised. "Why didn't you tell me you played guitar?"

"You didn't ask." A little peppery in his reply.

Howdy stepped a little closer and said to the man, "Did you steal his guitar?"

"Yeah, but only after he stole my girl."

"Tch." Howdy looked at Slim with a hint of disapproval. "You stole his girl?"

"Not stole so much as . . . ended up with," Slim said. " And not for long, either. Fact, if I knew where she was, I'd bring her back for a trade. But she wasn't big on forwarding addresses."

Howdy smiled and said, "I think I know that girl, or somebody like her anyway." He began to think about Marilyn Justine and her margarita recipe again before he pointed the .32 at Brushfire Boone and said, "You know, in my experience, if you steal a musical instrument every time a girl leaves you for another man, you're gonna end up with a damn symphony orchestra or something." He pointed at the television. "Dr. Phil probably tell you to find some other way to express your anger." Howdy nodded toward the Martin, said, "Slim, go on and get it."

Slim took the guitar, put it in the case, and said, "I think I'm entitled to gas money, having to come all this way to get what's mine."

In the distance, Howdy heard a siren. "Well, I can see your point, but I think you might just have to write that off, unless you want to continue this in the lobby of the Gray Bar Motel in beautiful down-town Beaumont."

Slim heard the siren too. "Yeah, all right. Let's go." He made to throw a punch at Brushfire Boone but pulled it, just wanted to make him flinch. "Far as I'm concerned, we're square now," Slim said. Then he turned to follow Howdy out the door.

Last thing they heard was Brushfire Boone yelling, "This ain't over yet!"

With the sirens approaching, Slim and Howdy left the apartment complex a little faster than they arrived. Howdy tipped his hat again when he saw those two girls from the pool. They were stuffing their towels and whatnot into tote bags, fixing to leave, almost as fast as Slim and Howdy. But they took the time to smile and give another friendly wave.

As they passed a trash can, Howdy dropped the .32 in like it was an empty soda bottle.

Slim couldn't believe it. "You just gonna throw that away?"

Howdy shrugged. "Ain't mine."

"What do you mean it ain't yours?"

"Oh, it was on that fella's kitchen table. I was just borrowin' it."

5

AS THEY WERE SCOOTING BOOTS DOWN THE SIDEWALK, HOWDY noticed the Mexican guy rooting through the tools in the bed of his truck like he'd lost something. Howdy nudged the guy and said, "Hey, if you're looking for them hedge clippers"—he pointed back at the apartments—"that fella up in 206 stole 'em."

The man gave Howdy a funny glance and a suspicious "*Gracias.*"

"*De nada.*"

As they approached their truck, Slim held out his hand. "Gimme the keys."

"That's all right," Howdy said, missing the point. "I don't mind driving."

"I think we oughta alternate."

"What?"

"It means take turns," Slim said, putting his guitar case in the back. "Truck's half mine, ain't it?"

"Fine by me." Howdy tossed him the keys. "Just don't drive outta here too fast."

Slim started the truck and said, "Cops are responding to shots fired, and you want me to dawdle?"

Howdy hung an elbow out the window and said, "We don't wanna draw too much attention's all I'm saying."

"Here's a tip," Slim said as he pulled away from the curb. "When you're trying to be inconspicuous, don't be taking potshots at people's appliances."

Despite the truth of the observation, Howdy seemed a little insulted by it. "Now, first of all," he said, "I didn't know the gun was loaded. And second—" He stopped when he saw the two cop cars come racing around the corner heading in their direction. Howdy pulled his hat down a bit and looked the other way until they'd passed, then he said, "And second, I probably saved your life back there." He shook his head. "Did you *not* notice the big knife that boy was waving at you?"

Slim looked a bit chagrined and nodded slightly. "Yeah, all right," he said. "And I appreciate what you did. I'm just sayin'..." He shrugged without finishing the thought.

"Don't mention it." Howdy waved a dismissive hand before jerking a hitchhiker's thumb behind them. "Interesting friend you got back there."

"He's neither one of those things."

"Okay, interesting nickname though," Howdy said. "Brushfire." He pondered that for a moment. "Arsonist? Garden variety pyromaniac?"

"A drunk," Slim said. "And a mean one. Got the nickname after an incident at a bar. Tried to impress some girl by ordering a Flaming Blue Jesus."

"A what?"

"Schnapps, Southern Comfort, and tequila, with 151 rum floated on top, lit on fire," Slim said.

Howdy shook his head as he made a distasteful face. "That's not a proper drink."

"Not a safe one either, especially if you're already drunk and you have a big bushy beard."

Howdy winced. "No."

"Yeah," Slim said, almost reluctantly. "You're supposed to wait for the flame to die down, but that girl challenged his manhood, so he hoisted it."

"Caught his beard on fire?"

"To his eternal surprise," Slim said. "And, drunk as he was, his natural reaction was to splash the rest of the drink onto the flames, like it was water instead of alcohol." Slim just shook his head. "Went up like the Hindenburg."

Howdy, looking for the silver lining, said, "I don't suppose he got the girl after all that."

"He got the girl all right," Slim said. "Blamed her for what happened and put her in the hospital. Ambulance that was coming for him, took her instead. Old Boone got his burns treated at the county jail."

Howdy nodded. "Just goes to show, friends shouldn't let friends drink anything that's on fire."

"Amen."

Howdy gestured at Slim's guitar case. "Well, anyway, glad you got your guitar back. That really is a beauty."

Slim gave a nod, said, "Yeah."

"You a pretty good picker?"

Slim shrugged. "Ain't Chet Atkins," he said. "But I'm all right."

"Write your own stuff?"

"I got a few."

"Yeah? Me too," Howdy said. "You make a living at it?"

"Ain't exactly getting rich."

Howdy laughed. "Yeah, well, I figured that much out based on that car you unloaded on Red. I just wondered if you were making a living at it, that's all."

"I get by."

They drove a few more blocks before Howdy was seized by a sudden enthusiasm. He said, "Sing me one of your songs."

"What?" Slim turned and looked at Howdy as if he'd passed a honeydew through one of his nostrils. "I ain't gonna sing you a song."

"Oh, c'mon," Howdy urged. "Radio's busted and I'm curious what kinda song you'd write. Maybe something about lawn and garden equipment?"

"I ain't about to sing you a damn song."

"I'm not asking for a love song, for Pete's sake."

"Doesn't matter," Slim said. "Ain't gonna happen."

Howdy shook his head. "All right then," he said. "You want me to sing one of mine?"

"Not particularly."

Howdy started to hum a tune anyway. After a couple of bars, Slim gave him a look like fingernails on a blackboard. That shut him up. After that, they drove along in silence for a while before Howdy put a boot up on the dash and said, "You have any idea where you're going?"

"Yeah," Slim said. "Away from the cops." He glanced at the rear-view mirror but failed to notice the Trans Am that had been follow-ing since they left the Settler's Cove.

"I tell you what." Howdy pointed ahead of them. "Take a right at the light up there."

"Where we going?"

"Place called Lucky's," Howdy said. "Good pulled pork and cold beer at a fair price. You hungry?"

"I guess."

"Me too."

Slim pulled into the parking lot underneath a flickering sign with two neon cowboy boots and a pair of tumbling dice that rolled out to snake eyes. Slim looked at the losing roll, then turned to Howdy and said, "Lucky's?"

Howdy shrugged as he walked past Slim. "Don't ask me," he said. "Maybe they're being ironic." He held the door open. "After you." Like he was the maître d'.

"That's all right," Slim said. "You go ahead."

As they stood at the door, neither of them gave any thought to the car pulling into the parking lot behind them. If they had, they might have noticed the girls inside giggling and slipping jeans over their bathing suits.

6

SLIM AND HOWDY WERE LEANING WITH THEIR BACKS against the bar, drinking beer, waiting for their food. George Jones was on the jukebox covering Haggard, a tune about a guitar player working the Holiday Inn in downtown Modesto. *Yeah*, Slim thought. *Been there. Done that.*

It was a slow night, maybe a couple dozen customers in the place, mostly couples, mostly happy. But there were a few in there by themselves, heartbreak written all over their faces, hunkered over their doubles, wishing things had turned out different. Man at the end of the bar, for example, sorry he'd cheated on his wife. Even sorrier he got caught. Kept telling himself she'd be back, and each drink made that seem more likely. Then there was the old guy in the booth in the back mumbling under his breath about not having that kind of money and cursing the Cowboys 'cause they didn't cover the spread. Again. "Go on," he mumbled. "Break my damn leg. See if I care."

These were the people Slim couldn't help but notice. Hard-luck cases and those prone to making bad choices. Sad faces and tragic lives. People who needed praying for 'cause they didn't have a prayer to begin with. Things you could write songs about. It was a honky-tonk truth: heartbreak came by the case in a place like this.

Just then, an old B.W. Stevenson song came on the jukebox. The catchy up-tempo melody pulled Slim out of the dark and he started to hum along.

"That's a good song," Howdy said. Then, singing, "She takes my blues away."

"Always liked it." Slim nodded. " 'Shambala' too."

That's when the two girls blew through the door like TNT, their hips swinging like church bells in the tower. Everybody looked up for a moment. Howdy nudged his new pal and said, "Well now, maybe *this* is why they call it Lucky's."

Howdy didn't recognize them as the girls sitting by the pool at the Settler's Cove. He'd only seen them from a distance then, with their hair tucked under baseball caps and those skimpy two-piece suits that would barely cover two big apples and a slice of pie. And, truth be told, he hadn't been studying their faces at the time.

Slim had been so focused on getting his guitar back that he couldn't have said whether the apartment complex even had a pool, so, as far as he was concerned, they were just two gals who, in the dim light, weren't out of the question.

One was blonde, the other chestnut. They looked a little old for their age, which appeared to be midtwenties. If you were a betting man, like the guy in the back booth, you wouldn't put money on either one being a debutante or a recent pledge for Kappa Kappa Gamma. Both wore tight low-riding jeans and skimpy half-shirts that revealed pierced belly buttons, little muffin tops, and those sexy little tattoos in the smalls of their backs.

"It's like a welcome mat," Howdy said wistfully.

Slim gave a derisive snort at that. "Just 'cause a girl's got a tattoo there doesn't mean she wants to have sex with you."

Howdy peered out from underneath his hat with a look he reserved for those who just tumbled off the turnip truck. "Slim," he said, "there's an arrow pointing right down the middle there, underneath where it says 'Visitors Welcome.'"

Slim took a closer look. "Not on both of them."

"No," Howdy said. "You're right. The other one's with the Sisters of Mercy."

Actually not. Tammy, it turned out, had done a short stint one time for check kiting. Crystal, for felony shoplifting. In fact the two of them had met while taking advantage of the hospitality at the East Texas Correctional Institution for Women. But that was a few years back and neither had been caught doing anything lately. Didn't even have a current parole officer.

"These two look right up our alley," Howdy said. "In fact, the one with that little turned-up nose has the potential to be my next broken heart. What do you say we buy 'em a round?"

Slim looked like the idea had crossed his mind first and was about to weigh in on the subject. But that's when the bartender delivered the pulled pork sandwiches, distracting Slim with the aroma. He was hungrier than he thought. "Lemme have another beer," he said, turning around, belly to the bar.

"Make it two." When they got their bottles, Howdy held his up for a toast. "Here's to gettin' your guitar back."

The girls got a pitcher of beer and shot some pool while the boys ate. When Crystal went to the jukebox, Tammy hollered, "Play something country!" And she did. And for the next fifteen minutes there were lots of exchanged glances, coy smiles, and the occasional wink. At one point, as Tammy lined up the eight ball in the far corner pocket, Howdy ducked his head toward Slim and said, "Is it my imagination or do they both seem to take a lot of shots requiring them to bend over that way?" He shook his head and almost whispered, "Bless their hearts."

"I'll say this." Slim tipped his beer toward Tammy, making sure she saw him. "That girl there is wearing the hell outta those pants."

It came as a surprise to no one that Slim and Howdy soon bought a pitcher of beer, carried it over to the girls, and challenged them to a little bit of eight ball. Over the next two hours they fed the jukebox, shot pool, and drank beer. Even two-stepped once when somebody played something by the Derailers.

Crystal let Howdy get the impression that he was picking her up. Like when he offered to show her how to hold her cue stick so she could put that funny spin on the ball the way he did. She just let him reach right around her and brush his hands up against any and everything while she wiggled herself in the general direction of his belt buckle.

Tammy, who upon closer examination looked slightly harder than a federal tax form, came up behind Slim and slipped a hand into where he had the truck keys. His eyebrows sprang up as she lingered, like she was trying to find a small bit of lint or something. She was hard to resist, despite the rough edges. Or maybe because of them, Slim wasn't sure which. But he was thinking he ought to examine her under a brighter light before making any decisions.

A little bit later, when the girls disappeared to the ladies' room, Howdy pulled Slim aside and said, "Whatcha thinking there, partner? Hotel, or see if they've got a two-bedroom?"

"Hotel? You crazy?" Slim shook his head. "I spent enough on beer, pork, and the jukebox already. I ain't springing for a damn hotel."

Howdy leaned on his pool cue, tipping his hat back with the chalky blue tip. He said, "Well, just for the sake of conversation, where were you planning to sleep if these two honeys hadn't showed up?"

Slim waved his hand toward the outskirts of town. "Hell, I don't know, I figured we'd swing by the Wal-Mart, grab a couple sleeping bags, and head out to a state park or something."

Howdy seemed incredulous. "You wanna go *camping*?" He gave Slim a sideways glance. "That's a little broke back, don't you think?"

"What'd you have in mind, the Four Seasons in Houston?"

"Doesn't matter what I had in mind...before," Howdy said. "What I have in mind now is finding out what kind of sheets Crystal's got and how she takes her coffee in the morning."

Slim lowered his voice and said, "Yeah, well, if I was with Crystal I might be thinking the same thing, but—"

It was almost too late when Howdy saw the girls approaching fast. He shoved Slim in the chest and said, "Awww, man, don't say that." Real loud, keeping Slim from putting his boot in his mouth.

Tammy came up and hooked a thumb into one of Slim's belt loops. She said, "Don't say what?"

Howdy acted like he hadn't seen them coming. "Oh, Slim was saying he thought we might oughta hit the road if we're gonna make it to where we're going."

"Hit the road?" Crystal sounded genuinely disappointed about this.

"Yeah," Howdy said. "We got...uh...we got auditions."

"Auditions? Where at?"

Slim said "Nashville" at the same time Howdy said "Austin." They glared at one another before fumbling through some sort of story about how one of them had told the other that the Nashville audition got put off until next week and they had the thing in Austin first.

Not that anybody was buying it.

Tammy smiled and slipped her hand back into Slim's pocket. She pulled out the truck keys and said, "Well, either way you go, it's too late to be making a long drive like that. Why don't y'all just come on over to our place and stay the night?"

7

WHEN THEY HIT THE PARKING LOT, HOWDY WAS GRINNING like he'd just been crowned homecoming king. Crystal had given him the keys to her car, a Twentieth Anniversary Trans Am, the one with the turbo installed on a 3.8-liter V6 with ported heads and a Champion intake. A very bad boy delivering in the neighborhood of 280 horses.

Howdy pulled up next to the truck, leaned across Crystal's welcoming lap, revved the engine a couple of times, and shouted to Slim, "Try to keep up!"

Slim said, "All right, just gimme a second."

But it was too late. Crystal popped in a cassette of Chris LeDoux and let out a Rebel yell as Howdy fishtailed out of the rocky parking lot onto old Highway 90, spraying the truck with gravel as Slim and Tammy ducked into the cab to avoid being peppered. Howdy pulled a quarter mile in what he told himself was just over fifteen seconds but was probably closer to twenty, men having a tendency to misjudge such things in their favor.

Half a mile later they slowed down, waiting for Slim to catch up. After a few minutes, they passed the Beaumont city limits and soon after that they were far enough out of town that the sky wasn't washed yellow-pink from the high-pressure sodium street lights.

The bucket seats and the console between them seemed to be the only things keeping Crystal from actually crawling into Howdy's lap as they drove down the dark country road at sixty miles an hour. Figuring they'd have a lot more fun if they got home alive, Howdy made sure she kept her seat belt buckled while he talked up the virtues of patience and delayed gratification. She started to argue but stopped all the sudden, pointed across Howdy's chest, and said, "Oh, take this left!"

"Hang on!" Howdy managed to keep it out of the ditch as he made the turn, though he almost hit the big entrance monument for Lake Creek Estates, a new subdivision where none of the houses were on wheels or blocks, a fact that lifted it several demographic notches above where either Slim or Howdy had imagined they were going.

A few minutes later they were parked in the driveway of a stately four-bedroom, three-bath Georgian Colonial-style home. Howdy found himself wondering if one of the girls had taken possession in a nasty divorce settlement or maybe they were just renting in a depressed real estate market. He wasn't about to ask, but he was starting to think that Beaumont or, more specifically, Lake Creek Estates might be the sort of place where a guy could get comfortable for a little while. Depending on how things worked out over the short term, of course.

Crystal was first to the front door with her keys out. She was giggling and fumbling and having a hard time seeing what she was doing, not just because she was tipsy, but also owing to the fact it was pitch black on the porch. "I told you to leave the lights on," she said.

"I thought I did," Tammy responded as she rooted through her own purse like she was trying to find her keys or a flashlight or who knows what women are looking for when they do that, Slim thought. Could be a Tic Tac or lipstick, there was just no telling.

Then, everybody heard something snap. "Oh, damn," Crystal said. "Finally got the key in there and the stupid thing broke off. Now we're screwed." Just like it was an accident.

Howdy put his hands on Crystal's slim hips and gently moved her aside. "Not just yet, honey. I have a little experience with this sort of thing. Old girlfriend used to lock me out of my house all the time." He pulled his pocket knife, slipped the thin blade to just the right spot, and popped that door wide open. "Viola!" He bowed slightly and made a sweeping doorman's gesture. "After you."

When they stepped inside and flipped on the light, Slim and
Howdy looked around in what might be described as bewilderment.
They'd been expecting anything from a standard Thomasville living
room set to Pier 1 hodgepodge, but what they got looked more like a
cross between the showroom floor of a Circuit City and a pawn shop.

"Just moved in," Crystal said, looking at Tammy with a big grin
and another giggle.

"Yeah," Tammy added. "Ain't had time to get everything unpacked
and put away just yet."

Crystal was already pulling Howdy down the hall toward what
they both hoped was a bedroom. Tammy headed for the kitchen
saying, "I'monna see if we got a coupla beers in the fridge."

Slim gave a nonchalant wave as he stood there taking inventory.
There was enough home entertainment gear for two city blocks, let
alone two country girls. Big screens, flat screens, speaker systems,
amplifiers, digital this, that, and the other. Tammy came back with
two bottles, handed one to Slim, and nodded toward the hallway.
"C'mon, cutie."

They heard lots of giggling as they passed the closed door where
Crystal had led Howdy into temptation. They got to the master bedroom at the end of the hall. It featured a king-sized water bed, mir-
rors all over the place, and more expensive electronics still in the
boxes. Tammy went to the bed and yanked off a pillowcase, then
disappeared into the dressing room. Slim wasn't sure what to make
of that but he heard sounds like she was going through her dresser
to put on something slinky. So, despite an ominous feeling to the
contrary, he started to undress.

Just instinctive.

A moment later, Tammy came back to find Slim with a reluctant look on his face and his pants about halfway down. She smiled,
and a tiny laugh escaped her lips before she said, "Slow down there,
cowboy."

"What?" Like a deer in the headlights.

She pointed at a flat-screen TV still in the box. "Grab that," she
said.

In his heart Slim suddenly knew the house didn't belong to either
Tammy or Crystal. But he didn't want that truth to get to his brain,

let alone any other part of his body. He was still half hunched over, holding his pants, when he repeated himself. "What?"

"I said grab that TV. Take it out to the living room."

He looked around. "The living room?"

She smiled again, crossing to where Slim stood stiff as a statue, nor was he moving. She rubbed him in the right spot and said, "Don't you worry, honey, I'll take care of you when we get back to my place." She winked. "Promise." She touched his lips with her finger before she noticed a change tray full of coins on the table. She dumped the contents into the pillowcase, then looked over her shoulder at Slim. "C'mon now, get busy."

Slim pulled up his pants and zipped them indignantly. "You brought us here to help you rob this place?"

"Well why not? You got that damn truck," Tammy said gesturing toward the driveway. "I mean, I can't get *shit* in the back of that Trans Am. I was thinking about rentin' something, but then you two cowboys showed up and, well, anyway, grab that TV so we can get on out of here."

Slim pointed at all the boxes. "Who's all this belong to?"

"Technically it belongs to that Transistor Town up in Shreveport, but we're taking it from a guy name of Black Tony."

"Black Tony?" Slim didn't like the sound of that one bit. He turned and headed for the living room, empty-handed.

Tammy followed. "Whoa now, cowboy, where you going?"

Slim knocked on Howdy's door as he stalked down the hall. "Let's go," he said without breaking stride.

Howdy glanced over at a clock, mumbled, "Damn, that boy's quick."

8

TAMMY FOLLOWED SLIM TO THE LIVING ROOM. "WHAT'S funny," she said, "is that he ain't black and his name ain't Tony."

"Yeah, that's hysterical all right," Slim said, looking past her, waiting for Howdy.

Tammy explained that Black Tony was a guard at the East Texas Correctional Institution for Women. She wasn't sure where he got the nickname, but she knew from personal experience that he was fond of offering privileges to the incarcerated in exchange for certain types of favors. Problem was he didn't always come through on his end of the bargain, which is how he had earned more than a few enemies, including Tammy and Crystal.

"So anyway," she said, "he jacked this truck heading for the Transistor Town and, as always, had to brag about it to somebody and you know how word gets around and, well, here we are." She gave him a wink and a sexy little smile. "Whaddya say we get one of these big screens in the back of the truck?"

"Not interested," Slim said. "Howdy, let's go!"

That's when Tammy started rooting through her purse again.

Slim looked at her and said, "What the hell made you think we'd go along with this?"

She pulled a gun from her purse. "This," she said, not showing it to him so much as pointing it at him.

Slim held his hands up slightly as he stared at the .32. It looked familiar. "Where'd you get that?"

"The trash can where your partner tossed it after y'all shot Brush-fire Boone."

"We didn't shoot him."

"Well, you should have," Tammy said, a little irritated. "That creepy shit's always coming down to the pool when we're tannin', hittin' on us, like we'd even consider it." She shuddered. "Can you imagine kissing those lips?" She shuddered again, but kept the gun on Slim. "Anyway, I figured anybody who'd just kick in a man's door and shoot him in the middle of the afternoon would be happy to get in on a sweet little deal like this," she said, gesturing at all the stolen goods.

"We didn't shoot him," Slim repeated.

"Well, why not?"

"Wasn't called for," Slim said. "We just . . . shot his fridge."

This tidbit seemed to come at Tammy like a knuckle ball. She ducked her head a bit and said, "You shot his fridge?"

"Not me. Howdy." Gesturing down the hall, wondering where the hell he was.

"Howdy shot his fridge?"

"Yeah. All I had was hedge clippers."

"Uh-huh," Tammy said, looking at him like he was nutty as a Stuckey's pecan log.

"Well, he stole my guitar."

"So, naturally, Howdy shot his fridge." She gave a wise nod. "It's all startin' to make sense."

Slim turned and yelled down the hall again, "Howdy!"

"Howdy is right." Tammy and Slim both jumped when Black Tony's deep voice came from behind them. He was standing in the doorway with a twelve-gauge pump. Black Tony was big enough to have played football for the University of Anywhere. The only thing that kept him off the team was his lack of speed, both in the forty and on the SAT. And, considering how much academic lee-way football programs give their athletes, this didn't speak well of Black Tony's chances of winning the Nobel prize in anything. He spit on the floor and gestured at Tammy with the shotgun. "I mighta guessed it was you up in here."

Tammy turned the .32 on him. She sounded angry and betrayed when she said, "You supposed to be working tonight!"

Black Tony smirked. "Yeah, well I meant to send you an e-mail about that but—"

Then she shot him.

Slim dove behind a boxed-up big-screen television as the .32 slug spun Black Tony a little sideways. But he still managed to squeeze his trigger. The shotgun boomed like a thunderstorm in the living room. Glancing up at the pattern of holes in the wall, Slim figured he was shooting triple-ought buck. Probably a riot gun from the prison.

Howdy came tumbling out of the back bedroom. The only thing he'd managed to put on all the way was his hat. The socks he'd never bothered to take off. He had his boots in his left hand and his jeans were dangling around his right ankle as tried to hop into the other pants leg while he hollered, "What the hell are you two doing out here?"

Tammy had taken cover behind a stack of microwave ovens. She was cussing Black Tony between each shot she fired. He was bleeding a little from his shoulder but didn't seem too bothered by it. When Tammy started to make disparaging comments about the lineage of Black Tony's mother's side of the family, Slim took the opportunity to scamper down the hall where Howdy was still hopping around like the one-legged man in an ass-kicking contest. "I told you to come on, didn't I?"

"The hell's going on?"

"Some guy named Black Tony," Slim said. "It's his house. Let's get the hell outta here."

Howdy did a one-leg lean against the wall and caught a glimpse of the big man with the shotgun. "That man's not black," he said.

"His name ain't Tony either," Slim said. "You wanna go ask him about it, I'll be waiting in the truck somewhere near Dallas. Now get your pants on!"

Howdy started to hop again just as Crystal came charging out of the room, a blur of bra, panties, and chrome. What looked like a .45. She knocked Howdy over like a ten pin, without so much as a "pardon me." She fired a blind shot toward the living room, yelling to Tammy that she was on her way and needed cover fire.

Damndest thing either one of them had ever seen.

Howdy managed to get his pants and boots on real quick once he was lying on his back. He popped to his feet and said, "We can't just leave those two in there with that big sumbitch and his shotgun."

"We ain't got a dog in that fight, c'mon!"

Howdy shook his head. "Wouldn't be right," he said.

Slim rolled his eyes and said, "Fine." He ducked into the bedroom and found Crystal's purse. "Where're the keys to the Trans Am?"

Howdy fished them out of his pocket. Slim snatched the keys and said, "Come on." He opened the bedroom window and jumped out. Howdy was about to follow, but when he saw that brand new Viper RX-650 radar detector, still in the box, he paused long enough to snatch it before slipping outside while the shooting and cussing continued in the living room.

When they got to the front yard, Slim noticed the box. "You just stole that?"

"You kidding? From the looks of things, I'd say it's already been stolen. I'm just gonna try to find its rightful owner."

"Uh-huh."

Another round of gunshots caused Slim and Howdy to look toward the house. They could see Black Tony's silhouette in the bay window as he stalked the girls with the shotgun poised in front of him. "Come on out, ladies," he said. "The gig's up."

Black Tony paused for a second when he saw headlights cut across the wall. He got the feeling it had something to do with him. He stood there, trying to do the math on the whole thing when, much to his surprise, that Twentieth Anniversary Trans Am came crashing through the bay window behind him, caught him on the hood, and proceeded to pin him against the brick fireplace like a big Christmas stocking.

The horn started to sound. This was followed a second later by a couple more shots.

On the street out in front, Slim said, "That sound like a .32 or a .45?"

Howdy got in the truck and started the engine. "More like a .32," he said.

"Either way, I guess they're all right now."

Howdy nodded. "Shame to wreck that Trans Am though," he said as he put the truck in gear. "On the way out here, I got that puppy down a quarter mile in fifteen flat."

9

HOWDY WOKE UP THINKING ABOUT HOW NICE IT WOULD HAVE
been to spend the night with Crystal or, lacking that, just to have
spent the night in a bed that wasn't the back end of a pickup truck.
As it was, he felt like he'd been trampled by a bull and pinned against
a fence.

Stiff, sore, and hungry, he sniffed the air and caught the scent of
coffee brewing, so things weren't all bad.

Howdy lifted the black Resistol from his face and squinted against
the early-morning sun. He rubbed his mustache, then propped himself on an elbow and peered over the side of the truck, clearing his
throat in the process.

"Got coffee if you want it," Slim said without bothering to turn
around. He was sitting on a log by the fire pit, a good bed of coals
heating a percolating coffeepot.

Howdy said, "How 'bout three scrambled with bacon, toast, and
hash browns?"

Now Slim turned around, aimed his dark glasses at Howdy, and,
without a trace of humor in his voice, said, "This look like a Waffle
Ho to you?"

Howdy had to admit it looked more like a campsite at the Village
Creek State Park which is where they'd spent the night. It was about
ten miles north of Beaumont, in the middle of nine hundred acres of
dense bottomland forest and a fine float stream smack in the middle
of what's left of the Old Texas Big Thicket.

Howdy put his boots on and slid out the back of the truck where he stretched a bit while glancing around at the noisy woods. Willows, beech, black gum, and oaks filled with chatty bluebirds and woodland warblers, while woodpeckers machine-gunned at the bark of evergreen pines. He took a deep breath, savoring the smell. Olfactory memories of days spent in the north Louisiana woods where he used to hunt and hike with his dad and his cousins.

"Be right back," Howdy said as he wandered off. "Gotta check the timber, as they say." He came back a minute later, sat down on a stump opposite Slim, and poured some coffee. He tipped his cup in a show of gratitude.

The inscrutable Slim, always lurking behind his shades, gave a slight nod that seemed to say, "No problem." Slim sipped his coffee, sitting quietly, looking off toward the horizon, occasionally combing his fingers through his goatee while grooming the edges with his tongue and lips. After a minute, he pointed off in the direction opposite of where Howdy had come from and said, "For future reference, there's a proper restroom over there."

Howdy looked where Slim had pointed. "Sure enough," he said, wondering why Slim hadn't bothered to say something about it earlier.

Another five minutes passed where the only sounds in the camp came from the birds or the fire, snapping and cracking after Slim laid on some fresh dry wood.

At one point Howdy glanced at Slim's sleeping bag, rolled up next to him, all ready to go, as if he had a notion of where he was going. Howdy thought back on their late-night shopping spree after leaving Black Tony's House o' Stolen Goods.

They got to the Wal-Mart just as it was closing. The manager, an efficient-looking girl by the name of Dee who displayed a fondness for mascara and hair coloring products, was in the process of locking the door when—much to Howdy's surprise—Slim opened up a six-pack of sweet talk that got 'em into the store for two sleeping bags, the graniteware percolating coffeepot, a couple of tin cups, and a half a sack of groceries.

Howdy let out a chuckle.

Slim said, "What's so funny?"

"I was thinking about how you smooth-talked Dee at the

Wal-Mart last night," Howdy said. "You don't say much, but when you do, I swear, I bet you could talk a priest off an altar boy."

Slim just lifted his cup and sipped his coffee, not arguing the point and not showing the slightest interest in having a discussion about it. He maybe gave a nod, it was hard to say for sure. He knew he had a silver tongue, just didn't see any point in bragging on it. Just a gift.

Slim's reticence wasn't enough to quiet Howdy. Apparently it only took one cup of coffee to get his motor going, at least the one for his mouth. He shook his head wistfully. "Yeah, you know, I sure wish Black Tony could've waited another five minutes before showing up last night," Howdy said, his nod inviting agreement. "That Crystal was just starting to get enthusiastic." He cocked a dark eyebrow and looked over at Slim to see if he would engage in a smutty conversation.

Slim showed no signs.

Howdy decided to change tack, trying to get his new friend to open up a bit. He bent his torso left and right and stretched like he was warming up to run a mile or something, grimacing as he worked the sore from his muscles. After a minute of this he said, "You know, I think if I had it all to do over again, I woulda got one of those sleeping pads at the Wal-Mart. Bed of the truck ain't exactly a Spring Air mattress." He gestured at the ground. "How about you? You sleep out here?"

Slim tossed the last trace of coffee from his cup. "Started in the cab," he said, shaking his head. "Wasn't long enough." He stood up, six feet and change, damn near gangly. He gave Howdy the once-over and gestured at him with his cup, saying, "Probably be all right for somebody your size though."

Howdy made a show of looking down at himself, as if to see if he'd shrunk or something overnight. The snarky comment had taken him by surprise, but he decided to let it slide.

Slim grabbed his sleeping bag and tossed it in the back of the truck next to Howdy's saddle. "You about ready to go?"

Howdy poured himself another cup of coffee and said, "What's your hurry? Have another cup." He motioned at the log where Slim had been sitting. "I was just thinking, with all the fun we had last night, we didn't get a chance to find out much about each other."

"So?" Slim checked his goatee in the truck's side mirror. "We ain't datin'."

"No." Howdy shrugged. "But I figure we're going to be running together, we oughta get to know each other, at least a little. You know, get our story straight if it comes to that."

"Listen," Slim said. "I've known you for all of what, eighteen hours? All the sudden you want me to start divulging personal details of my life? Bare my soul like you're Oprah or something?" He shook his head.

"Okay," Howdy said, pointing at Slim. "You're not a morning person. See? That's a start. Getting to know each other already. And I know you make a decent cup of coffee." He held his up in the air as proof. "So, you know, like, I'm from Shreveport, how about you? You wanted in any of the lower forty-eight?"

Slim was still shaking his head. "I'm startin' to think this was a bad idea."

"Oh, c'mon," Howdy said. "If the last eighteen hours ain't the most fun you've had in a long time, I sure want to hear about your week."

Slim folded his arms over his chest, leaned against the truck, and said, "Nearly getting killed is your idea of fun?"

"Hell no," Howdy said. "Crystal was my idea of fun. All the shooting and running around just added to the excitement, that's all." He pointed an imaginary gun at Slim and said, "I learned the hard way that gettin' shot is something you want to avoid, if you can. But gettin' shot *at* is pretty damn excitin'. I mean, that's the sort of experience can lead to a good song." His eyes got big and he pointed at Slim. "Hey! 'The Ballad of Black Tony,'" he said, all excited as he unsnapped his shirt pocket. He pulled out a little spiral notepad and a stubby pencil, like one stolen from a putt-putt golf course. "There's something there, don't you think?" He wrote it down. "'Ballad...of...Black...Tony.'" He looked up, wagging the little spiral pad for Slim to see. "Song ideas."

"No kidding." Slim was starting to wonder if this guy had escaped from the Louisiana Laughing Academy. "Are you crazy?" Not that he expected a crazy person's answer to make much sense.

Howdy smiled. "Let's just say I got a wild side." He paused as a thought came to him. "Hang on." He touched the tip of the stubby pencil to his tongue and wrote on the pad. "'Got . . . a wild . . . side' . . ." He looked off in the trees for a second, then continued. "'Just . . . about . . . a country . . . mile . . . wide.'" He stabbed the pencil at the page. "Hey! That's good. I'm on a roll."

"You're a regular Hank Williams," Slim said as he picked up the coffeepot and started kicking dirt on the fire. "Let's hit the road."

"Fine by me." Howdy dumped the rest of his coffee on the coals, then went to the truck, rolled up his sleeping bag, slammed the gate. Then he said, "All right, what's the plan?"

Slim paused. "Don't really have one," he admitted. "Nothing specific, anyway."

Howdy nodded. "I don't guess either one of us has any specifics," he said. "But generally speaking, I know you got a plan of some sort."

"What makes you say that?"

"Well, you drove across Texas to get your guitar," Howdy said. "Not only that, but you knew you'd have to deal with that lunatic when you got there and that didn't stop you. Then you sold your car, instead of the instrument, so I'm guessing that means something."

"Like what?"

"Like you're not aiming to be a doctor or a lawyer or the manager of a Waffle House," Howdy said. "Like you want to be a singer, songwriter, picker, something. Stop me if I'm way off track here, but it seems clear enough that neither one of us wants to spend the rest of our days hanging Sheetrock or pouring concrete."

"Nothing wrong with those jobs," Slim said, like he was a little insulted by the comment. "I've done 'em both."

"Hell, me too," Howdy said. "That's how I know I don't wanna spend my life doing it. Hell, I can ride, rope, hammer, and paint with the best of 'em, but I know I'd rather earn a living with my music. I'd rather call a honky-tonk my office and have my workday start at night." Howdy seemed to startle himself with that little nugget. He pulled out his pad again and wrote it down. "'Call . . . a honky . . . tonk . . . office . . . work . . . day . . . start . . . at . . . night.'" He stabbed the page with the pencil.

He looked at Slim, wagging the notebook as he said, "Ain't nobody gonna be discovered while nailing shingles on somebody's roof. You gotta get out there," he said with a sweeping gesture at the rest of America. "You gotta get out there and do your thing. Put your stuff out on the front porch where folks can see it. Get up on a stage somewhere and sing, show 'em what you can do. Tell 'em what's in your heart. Then you at least got a chance."

Howdy shook his head a little and reset his voice before continuing his sermon. "I got this buddy back home, plays guitar, says he wants to make records. But he won't quit his day job, won't take that chance, won't put himself on the line. Refuses to gamble with his life. Just gonna play it safe. I guess he expects somebody's somehow gonna hear how good he is and come knockin' on his front door, offerin' him a record contract, I don't know. But my point is, that's why I was going to sell my truck instead of my guitar, same as you. Next thing, if I have to, I'll sell that saddle of mine, but I'm keeping the Gibson. I'll busk on the sidewalk for change until somebody hires me to play indoors, but at least I'm gonna get out there and see if I can't make it happen. You know? Can't be waitin' for somebody to do it for you."

Slim stared at Howdy for a moment waiting to see if he was through talking. Then he said, "You ain't got to the plan part yet, have you? Or did I miss it?"

Howdy smiled and said, "I know a guy in Fort Worth. Heard he might be lookin' for a singer or two." He turned to head for the driver's side.

Slim stopped him, held out his hand for the keys. "My turn to drive."

10

BRUSHFIRE BOONE TATE WAS PRESENTLY STEWING IN THE
Beaumont city jail, a place that smells about how you think it would,
maybe a little worse. By now Boone had been there long enough that
he stopped noticing. Or if he noticed, he'd stopped caring, as he had
more important things to think about.

He was still waiting to hear back from his bail bondsman. There
seemed to be a holdup. Something about credit problems. Something that might leave him in jail indefinitely.

And all this thanks to those two cowboys. Shady Slim and his
trigger-happy chum.

What happened is that shortly after Slim and Howdy left the
apartment, it had been Boone's bad luck that the cops who responded
to the shooting went to the trouble of running his name through
their system. Not surprisingly, perhaps, there was a warrant for his
arrest for having failed to appear in court the day he was supposed
to answer a charge of simple assault stemming from an incident at a
local strip joint six months earlier.

As the cops led Boone away in handcuffs, he was heard saying,
"You're arresting *me*? What about those damn cowboys shot my
fridge?"

Adding insult to injury, Boone knew that even if he made bail, he
wouldn't have enough money left for so much as a bus ride home.
And, topping it off, Boone knew from experience that he could stand
by the side of the road with his thumb in the air all day long and no
one was going to stop to pick up anybody as damaged looking as

him. In other words, even if he got out, he was walking all the way home.

All thanks to Slim and Howdy.

For the past fourteen hours, Boone had been thinking hard about what he was going to do when he got out, if he got out. He wasn't the kind of man to live and let live or turn the other cheek. He was more the eye-for-an-eye type. Didn't care who got blinded, long as he wasn't the only one. He wanted payback.

Unfortunately Boone presently lacked the information, resources, and freedom necessary to set straight out after those two assholes that put him in jail.

So he just sat there, stewing on it, hour after hour.

11

"WHERE'RE YOU GOING?" HOWDY ASKED, AS HE PULLED THE radar detector from the box. "I-10's back that way." He threw his thumb over his shoulder. "You just shoot down to Houston, then hop I-45 up toward the I-20 loop around Dallas, take that over to Fort Worth." He clapped his hands once and pointed straight ahead like he'd sealed the deal.

"That's one way to do it," Slim said, as he shook his head. "But we're taking old 69 up to Lufkin and Athens and that route."

"You're crazy. That's two-lane the whole way. It'll take twice as long."

"*I'm* crazy? You want me to go south so we can turn around and go north."

"Houston's *west* of here," Howdy said.

"*South*west."

"Okay, fine, southwest, but at least you're on the interstate doing seventy or eighty." He held up the Viper RX-650. "What's the point in having a radar detector if you—"

"Look," Slim said. "When it's your turn, you can drive backwards at a hundred'n ten for all I care. But right now, I'm driving."

Howdy threw up his hands and tried to keep his mouth shut. Problem was, he had pretty definite opinions about the proper way to steer, accelerate, brake, pass, and signal. It took only about twenty miles for Howdy to discover that Slim shared not a single one of these opinions, and it damn near drove both of them crazy.

Howdy kept leaning over to look at the speedometer, telling Slim he could probably get away with eight over the speed limit instead of just the five he was doing and that he didn't need to keep four full car lengths between the truck and whoever got in front of them. "That just invites people to pass you," Howdy said. "And then they get in that space you left and then you have to back off some more and next thing you know, hell, we're going backwards."

"Nobody asked you," Slim said.

Howdy held up a hand. "Just trying to help." He got quiet for a couple of miles before he resumed his suggestions about when to pass and how to tell if another driver was going to make a turn without benefit of a signal. "It's all about their body language," Howdy explained. "That slight glance to the mirror as they decelerate but *before* you see any brake lights. And keep your eyes on their hands, they'll reposition 'em on the wheel—"

"I tell you what," Slim interrupted. "When we get to Fort Worth, you can open a damn driving school. Until then, I'd appreciate it if you'd just...shut...up."

Howdy was surprised by the depth of Slim's ingratitude and insulted by his disinclination to embrace all of his observations and suggestions. It got his blood up to the point he was tempted to compare Slim's driving skills to those of his own beloved grandmother who was eighty-three, half-blind, and timid to begin with, but, being the accommodating soul that he was and not wanting to get off on a bad foot, Howdy just pulled out his lyric pad and started working on rhyming the name Tony.

Slim observed the technique out of the corner of his eye. Howdy would kind of look up at the roof of the cab and mumble possibilities. "Bony...phony...pony...macaroni." Then he'd get quiet for a few minutes before trying something else. "Crystal...distal... distal? That's a medical term or something, innit?"

Slim just gave him a slow sideways glance like he couldn't believe how long it was taking him to find the word.

Finally, Howdy blurted it out, "Pistol!" He wrote that down. "Hell, yeah. Crystal with the pistol." Like he was the first one to think of it. For the next half hour, Howdy kept his nose stuck in that notebook, working on the narrative line for "The Ballad of Black Tony."

Slim, meanwhile, seemed lost in thought, as if considering one of the great truths. When Howdy finally closed his notebook, Slim said, "I been thinking."

"Never hurts," Howdy replied.

"I guess you're about half right."

Howdy smiled, glad to see Slim had finally come to his senses. "Hell, I'm completely right and you know it." He grabbed the radar detector and slapped it on the dash, said, "Now we're talking. Let's make some time."

Slim shook his head. "I'm talking about what you said earlier, that I must have a plan of some sort to be in the music business."

"Oh, yeah, well I just had a feeling—"

"But that's not why I drove across Texas," Slim said. "That Martin belonged to my dad. It means a lot to me."

"Well, okay." Howdy was momentarily at a loss on how to respond to Slim's sudden willingness to share personal information. But once he gathered his thoughts, he said, "Good to know that family's important to you. Says a lot about a man, I think." He waited for Slim to respond, but he didn't. He'd said all he was going to on the subject. Once Howdy figured that out, he said, "Does this mean you're not going to drive any faster?"

Over the next five hours, though Slim and Howdy were both sorely tempted on several occasions, neither one of them threw a punch at the other. Slim, because he preferred keeping two hands on the wheel at all times, and Howdy because he was smart enough to recognize that rendering unconscious the driver of the vehicle in which he was riding was the fabled cutting off of one's nose to spite one's face.

And his mama had taught him better'n that.

To Howdy's dismay, however, Slim stuck to the farm roads and the state highways and the speed limit, passing through old east Texas sawmill towns and mining communities whose promises were broken long ago, settlements that were killed when railroads or highways bypassed them or when the iron foundry turned unprofitable for one reason or another. Most of the current economy was based on the regional state hospital, a little bit of agriculture, some tourism, and naturally, the occasional bar.

Texas, of course, has a proud tradition of dance halls, roadhouses, and honky-tonks. And the one Howdy had in mind was called the Piggin' String, a watering hole and dance hall about halfway between downtown Fort Worth and the Texas Motor Speedway. It had been around since the early fifties and its modest stage had featured everybody from Ernest Tubb and Willie Nelson to Jerry Jeff Walker and James Hand.

The place was owned by a former champion steer roper by the name of Skeets Duvall who found he enjoyed cold beer and country music a lot more than wrestling with rampaging bovines in sawdust soaked with horse piss. Skeets also had the good sense to recognize that he could make more money and break fewer bones as a saloon owner than a rodeo rider. And get just as many girls. What he considered a win-win.

The Piggin' String was in the middle of nowhere when it first opened, but eventually the city sprawl had just about moved it smack into the middle of the suburbs. The wide red-plank building looked like an old seed-and-feed store with rusty Coca-Cola and Lone Star beer signs hanging onto the exterior walls for dear life. There was still a place to tie your horse out front.

As Slim pulled into a parking spot, Howdy eyed the key in the ignition. During the long drive he had come up with a new plan. He was thinking it would be more equitable for them to alternate based on number of miles driven instead of just every other trip. That way Howdy would get the next 350 miles. He figured he'd float the notion next time he got behind the wheel.

12

THEY WALKED INTO THE BAR LIKE A DANGEROUS PAIR OF
cowboy gangsters, guitar cases in hand. Howdy first, all serious with
his bold mustache, black Resistol, and matching duster draped over
blue jeans and a work shirt. Slim followed, tall and menacing behind
the dark shades, wearing his short brown leather jacket over black
jeans and T-shirt with that little silver cross at the neck.

They paused for a moment as Howdy looked around the place. Then
he nudged Slim and pointed toward the old guy sitting at the end
of the bar, skin like beef jerky and scars you could match to hooves,
horns, and a stirrup. "That's him," Howdy said. "Skeets Duvall."

Skeets had his head down, reading the paper. His right hand
rested on the bar within easy reach of an ivory-handled Colt six-
shooter, an old black rotary telephone, and a glass of sweet tea.

Howdy came to a stop and thumped the heel of his boot when he
did. He dropped his voice an octave and said, "FBI, Mr. Duvall." He
paused before saying, "I 'spect you're aware it's unlawful to display a
firearm in a public place in a manner calculated to alarm."

Skeets didn't even bother to look up, just licked the tip of his
index finger, flipped to the next page of the paper, and gestured at
the pistol with his thumb. He said, "If this alarms you, maybe you
need to go slip into a dress, missy."

Slim and Howdy looked at one another and laughed, causing Skeets
to look up. As the two men approached, Skeets waited for some light
to catch their faces. When it did, he seemed pleased enough at what he
saw. "Well if it ain't Howdy Doody and his...much taller friend."

Howdy made introductions.

"Pleasure," Slim said, shaking the older man's hand. "I saw you at the Mesquite Championships when I was a kid."

"How'd I do?" Skeets asked.

"The way I remember it," Slim said. "Whoever came in second was so far back, he almost got third place."

Skeets slapped his hand on the bar. "Glad to hear it," he said with a chuckle. "Ain't no shortage of stories where I managed to embarrass myself from the back of a horse or a bull or a barstool or any number of other places, come to think of it. In fact, there was this one time..." Skeets paused, gestured for his bartender, held up two fingers. "Bring my friends here something cold to drink."

Slim and Howdy nodded their thanks and pulled up a couple of stools as Skeets proceeded to weave a wild tale that he swore took place at a rodeo near Prescott, Arizona, involving a half-pint of whiskey in his back pocket, a Brahman bull by the name of Butt Pucker, and Zippy, a capuchin monkey in a cowboy outfit who, between events, rode around the ring on the back of a Scottish sheepdog for the entertainment of the crowd. "I was done riding for the day," Skeets said, "which explains why I was as drunk as I was. So me and some buddies was just messin' around and one of 'em dared me to get on the back of this big damn bull sitting in a chute, everybody knew was mean and sorry as the devil."

"So naturally you accepted the challenge," Slim said.

"Hell yes," Skeets replied. "What's a man gonna do? I got up on top of that big SOB and he acted like I wasn't even there. So I spurred him a couple of times, which tells you how drunk I was, but he just stood there." Skeets shrugged and said, "Well how much fun is that? So I started to get off, when all the sudden, the show started and that dog with the monkey on his back started racing around in the ring, ole Zippy shooting his cap pistols like Buffalo Bill or somebody."

"Lemme guess," Howdy said. "Old Butt Pucker spooked."

Skeets assumed a grave expression and said, "That he did." Skeets laughed and said, "Busted out of the shoot with me barely hanging on like dirty laundry. That little half-pint of whiskey broke in my back pocket, I got glass chewing into my ass, I'm cussing a blue storm, and you should've seen the look on that monkey's face when he saw us coming his way." Skeets did his best capuchin monkey impression, which just about brought tears to everybody's eyes.

When he could talk, Howdy said, "How many stitches you get?"

Skeets shook his head. "Damned if I remember," he said. "But I tell you what..." He stood up and gripped his belt buckle as if he might drop his pants. "You want, I'll show you the scar. Maybe you can count where the stitches were."

"Thanks," Howdy said. "I'll pass if it's all the same to you."

Skeets sipped his tea and looked down at the guitar cases. "So what brings you two to the Piggin' String? You on a tour to see all your old rodeo heroes? Sing us all a song?"

"Yeah, you bet," Howdy said. "That and lookin' for work."

Skeets scratched behind his ear and thought about it. He looked at Howdy. "You singing duets now?"

Slim was quick to say, "Naw. We're just traveling together."

Howdy added, "But I was thinking, if you had any openings we could split whatever you got."

"Well, the bad news," Skeets said, "is that I got Junior Hicks and his band coming day after tomorrow for a couple of weeks. Good news is, I ain't got nobody for the next two nights. Now I know it ain't much..."

"But we'll take it," Slim said.

"Well, now, hang on." Skeets gave his chin a rub, then pointed at Howdy. "I know from previous engagements that you can't carry a tune in a number nine washtub. What about your friend?"

Howdy figured it wouldn't look too good to say he'd never heard Slim sing, so he said, "What do you care? You're tone-deaf and everybody in this rat hole's a drunk. Not to mention how bad the sound system and the acoustics are in this place."

Skeets held up a patient hand. "Sweet-talk all you want," he said. "I still want to hear the boy sing before I commit to making both of you rich." Skeets looked at Slim. "What do you play, son?"

Slim pulled out his guitar, ducked his head under the strap, and gave it a strum. "What do you like?"

Skeets smiled at that. "I like you already," he said. "You do any Lefty Frizzell?"

Slim nodded as he tuned one string, then another. "Let me think how this starts," he said. After a moment he took a breath and glanced down at the fret board as his fingers started to jump like spider legs on hot strings.

The guitar had a beautiful tone, Howdy thought. It was no wonder Slim had driven all the way across Texas to get it back.

It took Skeets a moment before he recognized the opening guitar line, as Slim had done a sly rearrangement of the Harlan Howard/ Wayne Walker classic "She's Gone, Gone, Gone."

As for Howdy, he tried not to show it, but Slim's voice hit him like a freight train flying down a track. He'd never heard anything so pure, strong, and unexpected. Warm and gold as backlit amber, honey, or something akin to the real Frizzell but with an added edge that cut clean and deep. Howdy's reaction to the performance was electric and visceral. He wasn't sure if it was admiration or jealousy or, more likely, some of both.

Skeets knew he was going to hire Slim before he'd finished the first verse. But he let him sing the whole song 'cause it sounded so good. He smiled and nodded and sang along in his head until Slim hit the last note and laid his palm on the strings to still the vibration.

Skeets held out his hand to shake. "You're hired," he said. "Twenty-five bucks a night, any tips you can get, plus a hamburger and beer. You can do one night each, or alternate both nights, however you want to do it."

Slim just gave a grateful nod. "Fair enough."

"Skeets, you got a deal," Howdy said. "Now"—he leaned closer and tipped his hat toward a door at the far end of the room—"how's the action in the back these days?"

Skeets shook his head. "We don't allow that sort of activity on our premises," he said gravely. "It's illegal, the way I understand it." He looked at his watch. "And it usually gets started around nine."

"Anybody I know?"

"Most likely gonna be some regulars, Charlie Pepper, Mack Osborne, ole Gutterball for sure," Skeets said. "Last few nights, some old fella name of Dempsey Kimble's been playing. Probably be glad to have another wallet in the game."

Howdy looked at Slim and said, "If it's all the same to you, I'll do tomorrow night if you'll do tonight."

Slim didn't care one way or the other. He shrugged and said, "Fair enough."

13

THE FIRST THING HOWDY NOTICED WHEN HE WALKED INTO
the back room that night was a one-eyed pit bull with a black pirate
patch hiding the empty socket. The dog was strapped into some sort
of leather harness that, upon closer examination, turned out to be a
homemade contraption for holding the leg of an old coffee table to
where the dog's left rear wheel used to be. Judging by the happy and
vigorous sounds the dog was making as he licked himself, he didn't
seem bothered by his handicaps, but it was quite a sight to see him
try to scratch his ear.

Howdy wondered if the creature had come to be in this condition
as the result of a run-in with a machine of some sort or, worse, if it
was the result of forced employment in a violent wagering situation,
dog fighting being not entirely uncommon in this part of the world.
But instead of asking a bunch of complete strangers what might be
considered a rude or embarrassing question to which the answer
might be a threat with a knife accompanied by a "None of your
damn business," Howdy figured he'd just wait to see if it came up
in conversation, like, "Yeah, old Sparky here accidentally got tossed
into the cotton gin," the man might say. "Lucky to have any legs at
all, let alone three." Or, "That other dog just pinned him down and
chewed his leg off like it was a jerky treat. Thank God I'd spread my
bets around, still won a hundred bucks."

In any event, the dog was lying on the floor between two
men. One guy, wearing full hunting camos, leaning back in his
chair, talking on his cell, was patiently trying to make his point with-

out hurting somebody's feelings. "Now, honey," he said, "you know she and I ain't been divorced two weeks yet. You gotta expect I'm gone call her name out in the heat of passion now and then. It's just natural."

Other side of the peg-legged pit bull was a sour-looking old coot named Dempsey Kimble, the new guy Skeets had mentioned. Cross between T. Boone Pickens and Ross Perot, with ample ears angling out from the side like fleshy little satellite dishes. Looking over the top of some funny reading glasses as he poured a shot of pure brown whiskey from a bottle he'd brought. He threw back the shot and poured another while the others talked sports, counted chips, shuffled cards, and drank their own.

Next to him was Charlie Pepper, a big, open-faced beer drinker with a look of friendly determination about him, looked like the sort who'd plow to the end of the row every time and not expect a pat on the back for it.

Across the table from Charlie was a fellow, early thirties, whose colorful outfit seemed geared to make a statement, though probably not the one he ended up making. His name was Ed, but everybody called him Gutterball. He was, hands down, the best bowler in the county and maybe the worst dresser, it was hard to say since there was no known way of keeping score on that. Right now he was wearing a pair of maroon parachute pants, circa 1982, red Converse All Stars, and a T-shirt featuring a Confederate flag tied on a skull like a gangsta's do-rag. He wore a pair of wraparound gold-mirrored sunglasses and his hair was done in a classic Camaro crash helmet.

The overall impression was that of a mutant dragonfly with a mullet.

Howdy introduced himself to everybody and was told that the guy on the cell phone was Mack Osborne, owner of the local John Deere franchise and a man who was happily, and most likely temporarily, married to wife number four.

A waitress came in, took drink and food orders, and said she'd be back in a few.

Howdy set his guitar case against the wall and took a seat between Charlie Pepper and Gutterball. He looked around. The place hadn't changed since the last time Howdy was there. It was a storeroom for everything but the liquor (Skeets being many things, but a fool not among them). Chairs were stacked up against one wall, crates of paper towels and toilet paper against another, cleaning supplies against a third. There was a cot in the back where Howdy, and a lot of other musicians before and since, had spent more than a few nights. The center of the room was cleared for the table where they played cards.

They used to play a lot of five-card draw, seven stud, and some Omaha now and then. But these days, owing to the popularity of the televised poker tournaments, they usually played no-limit Texas hold 'em all night long.

"First ace deals," Gutterball said as he flipped the cards expertly around the table. "Six...deuce...ten...queen...five." Charlie Pepper won the deck. He shuffled. Dempsey cut. And then Charlie dealt two down to everybody.

Conversation was lively and strayed like unfenced cattle from one subject to the next. It started with a thorough dissection of the upcoming college football season, by which most of them meant the games to be played by the Aggies and the Longhorns. But Mack Osborne, proud booster of the Horned Frogs of Texas Christian University, managed to get in a few words about their hot young redshirt quarterback.

Howdy looked at his hole cards. Ten and jack of diamonds. He checked to Gutterball, who opened for twenty. Mack, Dempsey, Charlie, and Howdy called the bet.

After the flop and the turn, the best Howdy could put together was an outside straight. But he needed a queen or a seven. Dempsey bet big. Charlie raised. Howdy called. Sure as hell, he got the queen on the river and won himself a nice pot. He won the next hand too, with a pair of eights, after he bluffed Gutterball into folding trip nines. Next hand, Howdy and Dempsey Kimble both had two pair—both queens and tens—but Howdy took the pot with an ace kicker against Dempsey's jack high. "Easy come, easy go," Howdy said as he raked in another pot.

Dempsey Kimble poured another shot of whiskey, killed it, then peered over the top of his glasses and said, "Yeah, we'll see about that." None too friendly.

After a while, from out in the club, they could hear Slim onstage, tuning up. Even with the sound muffled through the walls, Howdy could hear the guitar's fine tone.

It was Gutterball's deal. He tossed two down for everybody and said, "It's up to you, Mack."

Out in the main room, Skeets came over the sound system, told everybody to give a warm Piggin' String welcome, which they did. It sounded like a pretty good crowd out there too.

Following the applause, Slim stepped to the microphone and said, "Thank you. Here's one you prob'ly know." A man of few words.

Howdy bet himself that Slim would open with the song that landed him the gig. "She's Gone, Gone, Gone." But he didn't. Instead, he went with a sly, winking arrangement of "Act Naturally" that clicked with the crowd and had them singing along with the familiar chorus.

All the sudden, Mack Osborne said, "Hey, cowboy. It's a hundred to you."

Howdy looked at his hole cards. Three, nine, unsuited. He tossed them into the muck pile and said, "Fold." As the rest of them played out the hand, Howdy listened to Slim do his thing. The guy was good, no doubt about it. He was eager to hear one of Slim's original compositions.

Meanwhile, back at the table, the hand came to a showdown between Dempsey Kimble and Mack Osborne. Mack won it with a jack high flush.

Dempsey Kimble muttered something un-Christian under his breath. As he gathered the cards, his elbow hit his shot glass, spilling the whiskey on the muck pile. "Ahh, shit." He pushed back from the table to keep his pants dry, then he gathered the wet cards and looked for a place to dump the ruined deck.

Charlie Pepper pointed at a cabinet and said there was probably a fresh deck in there. Dempsey dried his hands and looked in the cabinet. A second later he turned around and tossed a new deck—still in the cellophane—onto the table. Mack Osborne broke the seal, started shuffling, and said, "Okay, we're back in bidness."

They played a half-dozen hands, trading pots back and forth across the table.

Outside, Slim was still doing covers, a Haggard followed by a Jones, then a Buck Owens. Howdy was starting to wonder if the guy actually had anything original.

Charlie Pepper dealt the next hand. Two down around the table. Howdy had a good feeling about this one, even before he picked up the cards. He brought them close and slowly slid them apart. And there they were, gaudy as all Vegas—Siegfried and Roy, two big queens. Howdy did his best not to tell. He looked over at Dempsey, who was studying him through his reading glasses. When the bet came to Howdy, he threw in fifty, real casual, just to see what would happen.

The others checked their hole cards again, hoping they'd improved since the first time they'd looked. Whatever the strategies, one after the other, they all called the bet.

Out in the bar, Slim finished his set with "Who's Gonna Mow Your Grass," which he imbued with more sexual innuendo than Buck Owens tended to. After a hearty round of applause and a few "Thanks a lots," the room got quiet.

While Slim took a moment to tune a string and find a new pick, some girl yelled out, "You can cut my grass any day!" The crowd laughed and hooted. High fives all around.

Howdy could hear Slim chuckling into the microphone, that little half smirk no doubt on his face like he'd seen once or twice that night at Lucky's. Slim leaned into the mike, mothering it like some old FM rock deejay and said, "I trim hedges too."

The girl yelled something about needing to get her stump ground, but the crowd was making too much noise for Howdy to hear the exact details.

After the audience settled down, Slim said, "Here's one I wrote. Hope you like it."

Howdy perked up at that. Finally going to hear an original tune. Based on the pacing of his set so far, Howdy expected a bust- 'em-up honky-tonker but instead he got a string of lonely notes in a minor key, enough to soften a hard heart. Slim repeated the line before moving into some bluesy changes that took advantage of his vocal range, singing about the hurt of a long-suffering woman who had talked till she was blue to a man who wouldn't listen, a man who stood as living proof that some fools never learn.

By now, Charlie Pepper had dealt the flop. Ten, king, king.

Howdy stayed focused on Slim's song. The chorus had a sweet hook and, as the tune progressed, Howdy tried to imagine how it would sound opening with notes from a piano instead of the picked guitar.

Charlie said the bet was to Howdy, which brought him back from his role as imaginary record producer. Howdy looked at the flop. It gave him two pairs: kings and queens with a ten high. Not bad, unless somebody had a king in the hole. He looked around the table to see if anybody had a tell, but nobody looked like they were holding three kings. Howdy went with a modest bet, trying to flush the bluffs.

Gutterball and Mack called him and it went around to Dempsey. Howdy couldn't read Dempsey one bit. Just stared at you with those sour eyes, oddly distorted through the reading glasses. He couldn't tell if the man was bluffing, but Howdy was feeling good about this one and thinking the higher the stakes, the bigger the rush, so he saw Dempsey's bet and raised it to boot.

Gutterball folded like a pup tent. But Mack, Dempsey, and Charlie Pepper all called.

The turn was a beautiful thing if you were in Howdy's seat. The queen of hearts made him think of the old Juice Newton song. And just like that Howdy was living in a full house. Queens over kings. It was all he could do to maintain his poker face. He hemmed and hawed for a minute, fingered his chips, feigning uncertainty, and finally threw in a hundred.

Mack shook his head and folded. "Too rich for me," he said.

Dempsey took another shot of whiskey. Half the bottle was gone by now and it wasn't as if the man was sharing with anybody. By this point, Howdy figured Dempsey was so drunk he couldn't see through a ladder, but he didn't act it. Odd.

Dempsey squinted at Howdy for a minute, acting unsure about the bet. Finally, he tossed in a stack of chips. "I'll see your hundred," he said. Then he tossed in a bigger stack. "And raise you two." He smiled and said, "Easy come, easy go."

Charlie Pepper folded, saying, "Easy go is right."

There was something about how Dempsey had said it, rubbed

Howdy the wrong way. Or maybe it was the half sneer that came with it. Whatever it was, Howdy called Dempsey's raise, which just about cleaned him out.

The five of clubs was of no consequence on the river card. Now it was time for the last round of bets. Howdy was up first and it was all he could do not to shout, "All in!"

Out in the club, Slim had gotten to the final verse of his song and Howdy couldn't stop listening, even if he should've. It turned out that things were past the point of no return for the fool who wouldn't listen.

Howdy looked at Dempsey, then at his hand. Full house, queens over kings, was too damn good to fold. Like the man in Slim's song, Howdy was past the point of no return too. He'd invested too much to walk away. He wasn't sure if he was a fool or not, figured time would tell. He just put in the rest of his chips and hoped for the best.

Dempsey's smile revealed yellow teeth and gum problems. He waited, just to make Howdy squirm. Then he said, "I'll see that and raise you five hundred."

Howdy was out of chips and low on cash. He looked at his cards and the infected gaze of his ornery opponent across the table. Dempsey Kimble said, "Guess it's time to reach in your pocket."

Slim was out there singing about the fool pushing his luck to breaking while Howdy pulled his wallet. Only two hundred bucks left.

Slim delivered another line about the fool coming around to consider the possibility that maybe he'd gone too far this time.

Howdy said, "Two hundred's all the cash I got."

Dempsey nodded slowly. "Leaves you about three hundred short," he said, reaching for the pot.

"Well, hang on a second." Howdy nodded toward the parking lot. "I got a Billy Cook High Country Rancher saddle out in my truck, worth about a thousand."

Dempsey sat back and said, "You'd bet that?"

Howdy looked at his full house again and said, "Sure would."

Dempsey got calculating eyes and said, "So that would be a raise to me of, what, seven hundred? Right? I mean, you don't expect me to make change from a saddle, like giving you the stirrups and the girth."

Howdy could see his point. All he could say was, "All right, raise you seven hundred." Figured that would end things.

They were playing with a three-raise maximum, so there was still one left. Dempsey bared his yellow teeth and said, "I'll see that seven hundred and raise you another five." As you do when you have them by the short and curlies.

Howdy swallowed hard. He looked at his cards. The hand was too good and he was in too deep to turn back now. He looked over his shoulder at the guitar case leaning against the wall. He said, "I got a Gibson."

"Yeah?" Dempsey Kimble leaned on the table and said, "What's that worth?"

14

SLIM FINISHED HIS SONG ABOUT THE LUCK-PUSHING FOOL and the long-suffering woman, said he was going to take a short break and be right back.

A waitress put some quarters in the jukebox, and the joint kept jumping.

Slim propped his guitar in the stand, stepped off the stage, and headed for the bar. About halfway there he got intercepted by that girl who wanted him to grind her stump. They flirted for a minute before she slipped her number into his shirt pocket. "You better call me soon," she said, patting him on the chest. "Grass is getting pretty tall at my place."

Slim smiled at her. "Let me get my blades sharpened first," he said with a nod toward the bar. "You stick around till the end of the night, we'll talk about your landscape situation."

She turned and went back to her table where she huddled with her girlfriends, who giggled and drank and kept their eyes on the tall, good-looking stranger with the beautiful voice.

Slim tapped his finger on the bar, ordering a beer. Skeets was three stools down, in the same place he'd been all night, pistol within easy reach. He was talking on the old rotary telephone but paying enough attention to give Slim a wink and a thumbs-up, either for his set or for getting the girl's number, maybe both, Slim wasn't sure.

As he waited for his beer, Slim took a few peanuts from the bowl, shelled them, and tossed the hulls onto the sawdust-covered floor. He knew he ought to start working on his next set list, but he was distracted, thinking about how he ought to commit to taking care of that girl's patch of grass before somebody showed up with a riding mower. Before he could make his mind up one way or the other, he saw Howdy approaching with his guitar case.

"How's the game goin?" Slim asked. "You rich?"

"Not yet." Howdy shook his head, then nodded toward the stage. "Nice set, by the way."

"Thanks."

"Oh." As if something had just occurred to him, Howdy snapped his fingers and said, "Hey, listen, I need the truck keys."

"Sure." Slim reached into his pocket. "Where you off to?"

"Nowhere," Howdy said, avoiding eye contact and otherwise acting funny.

Slim stopped just before he tossed the keys. "Nowhere?"

"Yeah," Howdy said. "You ain't gonna believe what happened." He shook his head some more and forced a laugh that was a lot more nervous than infectious, which explained why Slim didn't catch it. "Check this out," Howdy said. "I opened with a pair of queens in the hole."

"Good start."

"Oh yeah, real good *start*." Howdy proceeded to give the complete bet-by-bet, card-by-card with some colorful asides about the peg-legged dog, Gutterball's parachute pants, and Dempsey Kimble's gum problems.

Slim listened with increasing curiosity—not because he wanted to know how it turned out but because, as he put it, "I still don't see why you need the keys."

Howdy, still assiduously avoiding eye contact, shuffled his feet a bit, shook his head, pushed his hat back, and said, "Aw, hell, I might as well just tell you. I lost the truck."

Slim's expression didn't change. He just stared, unblinking, at Howdy.

"Man, I had a queens over kings, boat," Howdy insisted. "Tell me you wouldn't have stayed."

"You bet the truck?"

"Yeah."

"Which half?"

"I know," Howdy said, ducking his head. "I'm sorry. I'm good for it. I swear."

"Good for it? How're you gonna be good for it? You gonna gimme a piggyback ride to our next stop?" Slim was aware that although they had agreed to put both their names on the title to the truck back at Red's Used Cars, they'd never actually gotten around to it. His mistake, looking back.

"Look," Howdy said. "If it's any consolation, I bet my saddle first. That was a damn seven-hundred-dollar raise. And by the way, remind me not to get into another no-limit game. Anyway, I figured seven hundred would put an end to it, but the sumbitch saw that, then turned around and raised me again." He shook his head. "It was like he knew what I had. Hell, I came this close to betting my guitar," he said, hefting the case. "But, well, I just couldn't."

"So you bet a truck you only own half of?"

In the vain hope that Dempsey Kimble's dishonesty would distract from his own stupidity, Howdy said, "I'm pretty sure he cheated."

"Uh-huh." Slim looked around the room, then back at Howdy. "Well, I'm pretty sure you gotta sell that guitar now."

"What?"

"Somebody's got to get the truck back," Slim said. "And I don't think it's going to be you. That leaves me. And if I'm going to get in the game to see if this guy's cheating, I'm going to need money. And I damn sure ain't gonna use my own, if you get my drift." He gestured at the crowd. "So you better find somebody in here to give you five hundred bucks for that thing."

It only took Howdy fifteen minutes to find a buyer but, desperation smelling the way it does, he only got three hundred for it.

He handed the cash to Slim and said, "Now what?"

Slim took the money and stuffed it in his pocket. He gestured at the guy who bought the guitar and said, "Now, go back and see if the guy'll loan it to you so you can do the next set." He turned and walked past Skeets, snatching the pistol off the bar, saying, "Need to borrow this for a minute."

15

DUCK HUNTING WAS ON THE TABLE WHEN SLIM WALKED INTO the room. The gun was in his waistband, hidden by his jacket.

Mack Osborne bet forty and said, "I smoke my quack with a Remington 1100."

Dempsey Kimble looked at his hole cards and chewed on his lower lip. "I like a Mossberg 935," he said before folding. "Points real good."

Charlie Pepper shook his head and said, "I never understood why anybody'd want to wake up that early in the morning to stand in cold water." He called Mack's bet. "But I tell you what," he said. "You bring me a cooler full of ducks and I'll cook 'em up right for ya."

Gutterball folded, drained his beer, and smashed the can against his forehead, causing the one-eyed pit bull to jump a little. Gutterball looked around, all agitated, and said, "Where's that damn waitress?"

Since nobody seemed predisposed to ask who he was and why he was standing there, Slim said, "Skeets told me a seat just opened up in here."

"That's right," Dempsey said, peering over his glasses at Slim as though he had just materialized. "Still warm, I think."

Slim pulled the cash from his pocket and somebody pointed at Howdy's old seat. He got his chips while Charlie Pepper carried on about his favorite way to prepare duck.

After a minute Mack Osborne was unable to contain himself any longer. He said, "Tea leaves? Oh, I ain't believin' it."

"I swear," Charlie Pepper said, hand up like taking an oath. "I tea-smoke them puppies. It's a Chinese thing. You start by making a rub outta Szechuan peppercorns, star anise, and salt, okay? Then take some fresh ginger, green onions, spread that on the bird, covered real loose, and let it set overnight."

As the recipe unfolded, Dempsey Kimble assumed the look of a man who was on the verge of having an old-school stroke. His face grew flush and he made a grunting noise to register his dismay at the emasculation of the American male.

Charlie continued, "Next day you mix about a third cup each of tea leaves and sugar. Of course, first you got to steam the duck for a couple of hours, then cool before you put it in the smoker for fifteen or twenty minutes over the mixture of tea leaves and sugar."

"Hell," Mack said. "That sounds pretty tasty."

Dempsey Kimble's expression revealed his scorn. "Used to be a man did the huntin' and was done with it," he said with pure contempt. "Woman's job was to make something to eat out of the thing. Now?" He shook his head in silent despair. Men at the poker table, talking recipes. What was the world coming to? He said, "We gone play cards here or have a damn Tupperware party?"

Nobody paid Slim much attention. He just played quietly, hand after hand, keeping his eye on that sour-looking Dempsey Kimble, the guy Howdy suspected of cheating.

After folding a two, nine, unsuited, Gutterball leaned on the table and looked at Charlie Pepper like he was fixing to ask a question about national security. He said, "What're you cooking on these days?"

Charlie Pepper held his hands out wide. "Son, I got that new Smokinator 3000 with that barrel square firebox and the forty-five-degree fixed-angle heat-deflector baffle."

"Get out!"

"Hell yeah, it's got three swing arms for jerky and sausage in the middle of the chamber, three air intakes, and a ten-gallon reservoir." He shook his head like he couldn't believe it himself. "Thing's so big you'd have to fall into a coma to end up with dry meat."

Although Slim had definite opinions about proper grilling and smoking techniques, he stayed out of the conversation. He just kept a careful eye on everybody as they played. It didn't take him long to see what was going on. After the deal had been around the table twice, he noticed that Dempsey Kimble never lost a hand that he played, though he didn't stay every time. He always seemed to know when to fold or when somebody was bluffing. It didn't matter who was dealing and there was nothing to suggest collusion among any of the other players. Dempsey Kimble simply seemed to have perfect knowledge of who had what every hand, and Slim figured there was only one way to do that.

Finally, Slim reached across the table toward Dempsey Kimble and said, "Hey." He gestured with his fingers. "Let me borrow your glasses."

Dempsey Kimble looked at him like he'd asked for a French kiss. "What?"

"Your glasses," Slim said. "Hand 'em to me."

"Get yer own."

Slim shot to his feet, knocking his chair over behind him. He pulled the revolver and had it right in front of Dempsey Kimble's red-veined nose when he said, "Now."

Dempsey looked at Charlie and Mack to see if they were going to back him up, but they had him pretty well fixed with suspicious eyes. When Dempsey heard the hammer pulling back to a click, he refocused his attention on the pistol. He pulled off the glasses and tossed them into the middle of the table like he was betting on a losing hand.

Slim put the glasses on and turned to Mack, who was sitting there with his mouth wide open and his hole cards in his hand. "Before you bet on that ace, jack," Slim said. "You might want to know that the Galloping Gourmet here is holding a pair of nines."

Charlie and Mack put their cards down, proving Slim was right. "How the hell'd you know that?"

Slim took the glasses off and held one of the lenses over the corner of a card, revealing the mark. "Special ink, can't see it without the glasses." Slim picked up Dempsey's whiskey bottle, took a sniff of it, then took a cartoon-sized guzzle that would've keeled most men over. "Speaking of tea," he said.

Everybody turned to look at the guilty party. Not a forgiving face in the crowd. Dempsey started to scoot his chair back, like he might be able to make a graceful exit somehow, but Mack pulled a .38 and Gutterball produced a hollow-handled survival knife with a curved blade that had what looked like small bits of dried animal flesh clinging to the nasty serrated edges. The one-eyed pit bull raised his head to sniff the air. Possum?

Slim wagged the pistol at Dempsey Kimble and said, "I think now would be a good time to get square with everybody."

16

EVERYBODY GOT THEIR MONEY BACK, AND THEN SOME.
Dempsey Kimble being the obvious exception. The players agreed
there was no point in calling the cops about the cheat, seeing as how
the game was illegal to begin with. Gutterball and Mack Osborne
said they'd take care of it in a judicious manner. And that was that.

Later that night, as Slim was finishing his last set, Howdy pulled
up a stool next to Skeets. He leaned his guitar case against the bar
rail and called for a beer.

"See you got your guitar back," Skeets said. "That's good."

"Yeah." Howdy nodded but didn't seem to pleased about something. "Guy wanted fifty bucks more than he paid for it, though."

"Damn. That's a little aggressive."

"That's what I told him," Howdy said. "Finally talked him down
to twenty-five."

Skeets snickered at that. "Yeah, well, I guess you'll have to write
that off as a rental fee for having to borrow it to do your set."

"I guess."

When Slim finished his set, the first thing he did was disappear
to the parking lot. Howdy noticed and said, "Wonder where's he
going?"

Slim returned a couple of minutes later, joining them at the bar.
"Skeets," he said, "you got a pen I can use?" Skeets pulled a ballpoint
from his pocket and slid it over.

Howdy looked to see what Slim was writing. "You got a song idea
or something?"

"Title to the truck," Slim said. "Thought I might go on and add my name to it."

While Slim did that, Howdy told Skeets about how Dempsey Kimble had spilled his drink on the cards so he could substitute the marked deck. "I guess he had that bottle full of tea so we'd pay attention to how much whiskey he seemed to be drinking, trying to make us think he was too drunk to be playing good cards, let alone cheatin' at it."

"Seemed to work pretty good too," was Slim's comment.

Skeets sucked on his teeth and said, "I almost hate to think what Mack and Gutterball are gonna do to the dumb bastard. They didn't seem real happy when they drove outta here."

"True," Slim said. "And based on all the hollerin' coming from the trunk of that car, I'd say Dempsey Kimble wasn't too tickled about things either."

"Hey, Skeets," Howdy said. "What do you know about that Mack Osborne? Did he put that dog of his in fights, like for money? Is that what happened to him?"

"Fights?" A moment of confusion crossed his face. "Oh, you mean the leg and the eye." Skeets shook his head. "No, the dog's diabetic. They didn't get it diagnosed till they had to amputate."

"I'll be damned." Howdy shook his head. "Never knew a dog could have diabetes."

"Oh yeah," Skeets said, apparently finding the whole thing fascinating. "Gets insulin shots, the whole nine yards. Mack says it's under control now. But it's still damn funny to watch him try to scratch his ear, ain't it?"

Howdy turned to ask Slim if he'd ever heard of a dog with diabetes, but he wasn't sitting there anymore. "Where the hell did he go?" Howdy looked around the club just in time to see the tall stranger slipping out the front door with some girl. Howdy said, "Well now, who is that?"

"Just some girl needs her yard mowed," Skeets said.

Howdy raised his beer in a toast. "Well, glad to see the old dog get a bone."

"Beats insulin," Skeets said with a nod toward the back room. "I guess you'll be sleeping on the cot."

17

SUNDAY MORNING BOONE TATE'S CELL DOOR JANGLED OPEN and they said he'd made bail. The terms were unreasonable but his options were limited. So he signed on the line. His bail bondsman told him not to even think about skipping out on him as he had a skip tracer name of Drake Dobson who would track him down and bring him back to face more hell than the devil himself could handle.

Boone got his belongings and started the long walk home, stewing over those two cowboys with every step. A couple hours later, as he turned onto his street, he still didn't know how he was going to do it, but he intended to track down Slim and that trigger-happy pal of his and make both of them sorry they'd ever crossed paths with Boone Tate.

The first thing he saw when he dragged his blistered feet into the courtyard of the Settler's Cove Apartments was the oily flesh of those two gals who were always sneaking in and using the pool like they lived there.

As usual, Tammy and Crystal were draped on the sagging lounge chairs, slippery with coconut oil. They had just turned over for the third time, rotating like meat on a spit.

It had been two days since they had escaped from Black Tony's—not only with their lives but also with a dozen portable audio players, ten of which they had since sold, using the profits to buy skimpy new bathing suits and the expensive tanning lotion with which they were now slathered. The remaining two units were attached to headphones clamped over Tammy's and Crystal's ears, which explained why they didn't hear Boone approaching.

The hip-hop was so loud he could hear it from ten feet away. The large tote bag between the lounge chairs was wide open, stuffed with their clothes, towels, purses, and who knows what else. Boone came around from behind, making sure not to cast a shadow across their faces. He glanced around to see if anyone was watching. No one in sight.

Crystal and Tammy remained oblivious as he slid the bag toward himself and fingered the last forty bucks from their wallets. He was about to make a smooth getaway when something shiny caught his eyes.

A moment later Tammy felt something tickling her jaw and waved a hand to brush away whatever it was. When she touched it, she got a sinking feeling. She felt the shape of the thing and the hand attached to it. She turned her head slowly, peered over the top of her sunglasses, and saw that waxy smile.

Boone licked his ruined lips and said, "You two smell like a coupla dang piña coladas."

Crystal remained unaware of the situation until Boone reached over and yanked on the string holding her top together. Considering her usual lack of inhibition, she moved with surprising quickness to cover herself as she sat up and said, "Hey!"

"Shut up," Boone said. "Where are they?"

"They who?"

"They who you got this gun from," Boone said.

Crystal looked down at the .32, then suddenly began groping around in the tote bag before she said, "Hey, that's ours!"

"Like hell it is," Boone said.

Tammy pointed across the courtyard. "We got it outta that trash can," she said. "Finders keepers."

Boone found it hard to believe that Slim's pal had just thrown the gun away, but he wasn't going to waste time arguing the point. He said, "I'm gonna ask nice one more time." He grabbed Tammy's arm and gave it a mean twist. "Where are they?"

"Oww!" She tried to jerk away but he had her good. "How am I supposed to know? They said something about auditions in Austin and Nashville, but I think that was just talk."

"You think?" He shook his head. "Don't make me break this little twig of yours." He twisted harder and looked at Crystal like it was going to be her fault if it happened. "You just gonna let me break your friend's arm?"

Crystal figured it wasn't any skin off her nose, so she said, "Howdy told me they were going to Fort Worth. Some club, looking for work."

"What club?"

Crystal squinted her left eye and said, "Pig on a String or something like that."

18

HOWDY WAS SITTING AT THE BAR THAT MORNING WHEN
Skeets showed up. TV was tuned to some bass fishing show, but
Howdy wasn't paying enough attention to even say what sort of lures
were working. "I found where you keep the coffee," Howdy said,
raising his cup. "Hope you don't mind."

"Not if it's still fresh."

"Just made it." Howdy noticed the paper sack Skeets had in his
hand. "Whatcha got there?"

"Breakfast," Skeets said. "And the latest news." He put the sack on
the bar and tore it open. Some biscuit sausage sandwiches tumbled
out. "Help yourself."

"Mighty kind," Howdy said, taking one. "What kind of news did
you bring?"

"The kind that'll warm your heart," Skeets said. "I ran into the
sheriff a little earlier down at the café where I got these." He held up
one of the biscuit sandwiches and took a bite. "He told me they got
a call first thing this morning from some woman said she'd seen a
man's body off the side of Old Agency Road."

"Dead?"

Skeets shook his head. "No, but probably wished he was. One of
his deputies drove out there to check and found a man handcuffed
to a fence in what I guess you'd have to call an awkward position.
Apparently one his legs had gone to sleep. Said it was too tingly to
stand on. Anyway, he didn't have any ID on him, but he told the
deputy his name was Dempsey Kimble."

"Is that right?" Howdy shook his head as a little smile danced across his face. "Handcuffed to a fence, you say?"

"Yeah," Skeet said, casually pouring himself a cup of coffee. "Oh, did I mention that he was buck-ass-naked and covered with bug bites?"

Howdy just about shot some sausage and biscuit out of his nose. "No, you hadn't gotten to that part yet," he said.

"Well, I guess that part of the story's important inasmuch as they arrested him for indecent exposure." Skeets added some cream and sugar, gave it a stir.

"Makes sense," Howdy said. "I mean, you can't just go around waving your giblets in public." He shook his head in a judgmental fashion. "Ain't proper."

"No, it ain't," Skeets agreed. "And you sure can't do it on other people's property. 'Cause then you also get charged with trespassing, which he did."

"Or shot."

"Which he didn't. So he got lucky there, I guess." Skeets sipped his coffee. "When they asked Mr. Kimble how he'd come to be in this unusual circumstance, he said he couldn't remember. Said he may have had too much to drink last night."

"Did they believe him?"

"No, they seemed to think he was lying," Skeets said. "Like he might be afraid to start pointing fingers at anybody on the off chance that it might just mean more trouble for him. So they let him call his lawyer and post bail. Gave him a shirt and pair of county-issue pants, sent him on his way. Told him not to show his face or his bare ass in the county again except to be at the courthouse to answer for his crimes. Just goes to show justice is blind."

"Well, if she wasn't before," Howdy said, "she would've wished she was after seeing Dempsey Kimble in the altogether."

19

SLIM GOT BACK TO THE PIGGIN' STRING JUST AS HOWDY WAS set to go onstage that night. He slipped through the crowd, didn't speak to anybody, except a waitress, then scooted into a back booth with his beer. He kicked back with the relaxed expression of a man who'd done a week's worth of yard work and now had the night off. Sitting there in a smoke-filled club where he felt at home, he thought about that lyric Howdy had been playing with the other day, the one about having a honky-tonk for an office and a workday that started at night. Slim liked it, thought Howdy might be on to something.

Across the club, Howdy ambled up onto the stage, sporting an impish grin like a cowboy trickster with something up his sleeve. He took the guitar from the stand, slung the strap over his shoulder, and gave the crowd the once-over. He offered a friendly nod here, a wink there. He pointed generally at the crowd and said, "Some awfully pretty girls here tonight." His eyebrows popped up. "Thanks for coming." He couldn't wait to see them dance, and he knew they would.

Howdy strung the crowd along for another minute, making them itch for it, as he tuned one string, then another. He'd act like he was about to play something, then he'd start the whole process all over again until finally some guy at the bar hollered, "Come on, Hank it up!"

Howdy gave him an upward nod of the hat like that wasn't a bad idea. But he just smiled and made them wait a few more seconds before he gently strummed the guitar, then picked a few familiar, sentimental notes that got everybody's attention as they collectively thought, *You got to be kidding.*

Howdy leaned toward the mike, his eyes nearly closed, his head tilted just so. Then, with all the sensitivity of a seasoned Ramada Inn lounge singer, he crooned, "Feelings...nothing more than...feelings." Then he stopped, as if to bask in the warm round of applause that signaled recognition. But there was nothing.

The Piggin' String had fallen into stone silence all the way back to the kitchen. A tomblike hush bordering on the explosive. The expressions on the faces in the crowd ranged from bewildered to betrayed to you-better-not-be-doing-"Feelings"-up-in-this-place.

Slim almost spit a mouthful of beer, thinking, *What?*

Standing there in the awkward silence, Howdy's mock-soulful expression dissolved into woeful anguish, like his feelings were genuinely hurt. Like he couldn't believe they weren't all singing along, swaying side to side, holding hands.

The moment seemed to last forever.

Finally, Howdy broke into a broad grin and said, "I'm just messin' with you." He chuckled a little. "Did you really think I'd do it?" He shook his head at the reaction he'd gotten. "C'mon now, y'all ready to have some fun?"

The crowd seemed a little suspicious but, after a second, they managed to work up a hoot, two hollers, and some applause.

"Well, all right then," Howdy said. "Let's do this thing!" And just like that, he attacked his guitar, shouting, "Yeah!" He whirled, one leg kicked out as he spun around, and launched a missile of swinging rockabilly that would've knocked the doors off the hinges if a screw'd been loose. The emphasis came on the offbeat with a hand thumping the sound board, like somebody slapping a stand-up bass, and it felt like somebody had opened the door to let in Carl Perkins and the Stray Cats. The crowd leapt outta their seats.

Slim's head snapped back. *Damn,* he thought. *This guy doesn't mess around.* He was belting it out like a muscle car with good handling, a high-octane voice like summer lightning with sharp teeth and horsepower to burn. *Hell yeah*—Slim took a long pull on his beer—*this is gonna be some fun.*

The floor was filled with dancers before Howdy was halfway

through the song. Those girls sure could two-step, and most of them kept their eyes on Howdy as he rollicked from one end of the stage to the other. He owned them. They'd follow him anywhere. And he didn't wait for applause at the end of the tune either, just lit the fuse on one skyrocket after another and *boom, boom, boom!* Pure fireworks, three songs in a row.

When he finally stopped, the crowd went berserk with applause and whistles and "Hell yeahs!" Woooooooooooooo!

"Thank you!" Howdy pulled a handkerchief and wiped his face. "Thought you might like that." As the crowd settled down, Howdy pulled up a stool from the back of the stage and took a seat. He let everybody catch their breath and get some beer while he snapped a capo on the second fret and got his tuning right. "If y'all don't mind, I'm going to slow it down just a little," he said. "Just for a minute." He strummed a few chords like a peaceful, easy feeling and started singing a story about a broken heart and a bloodshot sky.

Slim was about to take a slug off his beer when the song stopped him, his bottle hovering over the tabletop like a magic trick where you can see the strings. The way Howdy sang about the mortal sins of this wayward man rang true as a bell, with tender phrasing that was honest and steeped in real hurt. It caught Slim off guard and made him reconsider his preconceived notions.

Based on what he knew of Howdy up until a minute ago, Slim had an idea of the kind of performer the guy might be, the kind of songs he might do, and how he might do them. But now, as he found himself lost in the sound of the guitar and the world of a man searching for the memory of a woman in a mescal haze—a haze Slim had found himself in more than once—all he could do was shake his head and think, *You just never know.*

20

HOWDY'S REPERTOIRE COVERED A LOT OF STYLISTIC GROUND in a short period. In addition to a couple of originals, he kept the dance floor packed with a western swing medley, jumping all over the Spade Cooley classic "Shame on You," followed by Bob Wills and Tiny Moore's "Ida Red Likes the Boogie" out of which he made a smile-inducing segue into Louis Jordan's "Choo Choo Ch'Boogie" that sounded as close to Asleep at the Wheel as one man could get. To wrap up the set, Howdy grabbed his Louisiana roots and growled a furious and swampy version of "Diggy Liggy Lo."

"Whew! That's right," Howdy called over the applause that followed the end of the set. "Steal a kiss with every chance when you do the Cajun dance," he said. "I'm gonna take five." He took off his guitar and held it in the air to share the applause. "Y'all get a cold one and we'll get back at it in just a few."

The second he stepped offstage, Howdy was set upon by a cute little blonde who told him she loved his hat and his song about the guy who got lost in tequila town. She was too shy to say anything else and was gone before Howdy could say much more than thanks. Too bad, he thought, he had plenty more to say.

He headed over to the bar where Skeets was in his usual place, talking on the phone. Howdy chugged a cold glass of water, then got a beer and sat down to catch his breath and let his sweat-soaked shirt dry out a little. A minute later, Skeets hung the phone up and pointed at Howdy. "Son, you still got it," he said. "They love ya."

"Can't help it if the crowd's got good taste," Howdy said with a wink.

Skeets smiled and slapped his hands together. "Hadn't heard any Spade Cooley in a coon's age."

"Shame on you," Howdy said. "Fix your damn jukebox or something."

Skeets looked around the club and said, "Jew see Slim?"

"Can't say as I have," Howdy said, taking a cursory glance around the room. "Why?"

"Oh, doesn't matter. Just thought I saw him earlier is all. If he was here, I thought I'd tell you both at the same time. But I can tell you and you can tell him later."

"Tell him what?"

"You two might just be in luck."

"Good luck or bad?"

"Good," Skeets said, waving a hand at the telephone. "That was Jodie Lee I was just talking to."

"No kidding?" For the past seven years, Frank and Jodie Lee owned a honky-tonk called the Beer Thirty that was a few miles outside of Lawton, Oklahoma. They were good people. Howdy had played there a half-dozen times, though not in the past year or two.

"Jodie Lee, huh?" Howdy smiled, just hearing her name. A beautiful and funny woman, sassy and strong. She'd been a barrel-racing champion as a younger girl. Sat on a horse as good as anybody he'd ever seen. He'd always liked her. Thought Frank had married way above his station and had told him as much on more than one occasion. Frank was smart enough never to argue the point. He just told Howdy what an unbecoming thing jealousy was. "I haven't seen Jodie since…" Howdy thought about it a second. "I can't even remember when it was." He picked up his hat and rubbed a hand over his head. "Probably last time I played in Lawton, whenever that was. How's she doing?"

"Says she's doing all right for a widder woman," Skeet said, expecting that Howdy knew.

But he didn't and it hit him like an unpleasant surprise. "A widow?" He looked down at the bar, then up at Skeets. "Frank died?"

Skeets looked at him like he was the slow kid in the class and said, "You think of some other way she could be widowed?"

"What happened?"

"I told you, Frank died."

"We've already covered that," Howdy said. "You got any hows or whens?" He lowered his voice and said, "She didn't kill him, did she?" Like it wasn't completely out of the question.

Skeets gave a wry smile and shook his head. "Not that it didn't cross her mind a few times back when he was still drinking, but, no. It was cancer. 'Bout a year and a half ago."

That sucked the humor out of the conversation. Quietly, Howdy said, "Damn." His eyes closed in condolence and understanding, his head shaking slowly. "Cancer." He knew the kind of pain and suffering that rode in on that horse. He'd seen it up close, the disease having made two unwelcome visits to his own house. His mother when he was a young boy, his father a few years ago. Their faces came to mind and he said the little prayer he always did when he thought about them.

"Frank was as tough a man as I ever knew," Skeets said. "Hard to imagine anything slowing him down, much less stopping him."

"Yeah," Howdy said, thinking of his dad, his idol, bigger than life with that cigar jutting from between his teeth. "Hard to imagine, all right."

The thing that wasn't hard to imagine, since he'd seen it with his own eyes, was how much Jodie loved old Frank. He knew how much they'd been through together—the drinking, getting sober, all that and more. And he knew what they meant to one another. He hated to think how bad it must've hurt her. But there was no good way to ask that question, so he just said, "She's running the place by herself now?"

"The Beer Thirty?" Again Skeets shook his head. "She lost it, paying the medical bills."

Howdy rubbed a hand over his face. "Oh, man, that's tough."

"Not that he meant to, but Frank didn't leave her much more than a few good memories and a lot of bad debts."

The words echoed in Howdy's mind. A few good memories and a lot of bad debts. He couldn't help himself. He thought there might be a song in there. But he resisted pulling out his little pad to write it down. He just said, "What's she doing now?"

"Well, that's where the good luck comes in," Skeets said, slapping the bar. "She's got a place down in Del Rio."

"Del Rio?" Howdy acted like he would've bet good money that eight wild horses couldn't have dragged that girl out of Oklahoma. He said, "The hell's she doin' down there?"

"Pickin' herself up by her bootstraps," Skeets said. "You know Jodie. Ain't exactly the type to rely on the kindness of strangers. She somehow managed to take over J.D. Maddox's old club."

"The Lost and Found?"

Skeets gave a nod. "Don't ask me how, but she did. Anyway, she had ole J. Fred Hawkins lined up for a two-week gig, but that rascal ended up in jail somewhere south of Memphis. And it looks like he'll be there long enough to inconvenience her, so she's looking for somebody to fill in." Skeets shrugged. "She called me, asked if I knew anybody available on short notice. I told her about you two stumbling in here looking for work."

"'Preciate that," Howdy said. "What'd you tell her about Slim?"

"Didn't have to tell her anything. Turns out she knows him. Del Rio's his neck of the woods. She said he's worked for her a couple of times, glad to have him come back."

"The world keeps getting smaller, don't it?" Howdy said. He drained his beer, then looked at his watch. "I guess it's about time for me to get back to—"

The end of his sentence got lost in the sound of a table being overturned and glass shattering. A couple of girls sitting near the ruckus screamed and scattered, causing Skeets and Howdy to look toward the back of the room where they saw a big son of a bitch wrestling with Slim.

Skeets nudged Howdy and said, "I told you that boy was in here."

21

SKEETS WAS REACHING FOR HIS PISTOL WHEN SOMETHING dawned on Howdy. He gestured, palm out, for Skeets to leave the gun where it was for the time being. "I got this," he said, heading for the confrontation, like he already had a good idea. A couple of steps later, realizing it was a dumb rat what didn't have two holes, he stopped, turned around, and said, "But don't run off. I might need you."

The big guy's name was Buddy Cooper. About Slim's height but carrying an extra fifty pounds, mostly upstairs, rough as a cob with a jaw like a bulldozer. None of which would have mattered had Buddy not also been the jealous ex-boyfriend of the girl Slim had been kind enough to escort home the previous night. Her name was Ginger, actually named after the character on *Gilligan's Island,* if you can believe it, even had a sister named Mary Ann. In any event, it turned out Ginger had run into Buddy during happy hour over at the Pump Room earlier tonight. Well, Ginger had a few too many and couldn't keep her big mouth shut, just had to let Buddy know that other men found her irresistible. Including this tall handsome who had been singing at the Piggin' String the night before.

Well, once he got properly lubricated, Buddy, who had finished at the bottom of the anger management classes the court had required him to attend last year, drove over to the Piggin' String in a jealous, green-eyed rage to show this singing cowboy who the real man was in this part of Tarrant County.

As Howdy approached the mayhem, he could see it was a tight fight with a short stick, Buddy having the advantage, after jumping Slim without benefit of advanced warning. In such close quarters, both were reduced to throwing stunted punches at kidneys, noses, and the back of each other's heads. From somewhere in the middle of it all Buddy growled, "I'm fixin' to clean your plow, boy."

And not only did it sound like he meant it, but it looked like he was capable.

In the midst of all this, Slim managed to plant a boot heel in Buddy's gut, knocking him backwards over one of the pool tables. While prone on the green felt, Buddy kept Slim at bay by hurling the three, six, and eight balls in his direction. Although Buddy had been an all-state pitcher his senior year in high school, being drunk, horizontal, and twenty years older took a good bit of the mustard off his delivery. Slim, a good Pony League first baseman with that long stretch of his, ducked the first two balls, then caught the eight in his bare hand and threw it back, just grazing the side of that bulldozer jaw. Buddy reacted by grabbing a cue stick like he was going to step up to the plate with it. He rolled off the table and choked up on the stick, eyeing Slim's head like it was a big fat one coming over the plate.

Slim was trapped by overturned tables and was backed into a booth. He was looking around for a weapon—why the hell that dumb-ass Howdy had thrown that pistol into the trash can still escaped him—but there was little to choose from that matched up real good with a pool cue. So he grabbed a longneck, broke the bottom off, and started swinging it back and forth the way you do in circumstances such as this.

Buddy had a look in his eye that you can bet Ginger had seen at least once as he closed in and drew into his backswing. But the damn thing got stuck. He couldn't bring it around for a base hit, let alone a dinger. Confused, he turned and saw Howdy at the other end of the stick. "Who the hell're you?" he barked.

"I'm the one who came here to whoop that boy's ass," Howdy said, one hand on the cue stick, the other pointing at Slim. "Question is, who the hell *you* are."

"I'm the one who's *currently* whooping his ass," Buddy replied, tugging on the cue. "Let go of my stick and get in line. I got here first."

"I don't care when you got here," Howdy said, tugging back. "I got a reservation."

The confusion compounded like interest on Buddy's face. "How the hell you think you got a reservation to kick somebody's ass?"

Howdy jerked the stick out of Buddy's grip, poked him in the chest with the blue-chalk tip, said, "That guitar Casanova there took advantage of my girl a couple of nights ago while she was drunk and I was outta town. That's how."

Buddy swatted the stick away when Howdy tried to poke him a second time. "Well then your reservation musta been for *last* night when this sumbitch was in here taking advantage of *my* girl."

"What?" Like he was outraged by the notion of such sexual recklessness. Looking past Buddy, Howdy aimed the cue stick at Slim. "Boy, you best learn to keep that one-eye trouser trout of yours in its pen, you expect to see another birthday." He made a move like he was going to charge Slim, but Buddy shoved him back.

"Hey, asshole, like I said, get in line. You can have him when I'm done."

Howdy looked at Buddy, then Slim, giving the appearance of appraising the situation. Then he shook his head. "Nosir." Like it was one word. "I don't think there'd be enough left to make it worth my while."

"Ain't my problem," Buddy said. "Sloppy seconds is all you're gone get." He was rolling up his sleeves now.

The other patrons were watching like it was a Jerry Springer special: *Live at the Piggin' String!* Skeets was at the bar, smiling as he sipped a beer, enjoying the entertainment, like it was a hastily conceived floor show between musical acts. His pistol was right there, of course, ready to bring the curtain down on the whole thing if need be, but he had the feeling Howdy's plan—whatever the hell it was—was gonna do the trick.

All the sudden, Buddy lunged at Slim, who slashed and jabbed with the broken bottle, saying, "Don't come in here, less you want some stitches." It forced Buddy to back off.

When he did, Howdy poked him in the back with the pool cue again. Said, "Hey!"

Buddy jerked around. "You poke me with that one more time I'm gone stick it in wunna your ears and out the other."

Howdy tipped his hat back and tilted his head to one side, then the other, like he was sizing Buddy up. "Let me ask you something," he said, as if they suddenly shared a secret. "You by any chance a gambling man?"

Buddy kept one bloodshot eye on Slim so he couldn't get him with that bottle, the other was more or less looking at Howdy. "What do you mean?"

"You know, games of chance," Howdy said. "Wagering on a throw of the dice or the turn of a wheel or the choice of a card to determine the outcome of events."

Buddy gave a half-assed shrug, thinking about that weekend he'd snuck off to Laughlin with redheaded Wanda and won three hundred bucks at the slots. "Yeah, I guess," he said. "Why?"

"Let's cut for it."

"Cut for it?"

"Yeah," Howdy said, like it was only natural. "High card gets to kick Casanova's ass."

As he watched Howdy working on Buddy, Slim shook his head a little and tried to keep from smiling too much. He liked the way Howdy thought.

"I already told you," Buddy said. "I'm gonna kick his ass no matter what."

"Well, now I think we've agreed that whoever gets second shot at this, ain't gonna get no satisfaction. So I was thinking, we can turn it into a gamble, at least make it some fun for both parties."

"Ain't interested."

"All right," Howdy said. "I understand, stakes are too low." He pondered it for a second before saying, "What if we sweeten the pot? High card gets to kick Casanova's ass and gets paid for the privilege."

Buddy got to thinking about his truck payment and said, "How much?"

"I dunno." Howdy shrugged. "Fifty bucks?"

Buddy's cable bill was overdue too, not to mention his rent. He said, "Make it a hundred."

"Deal," Howdy said. "Cash on the barrelhead." He slapped his own

money on the pool table and turned to the bar, snapping his fingers, yelling, "Hey, Skeets, you got a deck of cards in this place?" As he walked
away, Howdy said, "And bring me my glasses while you're there."

As Skeets went to grab Dempsey Kimble's marked deck, Buddy
scraped together all his cash. He laid it on the table and said, "All I
got is ninety-six and change."

"Close enough." Howdy gave him a collegial chuck on the shoulder, then stepped past him to take a swing at Slim with the pool cue.
"You just keep your ass right where it is, lover boy," he said. "One of
us will be with you directly."

Figuring it was best to play along, Slim menaced Howdy with
the broken bottle and said, "Bring it on, you sorry-ass swamp cracker."
Gesturing with wiggling fingers. "I'll kick both your candy asses."

Skeets came over and tossed the deck to Buddy, let him pull the
cards out of their box, get the feeling they were legit. "Brand-new
deck," Skeets said. "Hardly been used."

By now a crowd had gathered around, and Skeets, not being one
to miss a good opportunity, was taking various side bets.

Howdy pointed at the green felt of the pool table near the money.
"Spread 'em out," he said. "You go first or second, I don't care."

Buddy smeared the cards on the table. "I got here first," he said.
"I'll pick first." He huffed on his hands and rubbed them together
for luck while he looked for a winning card. After a moment, he
paused, turned to Howdy, and said, "High card wins, right? Gets to
kick Romeo's ass and gets a hundred bucks from the loser?"

Howdy shook his head and said, "Casanova."

"What?"

"Romeo was the star-crossed lover," Howdy said. "Casanova, on
the other hand, was a famous seducer. I think that's what we got
here."

Skeets cleared his throat in a manner to suggest Howdy should
just get on with it. Slim just rolled his eyes.

"I don't get it," Buddy said.

"Don't matter," Howdy replied. "Romeo it is." He put the glasses
on, waved a hand at the fifty-two cards spread out on the Kelly green
felt, and said, "Go for it."

Buddy picked the jack of hearts and grinned like he was showing off new teeth. He turned to Slim, taunting him with the one-eye jack. "Your ass is mine, boy."

Slim taunted back with his jagged glass. "Fat lady ain't sung yet."

"All right," Howdy said. "My turn." He waved a hand slowly over the cards, hesitating, acting like he was going for one card, then another. Ratcheting up the anticipation, the crowd pushed in closer with each fake. Finally, he picked a card. "Ha!" He showed it to Buddy and said, "Jack of spades." Just screwing with Slim. The crowd loved it.

"What's that mean?" Buddy asked. "We both do it?"

"I think it means we tied," Howdy said with a wink and nod toward Slim. "Pick again."

Slim glowered.

Second time Buddy drew a nine.

Howdy picked a queen and that was all she wrote. Howdy scraped Buddy's money toward the corner pocket where his other hand waited to meet it. Folded it into his roll and put it away. Skeets was collecting on the side bets while the onlookers began drifting back to their tables. But after a minute it was clear that Buddy wasn't going anywhere, just stood there with arms folded across his chest. Finally he said, "Go on, then. Kick his ass." Nodding at Slim.

Howdy turned on a dime, got in Buddy's face. "I don't appreciate people telling me what to do." He didn't blink. Just two dark eyes staring from under the black hat, like a wild animal under the front porch.

Buddy held his ground.

Skeets, back at the bar counting his money, looked up long enough to see what was going on. He figured things might go south if he didn't bring the curtain down now. He slipped the pistol into his waistband and walked across his bar like he was Augustus McCrae. Howdy was saying something when he got there.

"Hey, cowboy, I won the bet," he said. "I'll kick his ass when I'm good and ready and not before. That's what it's like to be the winner." Howdy walked past him saying, "Better luck next time."

Buddy turned to follow but got blocked by Skeets, standing there with his hand on the ivory grip of his pistol. "Son," he said, "know when to walk away."

22

MONDAY MORNING SLIM AND HOWDY HIT THE ROAD WITH a sack of the sausage and biscuit sandwiches and a couple of large coffees. It was Howdy's turn to drive and he was looking forward to it, there being few things that lifted his spirit more than a clean windshield, a full tank of gas, and the open road. It was a four-hundred-mile drive, more or less, and they wouldn't be creeping through Bluff Dale, Rockwood, and Eldorado with Howdy behind the wheel. They'd be taking I-35 down through Austin and San Antonio before turning west on Highway 90, heading for Uvalde and finally Del Rio.

But that was a long way off. And, based on their history so far, they both knew there was no telling what might happen between where they were and where they were going.

Just have to wait and see.

They hadn't been on the road too long before they started chewing over the previous night's events, specifically the run-in with big Buddy Cooper. Even though Slim insisted he had the upper hand in the fight, had it all under control, didn't need any help from anybody, he was quick to give Howdy his due on stepping in when he did with the card trick.

"No problem," Howdy said, but not with all the conviction in the world. He had something else on his mind, something that had been bothering him since last night.

Slim didn't seem to notice. He said something about how his night with Ginger might have been worth a pair of ass-kickings, though he was glad it hadn't come to that.

"Yeah, well, next time, maybe I'll just keep out of it."

Slim couldn't help but notice that. He said, "The hell's got your feathers up?"

"Pardon me," Howdy said sarcastically. "That's just the way us sorry-assed swamp crackers get." Like his sensibilities had been trampled upon.

Slim couldn't believe it. "Are you kidding?"

"That was a little harsh, don't you think?"

"Hell, wasn't personal," Slim said with a shrug. "Just figured I should play along with your setup, that's all. 'Sorry-ass swamp cracker' was just the first thing to come to mind."

"That was the first thing?"

"I thought it sounded pretty good," Slim said. "You know, true to the moment."

"Like if I'd called you a seriously inbred hillbilly defective?"

Slim gave him a sideways glance as he sipped his coffee. "No, not really, because I think you'll find your hillbillies in the Ozarks and the Appalachians."

"That's not my point."

"I mean, I'm not even from Texas hill country, so..."

"You're missing—"

"And I'm pretty sure Louisiana's full of swamps, so at least I was geographically accurate, but, well, forget it," Slim said. "Next time I'll be more circumspect in my word choice so as not to step on your tender toes." It seemed counterproductive to get into a fight today over what had happened while Howdy was getting him out of a fight last night. So Slim said, "Good idea getting these biscuits." He stuffed half of one into his mouth and looked out the window.

Howdy was fine to let it slide. He'd brought it up, aired it out, and now he could let it go. He really wasn't that pissed about it. He just liked busting Slim's chops first thing in the morning. They drove along in silence for a while. Howdy hung an elbow out the window and turned his attention to testing the outer boundaries of the posted speed limit. After a few minutes he said to Slim, "What can you get away with in Texas, ten miles over? Fifteen?"

"Asking the wrong guy," Slim said. "And don't expect me to split any goddam tickets you get."

Howdy tipped his hat, chuckled a bit, said, "Yes'm, Miss Daisy." Then he took it up to seventy-five and started advancing on Austin just a bit faster than everybody else on the road. Not just because he figured it would grate on Slim, but that was part of it. After a minute he gestured toward the glove box, said, "Hand me that radar detector."

Slim popped the compartment, rooted around for a second, then shook his head. "It's not in there."

"What? Somebody stole it?"

Slim gave him a sideways glance. "Wouldn't be the first time," he said.

"Well, dog dammit!" Howdy shook his head as if disappointed in human nature. "You just can't trust people anymore." He shrugged, then gassed the truck up to eighty. "Guess we'll just have to do it the old-fashioned way."

Howdy took his driving seriously. Not the speed limit, of course, but the idea that cars and highways were designed to get you from one place to another as fast as possible without anybody getting hurt. He considered the notion that speed was the cause of most accidents nonsense. Hell, if that was the case, they'd never finish at Talladega, everybody'd be wrecked or dead. The real cause of most accidents was failure to maintain control, no matter what the speed. As far as Howdy was concerned, there were only two rules to driving. One: Never hit anything. And two: Never cause anyone else to hit anything. If everybody followed those rules, he figured, the world would be a safer place and everybody would get where they were going a lot sooner.

Howdy was so enamored of his driving skills that he sometimes imagined that with a twist or two of fate, he could have ended up on the NASCAR circuit instead of the honky-tonk circuit. He had wide peripheral vision, quick reactions, and the ability to read other drivers, anticipate what they were going to do before they even decided they were going to do it. His sense of where things were and how they were moving in relation to where he was, was uncanny. He knew if a space was opening or closing and whether he could fit in it or not.

He was never bored on long drives because he spent every moment measuring and adjusting and anticipating before making his move, improving his position, and looking for the next one. He imagined it was just like life, with every mile offering opportunities to get further ahead of the others, those not willing to make the effort, and it was that game of identifying the advantages and taking as many as he could that kept him engaged and made the time pass more quickly.

It was his way of enjoying the journey as much as arriving at the destination a little sooner.

It took Slim about twenty miles before he stopped reaching for the dashboard in a black panic and using the imaginary brake pedal on his side of the truck every time Howdy made a move in traffic. Eventually he realized Howdy knew what he was doing and that freed his mind to wander. And once you stopped fearing for your life, six hours on the road gives a guy plenty of time to reflect on things.

Slim had mixed feelings about his return to Del Rio. It wasn't like he had wants or warrants or unpaid debts or somebody waiting to kill him, nothing as concrete as that. If he'd been the superstitious type, Slim would have said the place just seemed to have it in for him. But that was crazy talk. He didn't believe that sort of thing. Shit, as the bumper sticker pointed out, just happened. But, in Slim's experience, it seemed to happen more frequently in Del Rio than other places. At least to him.

The place seemed more like a pair of loaded dice than a sleepy little border town across the Rio Grande from Ciudad Acuña. It was built around the customs station at the river, Laughlin Air Force Base to the south, and Devil's Lake recreation area to the north. Del Rio. Ask most people, they'd say it meant "the river." A few, with a better understanding of the language, knew it was "of the river," since the name had been shortened in 1883 by the U.S. Postal Department from the original, San Felipe del Rio, a name bestowed after Spanish explorers offered a mass at the site on Saint Philip's Day in 1635. Or so the legend had it.

But Slim had his own translation, based on his own history with the place. For him, Del Rio was Spanish for "the place things went missing."

Things like his favorite guitar, a certain woman, and his dad.

Slim wondered if something would go missing on this trip. Then he considered the possibility that maybe his luck had changed and maybe something would show up this time around. Only one way to find out.

23

ON THE OUTSKIRTS OF DEL RIO, HOWDY NOTICED THEY WERE low on gas, so he pulled into the Truck 'n' Go Quicky Stop. An oasis for the long-haul driver. Self-serve gas pumps in front, diesel pumps out back that came with full service, if you asked for it over the phone that was right there on the pole. The full-service attendants came in the form of some hardworking girls willing and able to do whatever to the truck you wanted. At a price, of course.

The Truck 'n' Go Quicky Stop even offered rooms with beds and showers by the hour. The convenience store inside had everything a trucker might need from toiletries and pharmaceuticals to cell phones and GPS systems, from fried chicken to chicken-fried steak. They even had a full aisle of the latest CDs and DVDs. Business was good.

After fueling up and scraping some bugs off the windshield, Slim and Howdy headed into town on the main drag, past greasy auto-repair places, rundown motels, check-cashing joints, and liquor stores. Howdy noticed an old mom-and-pop hardware store that was boarded up with plywood that he figured came from one of the nationally recognized home-improvement stores that had put mom and pop out of business in the first place.

Even under bright blue skies and sunshine, Del Rio wouldn't exactly stir the soul and fill its tank with hope. It was a dusty place, flat and struggling for air, hoping for the best against all odds. Like somebody had started with an idea for a nice town near that river with the grand name, then wandered off or died of ennui before they'd added any of the fine touches they had in mind.

Arriving under ominous gray skies, as Slim and Howdy were, the only thing to lift their spirits was the knowledge that they wouldn't be unemployed for at least two weeks. And that counted for something, ask any musician.

This being Howdy's first trip to Del Rio, and having arrived with higher expectations, he looked over at Slim and said, "I thought you said this was a paradise."

"I said a loaded pair of dice," Slim replied. "But I'll tell you what, you won't find a better enchilada anywhere."

Howdy figured that was reason enough to keep going. He drove on, past the fancy new shopping center anchored by the Dollar Tree, then over the tracks of the old Southern Pacific railroad where, off to the left, they saw a small, free-standing building, hard to miss with all the neon green and orange paint. The exterior walls were billboards of cartoon scorpions, tarantulas, cobras, and rattlesnakes, like some roadside reptile attraction that had escaped from Florida in the sixties and settled in Del Rio in a successful bid to avoid all the tourists. The crude hand-painted sign over the door read, "Rattlesnake Jake's—Exotic Pets."

A few miles later, near the far end of town, Howdy waved a hand at the great expanse of scrub surrounding them and said, "Did we miss it?"

"Keep going," Slim said, pointing ahead. "It's up there on the left."

And sure enough it was. A fine-looking old building, with solid timber beams, over a hundred years old, jutting from the exterior walls at the top like something from the days—and maybe even the architect—of the Alamo. Nothing fancy, mind you, but kept up and cared for as if by people with a sense of history, people who knew the value of the past and the importance of preservation. Over the decades, the building, which was surrounded on three sides by a plank boardwalk, had been a trading post, a general store, and even the headquarters of the San Felipe Agricultural, Manufacturing, and Irrigation Company. It had character and strength and, in its only exterior nod to modernity, neon beer signs in the window as tastefully as can be done. The building's façade arched smoothly upward in the center where the main crossbeam jutted out above all the others and pointed toward Mexico. In the space created by the arch, painted in bold script with drop shadows, were the words

Lost and Found

The parking lot was dust and gravel and empty for the most part when Slim and Howdy pulled in, just a couple of cars and trucks here and there. It was Monday and early enough that most folks were just finishing their day jobs.

"Nice place," Howdy said. "Looks like it could hold a crowd."

"Six or seven hundred I think," Slim replied. "Gets pretty lively on the weekends."

The dust hadn't settled from them pulling into the parking lot before some movement caught their eyes. A man roughly the size and shape of a buffalo was backing slowly out the building's side door, his hands raised in the air. His head was shaved and he had a gold ring through his nose. And though he was too far away for Slim and Howdy to make out any details, he seemed to have something shiny, stainless steely, riding the crest of his bald head from between the eyes to the first vertebra of his spine, like a metallic Mohawk, or an unusual zipper.

"Well now, that's something you don't see every day," was Howdy's observation.

"True." Slim nodded.

Howdy squinted at the bald guy, trying to bring his head into focus. "What the hell is that?"

"Looks like a bunch of silver studs or something." Slim was right. They were piercings, fifteen of them, looked like stainless-steel bolts holding an empty skull shut.

"Damn," Howdy said. "I think you're right." He shook his head in disbelief. "You know, every time I see something like that, it makes me wonder if everybody's nervous system is hooked up the same way."

Slim nodded again, then looked at the dark skies promising a thunderstorm. "I wonder if those things draw lightning."

As the bald guy continued backing out of the Lost and Found, he yelled, "You don't know what the hale you're talkin' 'bout," in an accent that sounded a lot more East Alabama than West Texas.

The next thing Slim and Howdy saw coming out that side door was the barrel of a blue steel .38 in the slender hand of the striking woman who followed soon thereafter.

Jodie Lee was already on the tall side, but with her hat and boots, she shot well past six feet. She wore an embroidered-eagle-design western shirt with front snap pockets and off-the-shelf jeans that fit like they were custom-tailored to every part she had. She was sporting a tribe's worth of turquoise and silver jewelry around her waist, wrists, and her graceful neck. Falling from under the hat was a silky ponytail, prematurely gray, that rested between her shoulder blades.

Jodie gave the impression of being handy with a gun as she wagged the .38 at the back end of a pickup with a hard-shell cover. "Open it up and let's see," she said.

The big bald guy glared at her, said, "I ain't gotta prove nothin' to you." He spit in the dirt in a desperate show of machismo.

Jodie pulled the hammer back on the .38, in a show of superior firepower. "Well, it's me or the cops," she said. "Up to you."

Slim nudged Howdy. "You think we ought to help?"

"Him or her?"

"I was thinking of Jodie," Slim said.

"Doesn't look like she needs any."

The bald guy finally opened the back of his truck, revealing several cases of whiskey and beer. "That shit's mine," he insisted. "And you can't prove otherwise." He was about to slam the top down when Jodie fired a shot, kicking up some rocks near the guy's feet. He jumped to one side and said, "The hell's wrong with you, bitch, you crazy?"

"A," she said. "Watch your mouth. B. Let's see the bottom of the boxes." She cocked the hammer again.

He tilted one of the boxes back and showed the L&F written in bold black marker on the bottom, the way she did all her stock when it came in.

Jodie smiled. "Well, they once were *lost* but now they're *found*," she said in mock revelation. "Put 'em up here on the porch." She tapped the place she meant with the silver toe of her boot, then backed up a step to make room. After the guy did what he was told, he slammed the hard shell down and said, "You just made a big mistake, honey.

You don't know who you're screwin' with." He stormed to the cab of the truck and jerked the door open.

"By the way," Jodie said. "You go tearing outta here kicking up rocks, trying to pop me or one of my windows, this weapon is likely to discharge by accident in your general direction. And you'd be surprised at how accurate that can be." She smiled, but not in a real friendly way. "So you better just ease on out and be sure you don't come back."

The guy mumbled something of the un-Christian variety, got in his truck, and pulled away without raising so much as a speck of dust.

24

JODIE EASED THE HAMMER DOWN ON HER .38 AND TUCKED IT in her waist just as the rain started coming down. She was stooped over to pick up one of the cases of whiskey when she heard boots on the boardwalk coming her way. Her hand went back to the gun's grip as she stood up to face whoever it was.

"Allow us, ma'am," Howdy said with a friendly smile and his hands halfway raised.

Jodie looked at the two men curiously. She hadn't seen Howdy in at least two years. Though she'd seen Slim more recently than that, she'd never seen him in the company of anybody else, let alone somebody she knew in the context of her old club in Oklahoma, so it took her a moment to put it all together. When she realized who they were and why they were there, she pointed at their truck and said, "How long you two been sitting out there?"

"Few minutes," Slim said, bending over to grab one of the boxes.

She tucked the gun back in her waist. "Fine couple of gentlemen you are," she said, yanking their chains. "Didn't you see I was involved in a potentially deadly confrontation with a hardened criminal?"

"Why do you think we stayed in the truck?" Howdy picked up a case of whiskey, then went all hayseed on her. "I mean, heck, we're just a couple of harmless ole gi-tar pickers."

She shook her head. "You mean to tell me you're still not carrying a gun, even after what happened in Lawton?"

"He had one for a minute back in Beaumont," Slim said, somewhat accusingly. "But he threw it away."

"Threw it away?"

Slim nodded like he agreed it was a dumb thing to do. Then he looked at Howdy with a curious smile. "What happened in Lawton?"

"Long story," Howdy said, trying to get everybody past it.

Jodie shook her head. "It's not that long." She turned to Slim, confiding, "See, your buddy here was—"

"I vote we save story time for later," Howdy interrupted. He gestured at Jodie the best he could with the case of whiskey in his hands. "Besides, if you'll recall, owning a gun wouldn't have done me much good at the time."

"I guess you have a point," she said. "They do you more good if you actually have them at hand when you need 'em." She turned back to Slim and said, "He was nekkid as a scraped hog at the time and both his hands were occupied with...what was her name? Mrs. uh...?"

"She told me she was divorced," Howdy said.

"She said her husband was in Canada for the month."

"What's the difference? The point is..." Howdy paused. "Shouldn't we get out of the rain?"

"Fine," Jodie said with a smirk they'd both seen before. "I understand. We'll change the subject if you want." She folded her arms, looked at Howdy, and said, "So exactly when, where, and why the hell did you throw away a gun?"

"Well, now that's actually a pretty good story," Howdy said. "See, Slim here had managed to get himself into a tight spot with this fella in Beaumont who was wavin' a knife that was about yea big." He held his hands about two feet apart. "So, there I was, in the kitchen—"

"I thought we voted to move story time to later," Slim said, nudging Jodie with a box. "Where you want these?"

"Inside," she said, leading them back into the storeroom. "Just set 'em on that table."

After they got all the boxes in from the rain, Howdy stood there looking at Jodie for a moment. She was the same strong, beautiful woman he remembered. But changed at the same time, burdened as she was by the sadness that came with being the one left to carry on without the love that had been her reason for living. Somehow, this just added to her beauty.

"Listen," Howdy said, softly. "I was sure sorry to hear about Frank." He stepped closer and pulled her in for a tender hug. After a moment, he eased back but kept his hands on her arms while looking in her eyes. "I didn't know till the other day when Skeets told me. I didn't even know he was sick." He shook his head, offering a sad smile. "I wish I'd heard before. I would have liked to come to the service. And you know I'da been there if I'd known."

"I know you would've."

"He was a good man."

Jodie cupped a hand on Howdy's cheek, her pale blue eyes taking in all the features of his face. "He sure was," she said, giving him a little pat. "Thanks, hun. That's sweet of you to say." She took a deep breath, said, "It was hard to let him go, but...what're you gonna do if the Lord decides to take him?"

Howdy nodded. "Only one thing *to* do," he said. "Either quit or keep on keeping on."

"Exactly right." Jodie smiled and held her arms out wide. "So welcome to keeping on at the Lost and Found."

25

A FEW MINUTES LATER THEY WERE SITTING IN JODIE'S office, shooting the breeze, listening to the rain come down. Jodie looked toward the ceiling and said, "Keeps up like this, it's gonna be a slow night." She had her boots propped on her desk, a cup of coffee steaming in front of her.

Howdy had made himself comfortable in a niche carved out of some of the boxes, his butt planted on a case of bourbon, arm resting on a case of beer. Slim was leaned back in a chair touching the wall behind him, his long legs helping him keep his balance.

Jodie tipped her cup toward Slim, said, "Hey, did you ever get your guitar back from Boone Tate?"

Slim and Howdy looked at each other and busted up laughing. Then Slim said, "Yeah, I got it back."

"That Brushfire's a nasty piece of work," Howdy said. "And I say that based on knowing him all of about five minutes."

"You're a good judge of character," Jodie said. "Boone Tate was born nasty. And after that fire, he just got nastier. Of course the liquor doesn't help."

"Doesn't seem to hurt his ability to hold a grudge though," Slim said. "He still seems to think he owes me for that business at Diablo's Cantina that night."

"Still?" Jodie shook her head. "That's not holding a grudge," she said. "That's clutching it to your breast and nursing it to maturity."

"What happened at Diablo's Cantina?" Howdy asked.

Jodie and Slim exchanged a look. "Nothing," Slim said. "Nothing worth telling, anyway."

Howdy shrugged it off, figured he'd get the answer later.

Jodie said, "So what happened with ole Brushfire?"

Slim and Howdy took turns telling her the story about the hedge clippers, the knife, the gun, and their wild night with Tammy and Crystal.

When they finished, Jodie said, "Well, I can see how two men might bond after an ordeal such as that. Skeets told me he wasn't sure how you two had gotten partnered up. I guess that's as good a way as any to do it."

"Well, now, I wouldn't say we're partnered up," Howdy said, as if a partnership with Slim or anybody else was the sort of idea he was unlikely to entertain. He was a solo act, a lone wolf, a solitary man. He thought about adding that particular Neil Diamond song to his repertoire.

"Yeah, we're just travelin' together," Slim added with a shrug. "Circumstances dictating the way they sometimes do."

"Uh-huh," Jodie said, understanding how circumstances will do that. She kept her eyes on Slim and said, "What about Caroline? Where'd circumstances take her? I mean if you don't mind my asking."

"Wait, wait, wait," Howdy said. "Who's this Caroline?"

"She was one of my best waitresses," Jodie said. "When I first came back to Del Rio."

"Well, well, well," Howdy said. "The plot thickens."

Slim casually waved a hand, like he was shooing a fly. "She was last seen headed east," he said with a shrug that was intended to give the impression he didn't care one way or another what happened to her. But he was unconvincing.

The poor performance perked Howdy right up. He slapped his hand on the case of beer and said, "Wait a minute. Is Caroline the girl you stole from Brushfire Boone? The one you said you'd gladly trade back for the Martin?"

Jodie smiled, looked at Howdy. "Did he say that?"

"He did," Howdy said, nodding. "Something about her not being real big on leaving a forwarding address."

"Well, he didn't mean it," Jodie replied. "That was just the hurt talkin', wasn't it, honey?" She did enjoy yanking a man's chain.

Slim held his legs straight out, tipping the balance until his chair listed forward and his boots hit the floor. He acted like he was going to stand up and leave. Take his ball and go home. He said, "You girls want to gossip about my love life, I think I'll go see a man about a horse or something."

"Oh, sit down," Jodie said. "We're just having fun."

"Yeah," Howdy added. "If it makes you feel any better, I had one just like that, name of Marilyn Justine." He smacked his lips and got a fond look on his face. "Made the best margaritas..."

Jodie said, "Did you get the recipe?"

"Nope. Girl didn't leave me so much as a good-bye on a sticky note."

"Ohhh, Howdy, that is so sad." Jodie rubbed an index finger back and forth over the top of her thumb, playing that little violin part to accompany his pitiful little story. "Still, you two will always have your night with Candy and Wanda."

"Crystal and Tammy," Slim said.

Jodie rolled her eyes. "Whatever."

Howdy gave her a wink and said, "Hey listen, I'm curious about earlier." He gestured out toward the parking lot. "Exactly who was that guy with the, uh, with the scalp situation?" He pointed at the top of his hat.

"Oh, that was Link," Jodie said.

"Link?" Howdy cocked his head at the name. "Like the sausage?"

"More like the thing that's missing between us and cavemen," Jodie said.

Slim leaned back in his chair again and said, "See now, I don't normally like to judge a book by its cover, but...he didn't exactly look like the brightest bulb in the marquee. The biggest, maybe, but not the brightest."

"That much is true," Jodie said, touching her finger to the side of her nose. "The boy has a bad case of the simples."

"I don't think he was here last time I was," Slim said. "He's the type I would've remembered."

Jodie shook her head. "No, he showed up a few weeks after your last gig," she said. "You remember Big John?"

Slim nodded, held his hand out kind of low to the ground. "Little guy, talked kinda funny?"

"That's him," Jodie said. "Well, he quit on me, moved up to Portland after some girl."

"The kind who leaves a forwarding address, obviously," Howdy said.

Slim held up the middle finger on his left hand and tilted it toward Howdy.

Jodie said, "So I needed somebody working the door, taking cover charge, counting heads, bouncing, all that. That's when Link showed up, looking for work. He was big and scary with those damn things in his head, especially the way it pinches that ridge of scalp along the crown. So it seemed like a good fit." She shrugged and took a sip of her coffee. "First couple of weeks he was fine. After that he started stealing everything that wasn't too hot or too heavy to tote. He set about robbing me blind without wasting a bit of gas trying to be slick about it." Jodie counted things off on her fingers. "The take at the door dropped off, cases of stuff started walking out the back, sound equipment started to disappear." Jodie shook her head. "So I got some cameras installed. Only took two days to get enough video to forestall any legal proceedings he might consider for me firing him without notice."

"So that was the business in the parking lot?"

"That was his termination interview," Jodie said. "Sometimes it's hard being the boss."

"It's a tough job, all right," Howdy said. "But I think not shooting him was a pretty generous severance package."

"My thought exactly," Jodie said. "Only big surprise is how ungrateful the son of a bitch seemed. Still, it's good news for the two of you."

"How so?"

"Now you'll both have jobs every night if you want. One of you playing, one of you on the door. Whaddya say?"

Slim and Howdy exchanged a quick glance and a nod. "Fair enough," Slim said.

"Deal!" Jodie slapped the desktop and opened a drawer. She pulled out another pistol and slid it in Howdy's direction. "So, let me ask you," she said. "Prior to throwing that gun away back in Beaumont, jew get a chance to find out if you're any good with it?"

Before Howdy could open his mouth, Slim pointed at Jodie and said, "I tell you what, we'll all be plenty safe if any major appliances come in here trying to cause trouble."

26

AS THE RAIN TAPERED OFF, THE CROWD TRICKLED IN. SINCE neither Howdy nor Slim cared one way or the other about who did what that night, they flipped a coin. Slim called it in the air and opted to take the stage when he won. Fine with Howdy. He'd work the door. They decided to alternate daily, keep from getting in a rut.

Hank Williams, Jr., kicked off the Monday-night game the way he always does with all his rowdy friends. It was Giants-Redskins, neither of which had what you'd call a substantial fan base in the greater Del Rio metro area. Still, it was football and guys'll watch and cheer for damn near anything where people get hit or where there's the possibility of a wreck, especially if there's cheerleaders and beer involved.

Of course nobody at the Lost and Found was wearing Giants or Redskins paraphernalia—or anything else from back east for that matter. Sports apparel was strictly Lone Star oriented. Cowboys, Longhorns, Texans, Aggies, Owls, Horned Frogs, and even a few old Oilers jerseys. The one exception being a chesty little blonde in an Arizona Cardinals T-shirt that nobody seemed to mind.

Otherwise, fashion broke down along the three usual lines. The majority wore jeans, western shirts, cowboy hats, and boots. Next most popular was T-shirts, jeans, and baseball caps. The third was a variety of air force dress.

Howdy was working just inside the front door, perched on a stool behind a rickety podium with a small light on top for checking IDs, and a shelf below where he kept the cash box for the cover charge and his little pad for writing down song ideas. Jodie's extra pistol was tucked in the small of his back. It was just a .22 but it was enough to keep most people from doing anything really stupid.

Every time somebody came through the door Howdy clicked his chrome counter, said, "Hey, howyadoin'?" and took their money with a smile. Flirted with the girls. Shot shit with the guys. It didn't take a high percentage of Howdy's concentration to do the job, so, as usual, he was thinking about other things.

In fact, ever since the conversation in Jodie's office, Howdy had been thinking about Marilyn Justine. Where was she? What was she doing? Why had she left? How much trouble would it have been to leave a note? What was in her margaritas?

Lacking, as he was, answers to any of those questions, Howdy moved on to thinking about that first night he tried to drink her out of his mind. Started with Corona, moved on to tequila. Margaritas, of course, in her honor, alternating with a shot of gold now and then. The margaritas weren't as good as the ones Marilyn made with that secret recipe of hers, but Howdy still managed to build a pyramid toward the ceiling with all the glasses he emptied.

The bartender that night kept saying that one more drink would make him forget. Howdy just shook his head, saying, "It's going to take more than a margarita to make me stop thinking about her."

Thinking back on it, Howdy pulled out his note pad. Wrote that down. That was a song as sure as he was sitting there.

The moment he put the pen down, the door opened. It was three gals looked like they'd just come from working in an office all day. Howdy tipped his hat, said, "Hey, how y'all doin?" He took their money and watched them wiggle off toward the bar, then turned his eyes back to the pad. Wrote down, "hurting, even while not feeling any pain."

That was how it happened sometimes. He'd be looking back over a page from his life or the life of someone he knew and something would jump out at him, give him a line to work with, a foundation to build on. Other times he tried to write from the perspective of someone he imagined or somebody he'd seen in passing and he'd try to project who they were, what they'd gone through. Like once when he saw an old man standing on the porch of a weather-beaten

house looking toward the sky. Or that time he saw a young woman
sitting on a bus bench crying, a sheet of paper clutched in her hand.
Was the man praying for rain? And what was that piece of paper? A
good-bye? Bad news from the doctor?

You write about life's trials, mama, how it's a hard row to hoe,
and the one who broke your heart so bad you thought you'd die.
Songs come from a snatch of language overheard at the coffee shop,
two people breaking up, maybe, one asking to be released from the
other. Released. What a choice of words. And then there's all the
good times and honky-tonk girls, the fast cars and the run from
the law. It's life, the stuff you go through.

And it has to come from the heart, not the head.

Howdy knew that writing songs was funny business. Sometimes
one'll squirt out like mustard from a squeeze bottle, other times it
can take months, drive you up a wall trying to find the point, or the
rhyme, or the perspective. And all that before you even try to tackle
a melody. But there was nothing like the feeling you got when you
got hold of a good idea.

While there was a deep satisfaction in adding a good song to your
catalogue, Howdy knew at least half the fun came in the actual writing. It was like life or taking a long drive—the journey itself meant
as much as the destination. It reminded Howdy of something somebody said one time about how chasing a dream is almost as much fun
as living it. And songs were like dreams, real and not real at the same
time, a version of reality that could reveal itself at any moment.

But you had to be paying attention.

Like the next time the door opened. A few more folks came in.
Howdy said, "Hey, how y'all doin'?" One guy wearing a John Deere
cap. Howdy'd seen a thousand of those in his life. The guy with him
was wearing a No Fear T-shirt. Howdy didn't think anything of it at
the time. But a minute later, one of the TV announcers said something about a guy in the stands giving a Bronx cheer over a dropped
pass. And a second after that, Howdy heard some guy call out for a
cold beer, and boom, just like that, Howdy had the idea for another
song.

Might start with a low swampy guitar rhythm, grow from there.
Howdy was thinking of J. J. Cale and John Fogerty and then the sly

groove of Commander Cody's version of "Hot Rod Lincoln." After eight or sixteen bars, the band might kick in, or maybe the instruments came in one at a time. Work that out later.

Cold beer, John Deere, no fear, Bronx cheer. He wrote it down.

Yeah, like that. A series of rhymes within the lines, each line about the variety of...what? People, places, and things Americana. Cold beer, John Deere, no fear, Bronx cheer. Covers a lot of ground fast, includes a lot of folks, coast to coast, border to border. How about Beale Street, Times Square, juke joint, state fair, homecoming, prom night, touchdown, title fight. He wrote it all down. It needed work—they all did—and something in between, a bridge to change it up and explain it, but it was a good start.

The door opened again. Two couples. Howdy looked up from his pad, said, "Hey, howyadoin'?"

27

EARLY MONDAY AFTERNOON, BOONE TATE SLIPPED HIS bowie knife and his .32 into his waistband and covered the grips with his shirttail. Then he walked to a nearby shopping center, stole a Ford Taurus, and headed for Fort Worth.

Foresight and preparation not being his strong suits, Brushfire still hadn't a clue what he would do when he got there. In fact, if all Slim and Howdy had done was to take the guitar and shoot his fridge, he might not even have bothered to go after them. But causing his arrest and the trouble that was flowing from that warranted retribution of a serious nature. But what, exactly? Gun 'em down in cold blood? If he thought he could get away with it, maybe. But if things went wrong, he knew that was the sort of trouble out of which it was hard to wiggle. The sort of trouble that might not be worth it. Maybe there was some other way to get their goats, maybe even some way that was profitable. Wouldn't that be nice?

As he drove out of Beaumont on I-10, Brushfire figured he had six hours in front of him to figure that out.

He got to Fort Worth around eight Monday night, found the Piggin' String in the phone book, and pulled into the parking lot just before nine. According to the sign by the door, Junior Hicks and his band were playing for the next week or so. No mention of Slim and Howdy. Still, this was his best lead, so he went in and took a seat at the bar.

As always, people stared when they saw him. His scarred face was one of those things people found it hard not to look at, like a car accident or Paris Hilton. Boone had two standard ways of dealing with this. Normally he'd get up in people's faces and cow them into an apology and a free drink. He'd raise his voice. "You want to see this? Huh? Here, take a closer look!" But not tonight. Couldn't afford to alienate anybody.

So he used his 9/11 story instead. Said he'd been with the New York Fire Department. Was at the Twin Towers. Saved a dozen people. Went back for more and got caught in a collapse. Had to be dragged out. Alive but scarred. People like to buy drinks for heroes, and they'll talk to 'em, too, tell them anything they want to know.

Skeets Duvall, among others, took Boone at his word. No reason not to. Had the bartender set him up, said, "Take care of him."

"That's all right," Boone said, waving a proud hand. "I got money."

Skeets shook his head. "It's no good here, friend."

"Mighty kind of you." He looked up at the tube. The Giants were thrashing the Redskins. He pointed at the replay of a touchdown, said, "That's what I'm talkin' about!" Like they were his hometown favorites.

An hour or so later, Skeets looked Boone in the eye and said, "Well, when that bull saw that monkey, he busted out of the shoot with me hanging on like dirty laundry. And you should've seen that monkey's face when he saw us comin'."

Boone faked a good laugh. Skeets's impression of that capuchin monkey was about the dumbest thing he'd ever seen. But he slapped the bar and shook his head and encouraged Skeets to do it just one more time. Brushfire knew people tended to like you even more if you laughed at their jokes.

A little later Junior Hicks and his band got up and started a lively set that got the house jumping. After the second or third song, Boone leaned over to Skeets and said, "These guys're all right. Singer kind of reminds me of my friend Slim who plays around these parts, or at least used to." He left it at that.

Skeets broke into a wide grin. "You mean Slim . . . out of Del Rio?" He pointed at his eyes. "Always wearin' sunglasses?"

"Yeah," Boone said. "Plays a real pretty Martin D-28."

Skeets slapped the bar. "Damn, son, you just missed him," he said. "Him and his buddy Howdy were playing here just a few days ago."

"Get out!"

"I swear."

"I'll be damned."

"Yeah," Skeets said. "They left here heading back to Del Rio, got a two-week gig at a place down there called the Lost and Found."

28

THE LOST AND FOUND WAS ABOUT TWICE AS LONG AS IT WAS wide, a big shoe box of a room with the stage at the far end. The main bar was along the long wall on one side, a second, smaller, bar was on the opposite wall toward the back. It was a big, open room with a pitched ceiling and exposed beams. The floor was smooth cedar planks covered with sawdust, peanut shells, and cigarette ash. Good for dancing.

By the middle of the third quarter, everybody had lost interest in the game. The Giants were spanking the Redskins like a child misbehaving at the grocery store. Jodie killed the sound but left the picture on the TV over the bar. She looked at Slim and said, "I believe you're up."

Slim sauntered onto the stage, adjusted the microphone to his height, and said, "Ev'nin' everybody. Welcome to the Lost and Found. My name's Slim and I'll be your entertainer this ev'nin'." He slung the guitar strap over his head and grinned like he was a waiter fixin' to tell them about the specials.

You'd never know by looking at him, but Slim was nervous as a frog on a busy road with a busted jumper. Always had been, couldn't help it. He'd been onstage hundreds of times and was never comfortable with it. His nerves twitched and jangled while his stomach knotted and churned. But he could wall it off, keep it hidden, using the dark glasses to create his façade of cowboy cool. You do what you can.

Slim paused and smiled at a table full of girls sitting near the stage. They smiled back. That always helped. As he started to pick something slow on the Martin, Slim looked out over the crowd, just over their heads, like he was trying to find something that wasn't in the notes he was playing. It was a simple melody and maybe not even that, just a vague melancholy pattern that repeated after so many bars while he talked over the top of it. A bittersweet vamp.

"It's good to be back in Del Rio," Slim said, prompting applause from the home crowd. "I'm not from here exactly but, back when I was a kid, I lived here for a few years. My dad, he worked down at Laughlin Air Force Base." He paused here to let the air force crowd give a hoot of recognition. He aimed the head of his guitar at them and said, "I'm sure a few of you will know what I'm talking about. I was about five or six, I guess, when we moved here. And one day I asked my dad what he did down there at the air force base, and he told me he was a jet pilot, one of the fastest in the world. And of course I believed him." Slim shook his head and smiled fondly as he continued playing the quiet acoustic bed that his words were laying on.

"He'd come home from work and tell me wild stories about being in dogfights at Mach three and all sorts of crazy stuff that I just loved to hear. I was wide-eyed and hangin' on every word outta his mouth. My mama, who had a thing about tellin' the truth, she'd fold her arms real tight, squintin' at him hard enough to crack walnuts, givin' him a look like he shouldn't be telling me stories like he was, but he didn't see the harm and Lord knows I didn't."

Slim did a little chord change and kept vamping, still quiet and sweet underneath it all. "Anyway it wasn't till years later that I found out some things about my dad. Among other things, it turned out he was a mechanic, not a pilot. But even when I found that out, I didn't care. Hell, I've seen a jet engine, and tell you the truth I think it's probably harder to fix one than it is to fly one."

Some of the air force guys gave a big shout of approval that made everybody laugh. Probably grease monkeys.

Slim slowed down his picking and grew more serious as he said, "Everything my dad got, he got by the sweat of his brow. Always showed up on time, never shirked a task. I can remember him saying sometimes that he felt like he was workin' overtime on a runaway train."

Slim stopped playing the guitar and let the last note fade. Nobody in the room made a sound. He stood tall and said, "He was a blue-collar guy, and he was my hero. Here's one I wrote for him. I hope you like it."

He gave it a second or two before he counted it down, "One-two-three!" And Slim ripped a rocking riff on those strings that sounded straight out of Bakersfield. He leaned into it and the crowd couldn't help but feel the goose bumps as Slim started singing, "He was a *hard*workin' man...wore a steel hard hat..."

The words struck a chord with everybody in the room, and his voice was an honest messenger. The riff was relentless and rollicking and it drew a dozen dancers to the floor like they believed the only way to live was burnin' the candle at both ends. Slim fed off their energy and they fed off his and every line in the song seemed like it was the true story of somebody in the place. Anybody who'd ever struggled to make ends meet and everybody who'd gotten real good at barely gettin' by.

Slim got 'em worked up and then he let 'em work it out on the dance floor, stomping a boot to keep the beat. Those not dancing were tapping their toes and drumming on the table tops. Slim repeated the chorus one more time before bringing it to a close. After the last chord, the crowd gave it up for him, big time. Cheers rattled the rafters. "Thank you! Appreciate that," he said, with a nod. They were still yelling when he continued, "Long as we're on the subject, let's do one from brother Merle. Here's 'Workin' Man Blues.'" And off he went.

For all the nerves and acid and knots in his stomach, Slim pulled it off one set after another, all night long, the way he'd done all his life. He mixed originals with covers of everybody from Buck Owens to Leon Russell to Hank Thompson. And, as usual, he had girls waiting on him every time he walked off the stage.

29

END OF THE NIGHT, AFTER SLIM FINISHED HIS SETS AND Jodie had given last call and turned the lights up to chase the stragglers out, Howdy put the cash box on the bar and started stacking chairs upside down on the tabletops. Slim was in a booth in the back having a beer with the blonde cutie in the Arizona Cardinals T-shirt when the door opened and a man walked in.

He headed straight for the bar, as if he expected to be served this time of night with the bright lights on and Howdy stacking the chairs. The guy's face was harder than getting the truth out of a senator, but he was dressed fine, not like some thug. He wore a tailored leather jacket, a tan wide-brim hat, and fancy ostrich boots. Boots to kill for. He had broad shoulders and not much room in the sleeves due to all the muscle. Except for his determined strut, he didn't seem like any trouble, though he looked capable of it.

"Sorry friend," Howdy said. "We're closing up."

"No problem." The guy waved him off like Howdy was new in town or mistaken and kept heading for the bar where the cash box sat. That's when Howdy saw the gun under the guy's jacket. Nine millimeter from the looks of it. Howdy stayed cool, put another chair on a table, and tried to catch Slim's eye to get a little help. He snapped his fingers and waved a hand in the air, but Slim was busy reading the girl's palm at the moment, no doubt explaining how that little branch off her lifeline meant that her future involved the horizontal two-step with a tall musical stranger wearing sunglasses.

Since it wasn't Howdy's style to interfere with another man's love life unless absolutely necessary, he figured he'd deal with this himself. He maneuvered around to a blind spot and started walking up behind the man, who was standing at the bar now, right by the cash box, real casual, like he was waiting for something he was entitled to.

Jodie was nowhere to be seen. She'd stepped to the back room for a minute. If she came out now, she'd be faced with this guy out of the blue. Howdy figured she had her gun with her, but the guy with the 9 mm would have the element of surprise.

Jodie walked through the door a second later. The moment the guy shifted his attention to her, Howdy took two quick steps, jerked the guy's jacket open, and snatched his gun. When the guy turned around, more than a little surprised, Howdy had Jodie's .22 and the 9 mm aimed where it counted. "I guess you didn't hear me," Howdy repeated. "We're closed."

At the precise moment Howdy made his heroic move, Slim and the girl reached the front door and were fixin' to slip out. But the action caught Slim's attention and he paused long enough to say, "Howdy, you got this one?"

"Yeah," Howdy said. "I got it."

"Good man," Slim said as he pushed the door open and ushered the blonde Cardinals fan toward the parking lot.

The guy smiled at Howdy, real friendly, not threatened in the least. His hands went up to disarm the situation. "Like I said, friend, no problem."

Jodie said, "Howdy, it's okay."

The guy's expression didn't change. Didn't get smug all the sudden now that Jodie was vouching for him. Just waited for the air to clear.

"You sure?" Howdy said.

"Yeah, I'm sorry," Jodie insisted. "I should've told you he was coming. This is Duke. He works for my uncle."

"Okay," Howdy said. "My mistake." He spun the 9 mm around and held it out, grip first. "No hard feelings."

"We're good," Duke said, taking his gun. "I'm sure Roy'll be glad to know somebody's got Jodie's back." He slipped the gun into its holster and turned to Jodie with a certain amount of expectation.

She reached under the bar, retrieved an envelope, and handed it to Duke. "Tell him I said hey."

"Will do," Duke said as he slipped the envelope inside his coat.

"And I'm sorry about all this," she said. "This is Howdy's first night in town."

Duke turned to Howdy and held out his hand. "Welcome to Del Rio." He nodded toward Jodie. "Take good care of her."

"Thanks," Howdy said, shaking Duke's hand. "I will."

Duke tipped his hat and left in the same businesslike manner as he had arrived.

30

HOWDY WAS ABOUT TO STACK THE LAST FEW CHAIRS ON THE last table in the place when Jodie said, "Whoa, cowboy, leave those down." She slid half a bottle of good tequila onto the bar. "That is, if you got time for a drink."

Howdy glanced over at the bottle and said, "Twist my arm."

Jodie hopped up on the bar, butt first, all that turquoise and silver jewelry jangling. She spun on her seat pockets, swinging her legs around, then dropped her boots onto the plank floor, her hands aloft like a gymnast coming off the balance beam.

"Nice dismount," Howdy said, admiring her ... everything.

And don't think she didn't notice as she grabbed the bottle, a lime, and two shot glasses before joining Howdy at the table where he was holding a chair for her. "Thank you, sir." She pulled a pocketknife from her jeans and sat down. "How you like the Lost and Found so far?" She popped a blade from the knife and started slicing wedges of lime.

Howdy sat down and said, "Great place." He licked his hand and sprinkled some salt on the wet spot. "Ya done good."

"Thanks. I'm glad you like it." Jodie poured a couple of shots, salted her hand, and held her glass up. "Your health."

"Back atcha," Howdy said, clinking his glass to hers.

They licked the salt, shot the tequila, and bit the lime like a couple of pros. "Whew!" Jodie made a face as she set her glass on the table. "Mmm that's good," she said.

Howdy was licking tequila from his mustache when Slim came

sauntering back in. He stopped just inside the door and held his arms out wide, saying, "Well, I'm livin' proof you can take the girl out of the honky-tonk but you can't make her take you home and get nekkid."

Jodie laughed as Howdy started to sing, "You can't...always get...what you want."

Jodie pointed at the door and said, "Throw the deadbolt on that." She aimed another finger at the bar. "Then grab a glass and join us."

"Don't mind if I do." As Slim crossed the room in his long, loping strides, he said, "Girl swore she had to get up early and go to work tomorrow. You believe that?"

"It *is* Tuesday," Jodie pointed out.

Slim acted like that didn't count for much. He said, "Well what's wrong with callin' in sick? Or just being a couple hours late?" He picked up an extra lime, long as he was at the bar, then he crossed to the table. "It's not like I was asking her to quit her job."

"Hey." Jodie leaned back in her chair with her hand on top of her hat and said, "What happened to all that reverence you had for the workin' man?" She jerked her thumb in Slim's direction before she realized he was already standing next to her and she was pointing south of his big belt buckle. "That don't extend to workin' women?"

Slim looked down toward his zipper and said, "Are you kiddin'? That definitely extends toward workin' women. That's why I wanted her to—" Slim paused, looked at Jodie who had him fixed with a look. "Oh, you meant the reverence, sorry." He sat down, did the salt, and they clinked glasses. "To workin' women," Slim said.

Jodie winked at him. "Amen to that."

Their empty glasses hit the table simultaneously.

Jodie said to Slim, "You sounded good tonight. I really like that one you did about bein' on the Hurt Train."

"Thanks," Slim said with a smile. "Wrote that with a friend of mine."

"It's a good one," Howdy said as he started slicing the second lime while Jodie poured another round.

"By the way," Slim said. "Who was that fella you were disarming in here earlier? I noticed you let him go."

"That was Duke," Jodie said. "Works for my uncle Roy."

"Oh." Slim nodded as if that explained it all. He turned toward Howdy and said, "Lemme ask you, after you took his gun, did you keep it or throw it away?"

Howdy shrugged as he lapsed into an imitation of Barney Fife. He brushed a finger under his nose and said, "Well, a man comes in after hours with a 9 mm and fails to identify himself, I just naturally spring into action." He gave Barney's trademark sniff and held his hands out in a silly karate pose.

Still half-embarrassed about the incident, Jodie put a hand to her face and said, "Sorry, I should've told you he was coming."

Howdy tipped his hat way back on his head. "Don't worry about me." He sniffed again and made a few silly karate moves with his hands. "My whole body's a weapon."

Slim said, "Hey, that's a pretty good Gomer Pyle."

"It's Barney Fife."

"Oh," Slim said. "Well, if that's Barney Fife, and if the guy earlier was Duke, then who the hell is this Uncle Roy?"

Jodie leaned back in her chair again and gestured around the room. "Uncle Roy is the man who made all this possible."

Slim and Howdy nodded as though they both had an uncle Roy themselves which, of course, neither one of them did. But after a second, Howdy held up his glass and said, "Well, then, a toast to Uncle Roy."

Slim shrugged, "Why not?"

Hoisting their shot glasses they all said, "Uncle Roy!" in unison, then drank their shots and bit their lime wedges.

Since the beginning, Howdy had assumed there was money in the envelope that Jodie had handed to Duke and, further, he assumed it was a cash payment of the under-the-table variety. But for what, he wondered. Protection? Was this Duke guy muscle for the local mob? Was Uncle Roy the head of organized crime in Val Verde County? Somebody had to be. Still, Howdy wasn't going to say anything about the transaction since it wasn't any of his business. But at the same time, he was too curious—some would say nosey—not to say something, so he said, "Not that it's any of my business, but is this like a real uncle, or a nudge-nudge, wink-wink kind of uncle?" Figured he could get in the back door asking this way.

Jodie gave him a funny look, only part of which could be blamed on the tequila. She said, "What?"

"I mean is 'uncle' a euphemism for something?" Howdy knew she'd been broke after Frank died, so he couldn't help but wonder how she'd come into possession of a fine honky-tonk like the Lost and Found. He was just wondering if this Uncle Roy was a loan shark or maybe just a sugar daddy of some sort.

"Nooo," Jodie said, slapping Howdy's arm. "He's my dad's brother. He's also my godfather, thank you very much." Then she slapped him again, just for good measure.

31

A SECOND LATER, JODIE WAS EXPLAINING HOW SHE'D BEEN forced to sell the Beer Thirty after Frank died. "By the time I paid off all the hospital bills I was so broke I couldn't pay attention, you know? When Uncle Roy found out, being my *godfather*," she said, slapping Howdy again, "he offered to help, said he wanted to buy the Lost and Found but needed a partner he could trust to manage it. Asked if I was interested." Jodie shrugged at her inevitable decision. "I had experience, and I sure wasn't going to find any better work in Lawton, so I moved." She gestured at the bar. "Duke drops by every night to pick up Uncle Roy's portion of the cash proceeds." She smiled and gave a slightly naughty wink. "He doesn't like to involve the IRS where he can avoid it."

Slim nodded, said, "Figures they've got better things to do."

"Exactly, like chasing after Willie Nelson."

"That's damn considerate of old Uncle Roy." Howdy held up his glass, about to make a toast to Willie's fabled tax problems, but he stopped and said, "You think Uncle Roy'd like a nephew? 'Cause I'm available."

"Already has one," Jodie said, thumping a fist on the tabletop. "My brother Grady."

"Oh, that's right," Howdy said. "I forgot all about him." Howdy seemed to search his memory banks for whatever information he had on Grady. After a second, he said, "He's got some sort of respectable job, doesn't he?"

"Oh, hell no," Jodie said. "He's a lawyer, here in Del Rio."

Slim knew about Grady but he'd never laid eyes on the man. He said, "You know, as many times as I've played here, I don't think I ever met your brother."

"No, he doesn't get over this way very often," Jodie said, shaking her head. "So you probably didn't meet." There was something in her tone that gave the impression they weren't the closest of siblings. But at the same time, it didn't sound like there was any real animosity between them, as indicated by the fact that she didn't refer to him as her "sorry-assed excuse for a brother" or words along those lines. If anything, there seemed to be a shade of regret in her voice when she said, "We don't actually see each other that much. He's always traveling for work, you know, pretty busy." Like she was making excuses for him.

"Still," Slim said, trying to put a sweet spin on things, "it's good having family around, even if some of 'em are lawyers."

Jodie answered with a shrug and a bittersweet smile.

They made an awkward toast to kin before Howdy motioned at Jodie and said, "You know, speaking of family and other personal details"—he used his shot glass to direct her attention across the table—"I been riding with Slim here for damn near a week and I can't get him to tell me a thing about himself."

"Really?" Jodie touched the oval turquoise pendant of her necklace, as if she were half-listening and half-thinking of something else. "Nothing?"

Howdy shook his head. "Nope. Every time I try, he makes a Dr. Phil joke and clams up like it's all classified information." He leaned toward Jodie, biting his lower lip in a way that was both confiding and accusing, and said, "But tonight he gets up onstage and shares tender moments of his childhood with a room full of complete strangers." Howdy picked up a lime wedge as he shook his head. "I mean, how do you think that makes me feel?"

"You poor thing." Jodie offered mock sympathy to go with Howdy's mock distress. "I just think Slim's a private person and you need to respect that." She rubbed her hand on Slim's forearm. He nodded appreciatively. "But I tell you," she said. "I know for a fact that if you get him liquored up enough he'll talk like a beauty parlor full of women."

"Is that right?"

"Oh yeah. All night long."

Howdy looked at the lime wedge pinched between his thumb and index finger. He rotated it like a roast on a vertical spit before he touched one end down on the table like he was playing flick football. He aimed it at Slim.

Slim just naturally made a goalpost with his fingers and thumbs.

"Three seconds left," Howdy said in a play-by-play voice. "It's a forty-yard field-goal attempt for the win." Howdy flicked the lime wedge with his middle finger, then thrust his hands in the air. "Iiiiit's gooood!"

Jodie, feeling fuzzier by the moment, shot to her feet in a one-woman wave. "Wooooo!"

Slim watched the lime wedge sail past and land on the floor behind him. "Nice kick, Dr. Phil." He retrieved the fruit, wiped off the sawdust, teed it up, and said, "All right, you wanna know something? Whaddya wanna know?"

Jodie poured another round and drank hers without waiting for the boys.

Howdy made a goalpost. "Well, like why didn't you tell me you grew up here?"

"You didn't ask." Slim flicked the lime. The kick was good. He held his fist out and Howdy bumped it with his own, as if to say, "Good one."

The five shots of tequila had Jodie suddenly feeling like one of the Dallas Cowboy cheerleaders. She did another one-woman wave. "Woooooo!" Then she poured another round, like a hole in the head.

"I'm asking now," Howdy said, reaching for the lime on the floor behind him, just out of his range. "Whoa!" He nearly fell over trying to reach it.

"New ball!" Jodie said. "New ball!" and tossed a fresh lime wedge at Howdy, who was laughing at how drunk she seemed to be getting.

"Asking now's too late, isn't it?" Slim said. "I mean, you already know, right? There's no reason to tell you again, unless you just like hearing the story."

"You're missing the point," Howdy said, teeing up his lime for the kick. "I'm talking about the nature of conversation here. Two people traveling together, heading for a small town, and it turns out one of them has a history with the place? Just seems like it would be natural for a person to bring that up in conversation."

While Slim held the goalpost for Howdy's kick, he looked at Jodie and said, "You've known him longer than me. He always talk this much?"

She gave a pained expression and nodded, keeping one eye on Howdy as he prepared to flick his lime. She was thinking about attempting a block.

Howdy lined up his fruit and flicked it. "The kick's away," he said. "It looks good. It's drifting a little. It's . . ."

Slim shook his head and said, "Wide right." He gave an official signal.

Howdy's head jerked back. "What?!" He rubbed his eyes and said, "Are you blind?"

Slim shook his head. "Wide right." He gave the signal again.

Jodie did another one-woman wave. "Wooooooo!"

"Are you outta your rabbit-assed mind? That was right down the middle."

"I call 'em like I see 'em," Slim said.

"Yeah? Well you see 'em like Ronnie Milsap."

Jodie grabbed her glass and held it up, spilling tequila on the table as she said, "Ronnie Milsap!"

Slim and Howdy looked at her and cracked up as Jodie wobbled in her chair. They clinked her glass, and downed the shot before Slim made the official signal again and said, "It's still wide right."

Howdy poked Jodie in the arm, said, "You know those cameras you installed? Can we use 'em for instant replay?"

They carried on like this for another hour or so, Jodie occasionally doing the wave before she finally came to a rest and said, "You know, as much fun as it is sitting here watching y'all flick fruit at each other, I think it's time we called it a night."

"And maybe a cab too," Howdy said.

"But first . . ." Jodie poured one last round for everybody. She looked at them and said, "It sure is nice to have you two here." She picked up her glass for a final toast. "To a fun couple of weeks."

Slim and Howdy said it together, "To a fun couple of weeks."

Little did they know the fun was only going to last for one.

32

LATE THE PREVIOUS NIGHT, IN THE PARKING LOT OF THE Piggin' String, Boone Tate stole a set of plates off another Ford Taurus and swapped 'em with the plates off the one he'd stolen in Beaumont. He got an hour out of town, then pulled into a rest stop for the night.

He got a late start Tuesday afternoon, stopped in San Antonio around five, went to a place he knew with a two-for-one drink special and free snacks. A couple of hours later he was headed west with a good buzz and a pocket full of chicken wings.

Boone got to Del Rio around nine Tuesday night. He knew the town well enough to drive straight to the Lost and Found. Got out there and saw Slim's and Howdy's names on the sign out front, but he didn't go in. He stayed in the Taurus. Didn't want to tip his hand. Wanted to figure out how he was going to make those two pay for the trouble they'd caused him before they knew he was there.

Boone sat there awhile, thinking. He knew the woman who ran the place, that Jodie Lee. He remembered her from when he used to live here. He never liked the way she looked at him. Like she felt sorry for him, like he was pitiful, and that chapped him good.

Boone started coughing and he hocked one out the window as he let his foot off the brake and pulled slowly out of the parking lot. He doubled back toward town and pulled into the lot at Diablo's Cantina. He stayed in his car again, looking at the front door with a mix of nostalgia and spite. He thought about going in—just to see their faces—but he wasn't sure if that restraining order was still in effect, so he decided against.

He was about to drive away when the front doors of Diablo's blew open and spit out these two big Mexicans along with an even larger Anglo who very quickly gave the impression of being mostly about brute force. Boone watched them swagger into the parking lot, getting ready to face off. Looked like they had ten or fifteen years in the prison yard between them. The fight was brutal. The hulking Anglo, who was known to police as Lloyd Brickman, aka Bricks, worked the two Mexicans over pretty good at first, but they got in their share of shots toward the end. Nobody walked away clean.

Eventually, Bricks stopped and spit a bloody tooth at his opponents. He huffed, then turned and walked off like he just remembered he had better things to do.

The two weary Mexicans caught their breath and limped back inside.

As Boone watched Lloyd Brickman lurch toward the main road, he had an idea, or at least part of one. Whatever he ended up doing to Slim and Howdy, it couldn't hurt to have some muscle and/or a fall guy. He pulled the Taurus alongside the lumbering brute and said, "Need a ride?"

Bricks leaned his cinder block of a head toward the window, blood trailing down the side of his face. He shook his head and said, "Need a drink."

"Hop in, I'm buyin'."

They went to a rundown watering hole under an overpass near the river, place called Whiskey Under the Bridge, a bar of last resort, a stinking joint swarming with tattooed miscreants and feral-eyed thugs.

Boone and Bricks fit right in. They sat at a table in a dark corner with two glasses and a pint of cheap whiskey. Turned out Bricks had just finished doing a nickel at Huntsville for a failed extortion scheme. "Just walked in, told the manager my partner was holding his wife hostage," Bricks said. "He popped that safe right open. I figured worse charge they could get me on was unarmed robbery." He shrugged. "You know, since I didn't have a gun or a partner." He shook his head like he still couldn't believe he got caught. "Seemed like a good idea at the time."

"Yeah," Boone said, "that's a good plan. Damn good."

"Yeah, except for the five years."

"Well, yeah, except for that." The scheme had given him an idea. Boone poured another glass of whiskey and said, "Maybe it just needs the edges smoothed a little."

"Might be."

Boone nodded, then drained his glass before he said, "So, I'm just thinking…"

"'Bout what?"

"A little business proposition."

The guy gulped his whiskey. "I'm listenin'."

33

IT WAS BUSINESS AS USUAL FOR THE REST OF THE WEEK. During the day Howdy hung around the Lost and Found, working on songs when he wasn't helping Jodie with one thing or another. He'd be hooking up a fresh keg or something when a lyric would occur to him, like on Tuesday afternoon when he turned to Jodie and said, "Can you think of anything that rhymes with Talladega?"

Slim helped out around the bar, too, except one afternoon when he took the truck and went across to Mexico, said he was just going over to do some sightseeing, by which Howdy figured he meant he was going for a stroll down memory lane, which he was, but there was no call for him to explain that, so he didn't.

Duke was the only constant. Showed up every night to collect Uncle Roy's envelope. Never had a drink, never made small talk, always polite, strictly business.

Tuesday night was typical. These three young bucks showed up, tails up and stingers out. Hardworking types ready for some middle-of-the-week fun. And why not? They'd started with a little sundown buzz, probably sucked down a forty on the drive into town and smoked a little of that homegrown too. By the time they hit the Lost and Found they'd doubled their personality and couldn't wait for some excitement. Figured if it didn't happen on its own, they'd do their best to make some.

They were shooting pool and shooting shit, drunker and louder by the hour. One of 'em, by the name of Bobby Earl, took to grousing about how he was always the best dressed but his buddy J.C. somehow always ended up with the prettiest girl. Wasn't fair, he said. J.C. just shrugged and asked what fair had to do with anything. Wasn't his fault he had that Eastwood grin. That Tulare swagger. Chicks dig it. You ought to get you some, he said.

Slim was up on the stage, just finishing a tender-sweet ballad he had written, not classic country, whatever that is, but something more in the realm of Willis Alan Ramsey than Bob Wills. It was a medium-slow acoustic ballad fueled by sadness, wisdom, and chord changes that made you close your eyes and believe this was the truth. It ended after a dramatic pause with the song's lyrical hook, which Slim rendered in his most wounded tenor: "Sometimes the heart heals faster than others...but there's alwaaays...a little...scar."

Just as the crowd was giving it up for the brokenhearted singer and his song, J.C.'s friend Billy got into it with this spunky—if somewhat undersized—cowboy who had something dumb to say that he would soon have to regret. One thing led to another, and before anybody knew it, Billy threw a punch and, *bam,* that cowboy's lights went out.

In an attempt to keep things from going bad to worse, as they tend to in circumstances like this, Slim hopped off the stage to help Howdy escort the boys roughly from the club. Left them out in the parking lot arguing about whether they ought to (a) go back in there and kick some ass, (b) go to that place down the road where Ricky and the Redstreaks were playing, or (c) head over to Cotton-Eyed Joe's for ladies' night. They finally settled on the latter but didn't get a mile down the road before they got pulled over by a Val Verde County constable who seemed intent on asking a series of embarrassing questions, the answers to which were both obvious and incriminating.

Wednesday night was different. It was the first time there was reason for anybody to think there might be trouble on the horizon. Problem was, no one noticed the two men sitting in the truck in the far corner of the Lost and Found's parking lot.

They were Mutt and Jeff on many levels. The older, smaller guy had to be considered the Boss Man, the brains of the outfit. That made the much larger guy the Big Goon. He did what the Boss Man said, but he didn't like having to do so.

The two of them had been out there watching a while, seeing who came and went, generally figuring things out.

At one point the two men saw this guy walk some big-hipped beauty out to her car for some sweet talk followed by what they figured was a little begging and a couple of hollow promises that didn't seem to be getting him very far.

After the girl deftly blocked a series of the guy's moves, Boss Man said, "Gotta hand it to that boy, he doesn't give up easy."

The Big Goon was unimpressed by the guy's gentle methods. He said, "Shit, it was me? I'd just thow the bitch in the backseat and bust a nut."

Boss Man gave the Big Goon a disapproving glance. "Yes, I s'pect you would."

The Big Goon sniggered while he thought things through. "Hell yeah," he said. "I'd stick my head up under that girl's T-shirt and see what's what. Just put my nose in between 'em and go—" He shook his bulbous head back and forth like a dog with a wet snake in its mouth making slobbery sounds with his rubbery lips. He laughed and said, "Hell yeah, I like me some big ones."

Even though the Boss Man was having similar, which is not to say identical, thoughts, he came off with an air of superiority when he said, "Shut up."

The Big Goon didn't like being told to shut up, especially by someone so much smaller than him, but he was stuck. He'd made his bed, as the Boss Man tended to point out on a regular basis, and now he had to sleep in it. Maybe he'd beat the crap out of him after their deal was over. *That'd* shut him up.

It was moments like this when doubt crept in and gave the Boss Man second thoughts about his whole idea. No, he thought, correcting himself, the idea itself was a good one. Solid gold. Easy money.

What gave him the second thoughts was his choice of partner or, as a district attorney might say in an indictment, his accomplice. There was no doubt he needed someone to do the actual deed. And while he knew the big, scary son of a bitch could pull off the physical aspects of the crime, there was always the distinct possibility he would screw up something else, something unforeseeable in its idiocy, something so pig-ignorant that no amount of planning could prevent it.

"What if she tries to get rough?" the Big Goon said.

"Do what you have to," the Boss Man said. "Short of killing her." As soon as he said this, he was hit with another wave of doubt. But, he reminded himself, he'd made his bed and now he had to sleep in it. If he tried to back out now, the big knucklehead would probably try to do it on his own, get caught, and roll over on him in a deal with the prosecutor. Jesus, he needed a drink. But first he wanted to go over things one more time in the hope that it would make a difference. He slapped the dashboard and said, "Let's get outta here, check her house one more time."

The Big Goon shook his head. "How many damn times're we gonna go through this shit?"

"As many times as I say."

"Hell, this ain't exactly brain surgery. All I gotta do is—"

"It's a got-damn federal crime," the Boss Man said between clenched teeth. "And you're not a two-time loser because you were so *scrupulous* in planning your previous escapades. Now start the got-damn truck and let's go check her house one more time."

The Big Goon keyed the ignition and mumbled, "You ain't exactly one to be talking about scruples."

The Boss Man gritted his teeth. He didn't want to explain the difference between the two words, so he said, "Just...drive."

34

THE OTHER NOTEWORTHY EVENT THAT WEEK HAPPENED around ten Thursday night when a guy, somewhere in his early forties, Slim guessed, walked in wearing a classic western suit consisting of a chestnut jacket with brown suede front yokes and drop-arrow detailing, a tan felt hat, and a gleaming silver bolo with the initials GH in raised gold letters. It was the first time Slim could recall seeing anybody wearing a suit in the Lost and Found, but that's not what made it noteworthy.

The guy gave Slim a slight nod and tried to walk right past him without paying the cover charge. Slim thought that was pretty cheeky since he figured it was plenty obvious that he was sitting there for the sole purpose of taking money from people, not to mention the large sign printed in perfectly good English that said it cost five bucks to get in the club. Slim held his arm out like a warning gate at a railroad crossing, said, "Just a second, Slick." He used a thumb to point at the sign but the guy didn't bother to look at it. He just stood there looking past Slim, toward the bar.

"Five bucks to get in," Slim said, aiming his dark glasses at the suit.

"Hmmm? What?" Now he looked at Slim and said, "No." He waved to Jodie and said, "I'm Jodie's brother."

Slim turned and saw Jodie waving at the guy like he was the sort of family that you didn't want to kill, at least not yet. Slim pointed at him and said, "You're the lawyer."

"Guilty," he replied. "Grady Hobbs." They shook hands. He pulled a business card from his pocket and gave it to Slim. "Pleasure's mine. Give me a call if you find yourself in legal trouble."

Slim gave a noncommittal nod. "Well, let's hope it doesn't come to that," he said, letting Grady pass. Still, he stuck the card in his pocket thinking that you just never know.

Jodie came out from behind the bar to greet her brother. She looked pleasantly surprised, but surprised nonetheless. She gave him a warm hug before stepping back to get a look at him. "You look great," she said, as if he usually didn't. "What brings you in here all dressed up?"

Grady put on a face like his feelings were hurt by the implications of everything coming out of her mouth. He said, "A man needs a reason to visit his sister's place of business?"

Jodie was tempted to make a snarky comment about how he hadn't been to the club more than two or three times since she took over the place and how he never even seemed to have time to meet her for lunch and how he always had an excuse for not accepting her invitations to Sunday dinner, but she held her tongue, gestured at the bar, and said, "Well, it's good to see you. Can I get you something?"

"How 'bout a Shiner Bock," he said, mounting a bar stool and reaching for his wallet.

She slid a cold one in front of him. "On the house."

"Thanks, sis." He tipped it in her direction, took a pull on it, then looked around the club and gestured with the neck of the bottle. "Business looks good," he said.

"Stayin' above water," Jodie said. "How about you?" She gestured at his suit. "You look like you're prospering."

"Can't complain," he shrugged. "Busy enough to keep the wolves from the door." He pointed at her as if he hadn't planned on mentioning it, but it had just dawned on him to say, "Fact, I'm heading up to Abilene tomorrow, take a bunch of depositions in this big class-action suit I filed against a pharmaceutical manufacturer."

From the corner of her eye, Jodie noticed a crowd gathering at the bar. "Hold that thought," she said. "I gotta go serve some drinks." She held up her finger to put Grady on pause. "Be right back."

Grady didn't miss a beat. He just turned to his right and engaged the stranger sitting next to him as though he would naturally be interested in hearing about his grand adventures in jurisprudence. "You mighta heard about this case on the news," Grady said, as if CNN had been all over this thing from the start. "Yeah, the damn president of the company knew from the get-go that the stuff caused kidney damage. You believe that shit?" Grady talked about how he'd probably be up in Abilene half of next week deposing witnesses and how he figured the settlement would end up in the range of fifty or sixty million dollars, not that he'd get all of it, of course, there were other attorneys involved, but his percentage was enough to make him waggle his hand. And yada yada yada.

Jodie listened to her brother with a mixture of amusement and recognition as she put up three drafts, two bourbons, and a margarita. Grady had always been a big talker. Had the same fondness for promise and disregard for delivery as a six-term senator. At fifteen, when he could finally jump high enough to touch the basketball rim, Grady swore he could dunk. And people believed him. He should've run for office. Jodie wasn't sure if all the big talk stemmed from insecurity or if Grady just liked to bullshit people because he was good at it.

The guy sitting next to Grady asked if he could somehow get in on the class-action suit, but then he added that he was just joking. Grady handed the guy a card and said, "Listen, you ever need a good lawyer, give me a call."

Jodie was drawing a pitcher of beer just as Howdy was finishing his second set with a song about a guy who gave up his job on a gas pipeline to go chasing a girl across the country in a westerly direction, which was a theme in more than one of Howdy's compositions. Over the applause that followed, Howdy said, "Thanks, y'all, that's one of mine called, 'Baby, When Your Heart Breaks Down.'" He propped his guitar in the stand, said he was going to take a short break, and headed over to the bar where Jodie introduced him to Grady.

"Hey, we were talking about you just the other night," Howdy said with enthusiasm.

"Uh-oh," Grady said. "Probably complaining about what a bad little brother I am."

Howdy waved that off. "No, she was saying she wished she got to see you more often. Said you're pretty busy with your work so it was hard for the two of you to hook up."

"Yeah, well that's all true enough," Grady said with a smile. "But here I am."

"Sure enough." Howdy slapped the bar. "Let me buy you a drink and get you to tell me some stories on your sister."

"Nothing I'd rather do," Grady said. "But I've got to get out of town at o-dark-thirty tomorrow morning. Gotta be in Abilene by ten, so if you don't mind, I'm gonna take a rain check on the drink." He slid off the stool and handed one of his cards to Howdy, said, "But listen, you call me if you ever need a good lawyer."

Jodie saw Grady preparing to make his exit. She said, "You can't leave, you just got here." She came out from behind the bar, knowing that he was leaving no matter what she said.

"I tell you what," Grady said, giving her a peck on the cheek. "I'll see you as soon as I get back from Abilene. We'll go out to dinner. My treat. I promise."

35

"THE EAGLE FLIES ON FRIDAY," JODIE SAID, QUOTING T-BONE Walker. She glanced at her watch. "Happy hour starts at four."

And by five-thirty everybody feels like money to burn and nothing to lose.

Better hang on to your hat.

Weekends at the Lost and Found. Time to let it rip and roar. Didn't matter if you'd spent the last five days working an oil rig or cooped up in a home or an office cubicle, all work and no play sucked. And when you *do* step out, it don't matter if you're high-rollin' or honky-tonkin', long as you're out.

There were low-cut dresses, knee-high boots, and tight jeans to be wiggled into and back out of later. If all went well, somebody might even be there to help. Lots of friendly people at the Lost and Found. There were drinks to be drunk. Rugs to be cut. Stick a whole roll of quarters in the boogie box, son, turn up the heat. Put a buzz in the joint.

"Let's get this thing rockin'!" were the first words Howdy heard come out of the mouth of the guy who walked in wearing a Can't We All Just Get a Bong? T-shirt. His buddy, trailing right behind, figured he was going to impress the chicks with his Git-R-Done hat and his ability to do the majority of Larry the Cable Guy's stand-up routine. Hey, it had worked before.

Howdy was on the door, checking IDs. Cover charge didn't kick in until later. Bong Boy and Git-R-Done were both old enough so Howdy just smiled and let 'em in, told 'em to have some fun. Thinking about his own younger, dumber days.

Slim was back in Jodie's office with his guitar and a legal pad, working on a song. It was an idea that had been percolating since the day he and Howdy pulled into Del Rio and stopped for gas at the Truck 'n' Go Quicky Stop. Slim had noticed this guy climbing down from the cab of his Kenworth, looked like he'd been on the road forever. Kidneys sore from too much coffee, back knotted like a rope. Then he pulled a picture from his shirt pocket and looked at it. He smiled and it was like dark clouds lifting off his face.

Slim didn't have to see who was in the picture to know there was a song in it. He figured the guy had deadheaded down from Tulsa or maybe Little Rock. His baby wanted him back home and he'd been in the fast lane since the last toll gate, haulin' nothing but high hopes and thin air. "Eighteen wheels singing home sweet home" was one of the lyrics he was working with. "For too many days, he'd been on the road, missing her more with every load, goin' broke one white line at a time." Yeah, it was coming together, but he still needed a title.

Out in the main room, Jodie and the rest of the staff were slinging hooch and wings and whatnot left and right. It was a thirsty crowd heading for a good night.

Later, at the front door, Howdy popped up straight and brushed his mustache when these four hotties came in, must've been around nine o'clock. Looked like they'd been locked up in an office all week pushing papers and somebody was going to have to pay for it on the dance floor tonight. A pack of she-cat tigers coming out of the cage, as it were.

Howdy allowed as how he was going to use his doorman's discretion to let the ladies in without a cover charge. "But I'm gonna have to see your driver's licenses," he said, tilting his hat at an authoritative angle. "Make sure you're not too young to be up in a place like this."

Well, you can't hardly find a woman who doesn't like to hear that she might look too young for anything, so Howdy immediately had one leg up with these ladies. And by the time he'd memorized all their names and told them the first round was on him, well, both legs.

Around ten, the girl of Arizona Cardinals T-shirt fame showed up straining the pearl snaps on a snazzy western shirt. In addition to that she was wearing a pair of old jeans and a willing smile. She paid the cover and drifted past Howdy, listening to her tall, mysterious troubadour who was up on the stage now playing a tender one at that very moment. As if he knew she was there.

"I like your shirt," Howdy said as she headed for the bar.

To Slim's credit he remembered her face and name pretty quickly, even without the distorted Cardinals logo staring at him. Just something about her. Next break, she said she'd hang around if that was all right. Slim insisted. Put her on his tab. Played her some songs. Shared her table between sets. Felt a firm squeeze on his thigh. Bingo. Give that man a cigar. Or maybe he was just happy to see her.

While all that was unfolding, Howdy bought a couple more rounds for the table of she-tigers, even stopped by their table once with a complimentary plate of nachos. Couldn't stay long though, he said. Had to get back to the door. But maybe later. Go to Mexico, one of those crazy all-night joints, something like that. Hell yeah. They were game.

End of the night, turning up the lights, Jodie slapped the bar the way she always did and said to the stragglers, "You ain't gotta go home but you *gotta* get outta here."

Slim was about to leave with Brianna, which turned out to be her name. Moved here from Phoenix two months ago. Renting a place up on Devil's Lake to which Slim had just been invited. He needed to borrow the truck to follow her out there, but Howdy had the keys and he was nowhere to be seen.

Jodie said she saw him heading for the parking lot, not two minutes ago.

Slim found him out there in the midst of the she-tigers and he called out, "Howdy, you gonna need the truck?"

Howdy tossed him the keys. "Nope." He put his arms around two of the tigers and said, "I got a ride . . . or two."

Brianna just had to ask, "Where're y'all going?"

Howdy shook his head like the whole thing was a shame and a sin but he had to tell the truth about it. "I wanted to go to Mexico," he said. "But the girls here have badgered me until I agreed to go back to their apartment to play a little strip poker." He reached to his pocket and showed Dempsey Kimble's deck of cards. "You two wanna come?"

Slim smiled and shook his head. "I think we'll pass."

As they headed off in different directions but with similar goals, neither Slim nor Howdy noticed the two men sitting in the truck in the far corner of the parking lot, watching.

36

BRIANNA PROVED TO BE A LOVELY AND SPIRITED HOSTESS. Unfortunately, the next morning she woke up bright and *way* earlier than Slim had in mind. He sat on the edge of the bed rubbing his eyes and working his moldy sock of a tongue like a cow chewing cud. After a second, he blinked a few times and croaked, "What're you doing?"

Brianna was busy packing a suitcase. She held up something silky, trying to decide, pack it or not? "I told you last night," she said.

"You did?"

"Yeah, I'm driving over to San Antonio for a wedding." She rejected the silky thing. "I invited you to come along."

"What did I say?"

"You didn't directly answer the question," she said. "Of course, you might not've even heard me. Looked like you were concentrating real hard on something at the time, like baseball or fishing." She paused and shook her head. "So, anyway, you wanna come?"

Slim's head moved like something small and surprising had hit his forehead. "Love to," he said with another couple of blinks. "But I gotta work." Again with the tongue.

"Well, Brianna isn't going to beg," Brianna said, suddenly referring to herself in the third person for the first time.

So that was that.

Later in the day, after a leisurely lunch, one of the she-tigers dropped Howdy back at the Lost and Found. Said she might come back tonight to hear Howdy sing. He said he'd like that, and then he smiled, and she smiled. But nobody expected any promises. Howdy said he'd be there, either way. She winked and drove off. He never saw her again. Wasn't the first time.

That night Slim worked the door while Howdy rocked the crowd.

Jodie said she felt a little headache coming on around eleven, nothing debilitating, really, just annoying. She took a couple aspirins and kept slinging hooch. She gave last call a little earlier than she might have otherwise. By the time they got the last customer out of the place, Jodie had hit a wall, exhausted. Still, she had the moxie to clean up, close the books, and give Duke the envelope for Uncle Roy. After that she said she was taking the remaining receipts to the night deposit at the bank, then she was heading home for a hot bath.

She left Slim and Howdy to lock up.

"Will do," Howdy said, stepping behind the bar. "Hope you feel better."

Slim walked over and laid the .22 on the bar. He climbed up on a stool and watched as Howdy started gathering bottles in front of himself. Curacao, Grand Marnier, triple sec, Rose's Lime juice, Cointreau, gold tequila, silver tequila, and premium tequila. Then a blender, a shaker, some sweet and sour, and a bag of fresh limes, which he pushed toward Slim. He said, "Cut those in half for me, would you?"

"With what?"

Howdy gave him a cutting board and a knife before he organized his ingredients on the bar, grouping the orange-flavored liquors, then the tequilas, then the sweet and sour and other ingredients. Then he clapped his hands, pointed at Slim's dark glasses, and said, "What do you know about the margarita?"

"I like 'em on the rocks," Slim said. "No salt."

"I'll bet you didn't know the margarita was invented in Hollywood, in the 1940s," Howdy said. "For Rita Hayworth."

"You'd bet on that?" Slim said. "Because the way I heard it was—"

Howdy pointed at the limes and said, "Just juice those for me, would you?" He slid the juicer across the bar. "You can tell your story later."

Slim snickered and started squeezing the fruit. "Yassah, boss."

Howdy continued by saying, "The story goes that a master bartender by the name of Enrique Bastante Gutierrez made the first margarita at the famous Tail o' the Cock in L.A, for Rita Hayworth, whose full name was Margarita, after whom he named the drink."

Slim dipped his head and looked over the top of his shades, saying, "Margarita Hayworth?"

"You can see why they shortened her name," Howdy said as he poured some cheap gold tequila into the shaker with some ice and a glug of pale-green prefab margarita mix. He shook it, then strained it into two glasses. He slid one to Slim. "Now that's the basic drink you'll get at bars all over America," Howdy said, giving his a sip and clucking his tongue to taste the thing. "Essentially, sugary limeade with a splash of tequila."

Slim tasted his. "Yeah, that's not very inspiring," he said. "About a C-minus."

"Exactly." Howdy tasted his again before dumping the remainders from both glasses into the sink. "It's not awful," Howdy shrugged. "It won't kill you to drink a few, but that's the best you can say for it." Howdy rinsed the shaker and added a new scoop of ice. "But people settle for it every day, like that's as good as it gets." He poured some 100 percent blue agave tequila into the shaker, measured an amount of Cointreau, then added fresh lime juice. He shook his head slightly and said, "I never understood that."

Howdy went on to make a brief, if haphazard, argument that it was the same way people seemed to settle for so many things in life. They settled for things that were easy and adequate but not perfect and told themselves they loved it because perfect took too much work and even then there were no guarantees. But otherwise, he said, and all too often, you end up one day looking back at a decision and thinking, Why didn't I hold out for something better than that?

"That's a cliché because it's true," Howdy said. "I mean, how many people you know who are miserable, and got nobody to blame but themselves, because they settled for something less than what they really wanted?" He put the top on the shaker as if to cap his argument.

"But not you," Slim said. "You're holding out for perfect, aren't you? No matter what the cost."

Howdy was squinting when he looked up from under his hat and said, "What?"

"You're holding out for Marilyn," Slim said. "Or *a* Marilyn."

"*A* Marilyn?"

"An imagined ideal," Slim said. "The search for which has left many a man as unhappy as anybody who ever *settled* for less."

Howdy chewed that over for a second before he rattled the cocktail shaker a couple of times. "What's your point?"

"Well, if you can't have Marilyn," Slim said, "you can at least have a part of her. Something almost perfect." Slim gestured at the bottles and said, "The margarita recipe."

Face to face with the truth, Howdy smiled and said, "Nah, it's nothing like that." He poured the chilled drink into the two glasses.

"I was just guessing." Slim hoisted his drink and said, "Here's to perfection."

Howdy joined the toast and they tasted the drinks.

"Now *that's* a damn fine margarita," Slim said. "A-plus." He drank some more.

"Yep." Howdy nodded at first, then shook his head. "But it's not Marilyn's."

Slim eased a concerned look over the top of his glass and said, "You're not going to throw it out are you?"

"Hell no," Howdy said. "Holding out for perfection's all good and well, but it's no reason to throw out premium tequila." Howdy was taking another drink when the phone behind the bar started to ring. He turned and looked at the caller ID. It was Jodie's cell phone. Howdy answered, "Lost and Found, now under new management."

"Yeah," Jodie said. "And I bet you're drinking all the good tequila."

"Hey, boss, you're the one left us here with the keys," Howdy said.

"There's a sucker born every minute," she said. "But that's not why

I called. I don't think I locked my office. Make sure it's locked before y'all leave, okay?"

"No problem," Howdy said. "Feel better."

After Howdy hung up, Slim said, "I know a guy in Corpus who swears the margarita was created for Peggy Lee at a bar down in Galveston by the renowned mixologist Santos Cruz."

"He can't prove a thing," Howdy said as he began working on a new recipe.

Slim said the margarita story he always thought had the ring of truth to it, involved a woman named Bertita who tended bar at a place on the cathedral square down in Taxco, Mexico.

"Bertita?" Howdy said skeptically. "So how come it's not called a Bertita-rita?"

Slim opened his mouth to address this question when the phone began to ring again. Howdy looked, it was Jodie. He answered by saying, "Why can't you just let us drink your tequila in peace?" He paused for the retort, but none came. "Jodie?" He could hear something coming over the connection but he couldn't tell what it was. Odd noises of indeterminate origin. "Jodie? You're break-ing up." The sounds were muffled, garbled, and disturbing in their uncertainty.

Somewhere in all this Howdy thought he heard Jodie's voice, though she wasn't speaking clearly, maybe she wasn't even speak-ing, but it was her voice making some sort of sound. Then a sudden crack followed by a grinding noise followed a moment later by what might have been a car door slamming or a gunshot. "Jodie?!" Howdy looked at the phone. They were still connected. "Are you okay?" But there was nobody at the other end. All he could hear now was what sounded like crickets chirping. Then the connection dropped and Howdy hung up.

Slim said, "What's going on?"

"I don't know." Howdy shook his head. "Something that...It sounded weird."

"Call her back." Slim stood up as if it might help.

Howdy punched in her cell number. After a few rings he looked at Slim and shook his head. "Voice mail," he said.

Slim picked up the .22 and said, "Let's go."

37

AS THEY RAN OUT TO THE PARKING LOT, SLIM YELLED,
"Gimme the keys."

"I don't think so," Howdy replied as he fished them from his
pocket.

"It's my turn to drive."

"We ain't got time to take the scenic route," Howdy said. "I'll
drive."

"You're the one wasting time," Slim said. "Gimme the damn
keys."

Howdy complied since Slim had beaten him to the driver's-side
door and had the sort of grip on the handle that he didn't look like
he was going to relinquish. "All right, you can drive," Howdy said.
"But I call shotgun."

Slim snatched the keys dangling from Howdy's hand, then jumped
in. He said, "Speaking of guns, Jodie carries that .38 with her all the
time doesn't she?" He turned the key and the engine chugged a few
times but wouldn't catch.

"I think so," Howdy said.

"All right, good." Slim pumped the accelerator a few times and
tried again, but it still wouldn't turn over. *Ruur-ruur-ruur.*

"She's not afraid to use it either," Howdy said, thinking back to
the day they saw her firing (and firing at) Link. He gestured at the
accelerator. "Ease up on the gas."

"Come on, you piece of crap!" *Ruur-ruur-ruur.*

"It's not the truck," Howdy said. *Ruur-ruur-ruur.*

Slim turned the key again and again as he pumped the accelerator like Buddy Rich on a kick drum. "Come on!" *Ruur-ruur-ruur.*

"Excuse me, Mr. Earnhardt, but I think you flooded it."

Ruur-ruur-ruur. Boom! Howdy just about jumped through his hat when the truck backfired and roared to life. He didn't need to look at Slim to know that he had one of those don't-tell-*me*-how-to-start-a-truck smirks on his face. "Ha!" He popped the clutch and shot out of the parking lot.

Much to Howdy's surprise, Slim was willing and able to drive like a bat out of hell when the occasion called for it. He ran lights, cut through lawns, and passed anybody not doing approximately sixty. "You know the limit here is twenty-five," Howdy said as he white-knuckled the door on one particularly hairy turn.

"Now you're going to complain that I drive too *fast*?" Slim could only shake his head. "Just shut up and hang on."

"No, I'm impressed," Howdy said. "Didn't know you had these kinds of skills."

Slim leaned into a wild left turn, jumped the curb, and clipped a couple of garbage cans, spewing wet, rancid trash over the hood, the windshield, and half the block.

"Watch those cans," Howdy said. He leaned forward to see what had landed on the windshield and found himself staring into the rotting eye of a Guadalupe spotted bass, or what was left of it, after being pulled from Devil's Lake and filleted. "Eww." He reached over, hit the wipers, and launched the fish carcass over the cab.

Howdy pulled the Lost and Found phone from his pocket and tried Jodie again. A second later he flipped it shut. "Still goes to voice mail," he said.

Slim took one hand off the wheel to point up the road. "Is that it?"

"No, the next one," Howdy said. "Ceniza Street."

Slim made the turn at forty with Howdy leaning out the passenger window like he was trying to keep a catamaran from capsizing.

Slim screeched to a stop in front of the house, a modest *rancheria* sitting on a half acre at the end of a cul-de-sac. The landscaping was the standard southwest mix of wild flowers, cacti, succulents, and native grasses. The prominent botanical feature was a mature century plant with its blooming rosette of spiny leaves.

The front yard was divided by a curving flagstone path. Jodie's truck was parked in the driveway. The only light came from the front porch, nothing on inside.

Howdy went to the front door and knocked. Slim peeked into windows and checked around back before returning. "No answer," Howdy said.

"Back door's locked," Slim replied. "Some windows are open but the screens are intact. I don't think anybody's in there."

They stood there for a minute looking at the scene, looking for anything that seemed unusual. But nothing seemed amiss at first glance.

"Maybe the headache was a ruse," Howdy said. "Maybe she was having a rendezvous she wanted to keep secret. Just met somebody here and went off with 'em?"

"No, she was eating aspirins like bar nuts," Slim said. "The headache was legit." He looked around then shook his head. "Besides, that doesn't explain that weird phone call." Slim shook his head again. "I don't think she was planning to go out, at least not voluntarily." He went back to the truck and grabbed a couple of flashlights, tossed one to Howdy.

Based on where her truck was parked, they figured Jodie would have walked past the century plant and hit the flagstone path about halfway to the house. They retraced this path using the flashlights. The ground was hard-packed so it was tough to make out any footprints. They walked around for a minute before Howdy's flashlight caught a reflection, and he said, "Got something."

Slim came over with his light, shined it where Howdy's was. "Damn," he said.

"Yeah," Howdy said. "Damn is right." He bent down and picked up the silver and turquoise necklace Jodie had been wearing that night. It was snapped in half.

"Now what?"

"No idea," Howdy said as he pulled out the phone and hit redial. Somewhere in the near distance they heard something strange, a haunting and oddly familiar melody. Slowly, Slim and

Howdy turned around until they were looking across the yard. In the darkness, a faint blue glow rose from within the gray-green leaves of the century plant as Jodie's ring tone—the theme from *The Good, the Bad, and the Ugly*—wafted from the leaves of the agave. The phone played the opening four bars before going to voice mail.

They walked over and peered into the plant. Slim said, "Where's Clint Eastwood when you need him?"

38

FIVE MINUTES FROM JODIE'S HOUSE THERE WAS A ONE-STORY brick building that looked like it could have been an appliance repair shop. The front was all plate glass, perfect for the display of second-hand washers and dryers but, as this was the Del Rio Police Department, the items on display were somewhat more tragic than Maytags with broken drive belts.

Slim and Howdy pulled into the parking lot and the wash of fluorescent lights shining through the big windows. Inside, handcuffed to a bench along one wall, they could see two drunks, a smacked-up hooker, and a sullen teenage runaway, all waiting for their dose of justice or whatever else was meted out at this place. Across the room, behind a battered desk, sat an overworked cop with a bitter cup of burned coffee.

When Slim and Howdy walked in, triggering the electronic door chime, Senior Patrol Officer Joel Hernandez looked up from processing some arrest reports. His expression landed him somewhere between suspicious and surprised. They didn't get a lot of walk-in business this time of night, and precious little that was sober.

The chime forced the hooker's opiated eyes open and she reacted as though Slim and Howdy were the character witnesses she'd been waiting on all her life. She pointed at them with the glue-on nails of her uncuffed paw. "Ask these two," she said. "I ain't been anywhere near Laredo in the past three weeks."

Officer Hernandez pointed at her. "Rosy, shut up."

She opened her mouth to respond but nothing came out. Then

she closed her eyes and rested her chin on her Dolly Partons, which were being supported by an industrial-strength bra.

Officer Hernandez pushed back from his desk, looked at the two men. "Can I help you?"

"Yeah," Howdy said. "We need to report a crime."

Officer Hernandez made a show of looking at the clock on the wall. It was two thirty in the morning. "Don't you have a phone?"

"We were in the neighborhood," Slim said.

Howdy nodded. "So was the crime."

"Great," the cop said. "Just what I need." He yanked a new form from one of the stacks in front of him, grabbed a pen, and said, "What're you reporting?"

"We're not sure," Howdy said.

Officer Hernandez stared at Howdy for a few seconds, twirling the pen. "Maybe you'd like to figure that out and come back another time." He put the pen down. "Like when I'm not working."

Slim shook his head, thinking about what Jodie might be going through. "You guys need to get on this now."

"Oh, we do?" Officer Hernandez gestured at his little rogue's gallery. "I actually got plenty to do right now, but thanks." He turned his attention back to his paperwork and said, "Next shift comes in at eight."

Slim leaned onto the desk, putting a hand over the paperwork. He said, "Look, Slick, this could be assault, kidnapping, rape, and/or murder."

That last word brought Rosy back to life. Her head hit the wall behind her when she lifted it up to say, "I told Antwan, I said, I'll kill that scumbag he ever try that again. Ain't nobody gonna pull that shit on Rosy. Noooo." She paused for a moment then nudged the drunk sitting next to her. "Hey, honey, you want a date? Rosy's the best in town."

"Rosy, shut up!" Officer Hernandez looked at Slim, reluctantly asking for more details on the crime. When they finished telling the story and all the evidence was sitting on the desk, the cop said, "That's it?" He poked at the broken necklace. "You found some jewelry on the ground."

"And the cell phone," Slim said, pointing.

"In the century plant."

"Right."

"Plus the weird phone call," Howdy said.

"Right," Officer Hernandez said. "But no witnesses to anything."

"Nope."

"No blood?"

"It's dark over there."

"I thought you said you had flashlights."

"We do, but . . ."

"All right, and you say there's no body."

"If we had a body," Howdy said, "we could rule out kidnapping, now couldn't we?"

Officer Hernandez glared at the sarcastic cowboy with the black hat and said, "I tell you what, Sherlock, you're so damn smart, you can solve your own crime." He put the form back in the pile whence it came, looked up, and said, "I can't help ya."

"What?"

"Why?"

"You mean other than the fact that there's no evidence of a crime?"

Rosy turned to the teenage runaway and said, "That's what I keep saying. Where's the crime? Ain't no eva-dence against me, 'cause I wasn't nowhere near there when it happened."

Along with a whiff of Rosy's breath, the sullen teenager caught a glimpse of his future and the kind of people he'd be rubbing shoulders with if he didn't get his act together. Years from now he would look back at this moment as the turning point in his life. But that's another story.

Howdy gestured roundly at the desktop as if it were covered with fingerprints, shell casings, and a half pound of DNA. He said, "Whaddya mean, no evidence?"

"What you have here is some jewelry and a cell phone," Hernandez said. "What you don't have is a compelling reason for us to act."

Slim held his hands out in disbelief. "What part of this don't you understand?"

"Look, *Slick*," Officer Hernandez said, throwing it back at Slim. "In our experience, very few missing adults are the victims of foul play. They mostly disappear on purpose. Besides—and this is something you need to know—being missing ain't a crime. For all I know she's trying to get away from you two for good reason."

After having given it some thought, one of the drunks looked over at Rosy and said, "Tell you what, how about a free sample? It's good as you say, you get all my business."

Rosy's head popped back again, hitting the wall. "I'll give you the business, all right," she said. "But not for free. You just wait till Antwan gets here. He'll show you what's free."

"Oh, c'mon, how 'bout just a Dirty Sanchez?"

"No!"

Officer Hernandez ignored the negotiations and pointed at Slim. "This woman who's missing, she your girlfriend?"

"No," Slim said. "I work for her."

"I'll be your girlfriend," Rosy said with a nod. "Do whatever you want. Best in town."

This time Howdy turned around and said, "Hey, Rosy? Shut up."

The drunk lowered his voice, nudged Rosy, and said, "What about uh Alabama Tight Spot?"

She just shook her head.

"A Toothless Tiger?"

As the drunk continued down the menu, Officer Hernandez sat back in his chair, scratched the side of his neck, then pointed at Slim and said, "Yeah, I'm thinking you're the boyfriend, gave her the necklace, y'all had a fight, she tore off the jewelry, threw it at you along with the phone. Now you're all pissed off and you and your buddy want us to help you find her. Something like that."

This bit of deductive reasoning took Howdy past the end of his rope. He looked at Slim and said, "What's the penalty for assaulting a police officer in Texas?"

Before anybody could address the question, the electronic door chime sounded again and everybody turned to see who it was. He was a mean-looking mutt in a shiny suit, closer to purple than anything else, with a wide-brimmed fedora that actually matched. No surprise, the man seemed completely unconcerned that he might be perpetuating stereotypes.

Rosy rattled her handcuffs and tried to stand as she called out, "Antwan! It's about damn time you got here."

"Shut up, bitch!" Antwan glared at Officer Hernandez. "Lemme ask you," he said. "How's a man supposed to make a living, you keep draggin' his hos in here for no reason? Huh? Hard enough out there for a pimp as it is. I pay you people good money to let these girls be. Now unlock those cuffs," he said, pointing at Rosy, "so I can put this thing back to work." He sucked on the toothpick stuck off to the side and pulled his jacket back so they could all see his gun. "I ain't messin' around, now. "

Howdy, who was having a hard time believing a man would be seen wearing a suit like that, said, "Yo, Huggy Bear, we got here first. Wait your turn."

Antwan turned his attention to the cat in the cowboy hat. "Yo, Cisco Kid, you best keep yo' punk-ass mouth shut till I get my business done."

Slim stopped Howdy from bull-rushing the pimp, then he pulled the .22. "Like my friend said, wait your turn."

Antwan didn't hesitate. He went for his gun in a flourish of purple.

The sudden shot surprised everybody in the room, but none more than Antwan, who hit the floor with his gun still in his waistband. "Sonofamutharatbastardshiteatingoddaaaaam that hurts like a muthasonofaawwww." He stopped cursing eventually and lay on the floor moaning, blood pooling around his foot.

Howdy stepped over to where Antwan was squirming around on the linoleum clutching at his leg. "You shot yourself, you dumb bastard." Howdy pulled the gun from the pimp's waistband and glanced at the man's bloody boot. "Looks like you took off a toe."

"Shoot him again," Rosy said. "Higher."

Officer Hernandez slapped his desktop. "Goddammit, Rosy, shut up!" He got on the radio and called for an ambulance. "It's gonna take me all night to do the paperwork on this."

The pool of blood gathering around Antwan's foot was more than one of the drunks could take. He leaned forward and heaved a quart or so of fortified wine and what might have been a couple of tacos. It was hard to say for sure.

Howdy stepped back, wincing, and put Antwan's gun on Hernandez's desk. He nudged Slim and said, "Let's go."

Hernandez, who couldn't believe how his night had gone so quickly from bad to worse, said, "Where you two think you're going? You're witnesses."

"I didn't see shit," Howdy said. "And my buddy here is blind."

"That's right," Slim said, putting his sunglasses on. "Besides, we gotta go solve a crime."

39

IT SEEMED LIKE EVERY FEW HOURS JODIE WOULD REGAIN enough consciousness to remember another detail, however fuzzy. It was like trying to work a jigsaw puzzle in the dark without knowing what the image was supposed to be. The whole thing lacked context. She'd try to fit the new piece into the puzzle before the guy lumbered into the room and sent her reeling off again.

She wondered how many times that had happened, let alone why.

Time and again she found herself in a murky area where she wondered if she was dreaming, and then she wondered if she could wonder if she was dreaming in her dreams. And she tried to pinch herself, but nothing changed because you can pinch yourself in your dreams too. At least that's how it seemed.

She was almost home. No, she was there. In her yard. Her head hurt. Was she in the bathtub when it happened? No, never got that far. She was on the way.

It was always dark. It felt like she was trying to put a stained-glass mural together with a few shards from a Coke bottle. She was never clearheaded enough to use the materials she had, and they were inadequate anyway.

He was big. Masked. Maybe. She wasn't sure. Came from behind her with surprising quickness. Standard nightmare stuff. Grabbed at her, but she dodged that first one. He kept coming. Determined. Something in his hand. Not a gun or knife. Nothing metal. Soft. White.

What happened to her gun? He must have known about it

somehow. Did he take it at some point? Must have. Not a clue.
Unless this was a dream and she didn't have the gun in her dream.

But her necklace. She had that in the dream. Broken, spilled on
the ground. So why not the gun? She gave up on that. Might as well
ask why can you fly sometimes in your dreams. But not always.

Tried to call for help. Made sense. Had the phone out. Managed to push a button. Hoped it was redial. All the while trying to
dodge her attacker and the century plant and the cacti in the yard.
He finally got a hold on her. He was angry. That's why her shoulder
hurt so bad. He just grabbed her and gave her a punch. More like he
wanted to than needed to.

She was kidnapped? Really? She was clear enough to wonder why
anyone would want to kidnap her.

He got her. A vice grip. Too strong to escape. Then that punch.
Twice her size, or so it seemed. The white thing in his hand over her
mouth. Soft cloth soaked in something. Struggle became useless.
She was a rag doll. Game over.

Regained semiconsciousness in the dark more than once, but how
many more? Hands tied. The big guy, again with the smelly cloth.
Then gently, back to sleep.

40

SLIM AND HOWDY LEFT OFFICER HERNANDEZ TO MOP UP
after Antwan and the heaving drunk. They spent the rest of the night
repeating their story to the folks at the Val Verde sheriff's station, the
Texas State Trooper headquarters, the Texas Rangers' station, and
the Border Patrol.

None of whom did squat.

The sheriff and the state troopers said it wasn't unusual, let
alone illegal, for a woman to get mad and go off without telling
anybody where she was going. The Rangers and the Border Patrol
said even if a crime had been committed, it was out of their juris-
diction. And, although neither Slim nor Howdy asked their opinions, the Rangers and Border Patrol guys said they had to agree with
the assessment of the sheriff and the state troopers about the way
women act.

Slim and Howdy returned to the Lost and Found around dawn,
bewildered and disappointed by their inability to spur the local con-
stabulary to action. Their expressions were as grim as their moods.
Neither of them wanted to say it out loud, but both were thinking
the same awful thing. If Jodie was still alive, she was probably being
put through hell. But there was the real possibility that she might
already be dead. Either way, they figured it was up to them to do
something about it. They weren't sure what, but they couldn't just sit
around doing nothing.

They left a message on Grady's voice mail, then looked through
Jodie's office until they found Uncle Roy's address. They grabbed

some breakfast to go, two large coffees each, then returned to Jodie's
house to see if they'd missed anything. They found another piece
of the necklace but otherwise came up empty, so they went to see
Uncle Roy.

He lived on the outskirts of South Del Rio in a sprawling old-style
ranch hacienda built in the 1930s when it was the main house for
a two-hundred-thousand-acre cattle ranch. Uncle Roy bought the
property thirty years ago, after previous owners had sold off all but
seven acres. But the house, surrounded by a tall adobe wall topped
with shards of glass, was a thing to see.

As they cruised up the long, cactus-lined driveway, Slim said,
"Nice place."

"Yeah," Howdy agreed. "The wages of sin look like they're pretty
good in this part of Texas." As they approached the apex of the
circular drive, Howdy pointed at the four men who were already
approaching the truck. "You think that's valet parking?"

"Kind of doubt it," Slim said.

The moment Howdy put it in park, the security guards pulled
them out and frisked them. "Gun," one of them said when he found
the .22. "But not much of one."

After explaining who they were and why they were there, Slim
and Howdy were escorted into a vast living room. It looked like a
museum of the old Southwest, the walls lined with an astounding
collection of weapons, saddlery, and artwork.

Howdy was drawn to a glass case featuring a pair of silver-overlay,
drop-shank spurs of the old California style, with heel chains and
large snake-and-eagle conchos on the straps. Across the room, Slim
admired a parade saddle with a thousand silver mountings, matching headstall, reins, breast collar, full-length serape, rump cover, and
a silver-mounted bit.

Slim and Howdy looked up a moment later when the large wooden
doors at the far end of the room swung open. The man who came in
was the last of a dying breed, like one of the antiques on display. He
was a tough-looking old coot, short and bristly, with an expression
about as welcoming as barbed-wire. His gait was hobbled, pain in
every step. Bad knees, bowed legs, ruined hips, and too much pride
for a wheelchair or even a cane.

Underneath his silver belly hat was a face that looked like it had been carved from old boot leather. He had their .22 in his hand. He set it on a table.

"I'm Roy Hobbs," he said, his voice craggy as his face. "What's this about my Jodie?"

"Sorry about the hour," Howdy said.

"Been up since five," Roy replied, tapping an unfiltered cigarette from a pack. "Ain't got much time left, don't see any point in sleeping it away."

"Yes, sir." Slim and Howdy crossed the room to introduce themselves. "Mr. Hobbs, I'm—"

"I know who you are," Roy said, lighting the cigarette. "Duke told me about that night at the Lost and Found when one of you took his gun."

"That was me," Howdy said. "I didn't know he was supposed to be there."

Uncle Roy blew a cloud of smoke and waved off Howdy's concern. "Hell, I was glad to hear you did it," he said, gesturing for them to sit. "Now, what's this about Jodie?"

They told him the whole story, from the odd phone call to all the cops refusing to help. Roy was quick to agree that there was something wrong with the picture. Then he fell silent, looking off to one side, his thoughts running while the cigarette smoke curled around his gnarled right hand.

Howdy tried, but Roy Hobbs was a hard man to read. Despite his current wealth, he had a lot of tough years and lean times etched in his face. He looked like a man prone to expecting the worst and all too often having those expectations met. At the same time, he looked like the sort of man who would put up a fight for things he cared about without concern for the odds.

After a minute, Uncle Roy let out a sigh and said the words neither Slim nor Howdy wanted to. "Seems like there's two possibilities," he said, his eyes cutting back and forth between his two visitors. "She's either dead or somebody's kidnapped her and she *ain't* dead. At least not yet."

"Yes, sir," Slim said. "I think that's about it."

"If it's some psychopath, you know, some damn serial killer, like that one up in Juarez a couple of years ago—what'd they call him, the *Campo Algodonero* Killer? Dumped all those girls' bodies in that cotton field…If it's something like that, there's nothing to do," Uncle Roy said. "Her body'll surface sooner or later and then all that's left is huntin' down the animal and killing it." He looked at his cigarette and said, "But if she's been kidnapped and she's still alive, there's a possibility it's somebody she knows. Somebody she pissed off. And that's somebody we might be able to track down."

Slim turned slowly to look at Howdy. He said, "Link." Howdy nodded.

Roy looked up at them. "Link? What do you mean, link?"

"A guy she fired last week," Howdy said. "Big scary-looking sumbitch, calls himself Link. She caught him stealing, had to let him go."

"At gunpoint," Slim added.

"It's a place to start," Roy said with a nod. "You know where to find him?"

"I suspect we can find out," Slim said. "Bound to have an address in the office."

As Uncle Roy stubbed his cigarette out in a standing ashtray, he studied Howdy. "Son, you look like you got something to add. Spit it out."

"All right," Howdy said. "I'm wondering if you can think of any-body might be pissed off at *you*. Somebody you, uh, do business with."

Roy nodded his head slowly as if the thought had crossed his mind already. He said, "What'd Jodie tell you about my business?"

"Not much," Slim said. "But that was enough."

"Look, we ain't got time to be coy about this," Howdy said. "Your man Duke collects an envelope of cash every night. But that ain't near enough to pay for this hacienda. Doesn't take a trained investi-gator to figure you for a man with a wide variety of business concerns, most of which are not openly discussed at chamber of commerce meetings. I figure you do some importing, some retailing, maybe some wholesaling. In other words, you're the guy in this neck of the woods who provides the sorts of products and services that a lot of people want but can't say they want to be legal."

"That about sums it up," Roy said.

Howdy looked Roy in the eyes, said, "And that means you deal with folks in some of the darker corners of Val Verde County. So I'm just asking if you can think of anybody who might try to get to you, using Jodie as leverage."

"There's always somebody," Roy said, no shortage of regret in his voice. He damn sure didn't want to bear any responsibility for whatever had happened to his godchild. "My boys'll be out rattling cages within the hour." He tapped another cigarette from the pack. "I guess one thing's for sure," he said. "If it is a kidnapping, a ransom note won't be far behind."

41

INDEED. WHEN THE TIME CAME, THE BOSS MAN SNAPPED on a pair of latex gloves and composed the ransom note in the standard fashion. He kept it to the point:

We have the WOman.
unharmed.
$50,000 U.S.
You have thirTy-Six HouRs.
Los Zetas.

Los Zetas being the name of an infamously violent criminal organization in northern Mexico that had lately taken to beheading those who failed to follow any of their directives. The Boss Man figured nobody would try anything cute if they thought they were dealing with those guys. Just pay the ransom and hope for the best, that's what they'd say.

The Boss Man slipped the folded note into an envelope he'd taken from the Posada Rosa Hotel months ago. Thought that was a nice touch, complete with a Mexican stamp. According to the plan, the Big Goon was to mail the ransom note in Piedras Negras, give the impression that maybe those black tar dealers down that way were branching out into the newest field of lawlessness. After all, kidnapping had become big business in that part of Mexico, might as well take advantage of their bad reputation.

He also figured a little geographical misdirection would throw any snoopy types off the scent. Even better, somebody follows the postmark down to Piedras Negras, starts sticking their nose in the wrong places, asking the wrong questions, even saying the words *Los Zetas,* probably ends up gutted on a dark side street, stuffed into a drainpipe, confirming, in a roundabout way, that *Los Zetas* actually *was* responsible for snatching Jodie.

Beautiful, he thought. Just beautiful.

And now the Big Goon was bouncing down a dirt road in a stolen El Camino, on his way to Piedras Negras to mail the note. He was just past Villa de Fuentes when he had what struck him, without doubt, as the best natural idea in his entire criminal career. It was so good it tickled him. So he started to laugh. He slapped the steering wheel and threw his head back like a braying mule. Ha! Boss Man wasn't the only one who could cook up a scheme.

The Big Goon now had a plan of his own.

He stopped at the first store he came across, ran in, bought a stack of magazines and a glue stick. Then he crossed the street to a dim bar, the faded sign over the door featuring a pair of dancing shrimp with castanets and sombreros. *¡Camaron Que Baila!* He ducked into the darkness, slipped into a back booth, where he sat, so giddy about his scheme that he was soon drumming his fingers on the tabletop to the rhythm of *"Abre los ojos"* blasting from the jukebox.

The Big Goon pulled the magazines from the bag just as the waitress came over. She set a cocktail napkin on the table and said, *"Hola, señor."*

Something about the way she said it gave the Big Goon a tingle. His eyes roamed all over as he took in her plentiful sights. She was patient and accommodating, full-bodied and brown as good whiskey, with long dark hair, and eyes to get lost in forever. Most important, she had *muy grande tetas.* Lord almighty, he couldn't help but stare. He said *"Mamacita"* in a tone that managed to be both reverent and leering. He meant to add something about her being *muy caliente* but, at the moment, his brain lacked the follow-through.

She smiled at him the way she did, the way she'd smiled at a hundred others before turning on them. It never failed. She took his order and gave a sly look over her shoulder as she walked away with a little extra sway in the hips because she knew he was still looking. At the bar she popped an extra button on her blouse, then brought his beer and his shot of Jim Beam on the side. She leaned way over as she served him, lingering, to give him an eyeful. She half-whispered, "Enjoy."

"That's what I'm talking about," he mumbled. The Big Goon put a twenty on her tray, said, "Keep the change, *mamacita*."

"*Ooo, muchas gracias*." She gave him a wink and, if he wasn't mistaken, she licked her ruby-red lips just so.

The Big Goon threw back the shot of Jim Beam and said, "*¿Como te llamas?*"

She ducked her head, feigning some modesty, before she said, "*Me llamo Carmelita*."

He tapped the twenty and said, "Well, Carmelita, there's gonna be plenty more where that came from, and soon too." He set the shot glass on top of the twenty and said, "*Uno mas, por favor*." Virtually exhausting his Spanish.

As Carmelita went to get the drink, the Big Goon started flipping through a copy of *Vogue,* had a girl on the cover looked like Angelina Jolie except without all the crazy in her eyes. After the first thirty pages of advertising, the Big Goon realized he wasn't going to find what he was looking for in a fashion magazine.

He was pulling the *Sports Illustrated* from the stack when Carmelita returned with two more shots. "On me," she said.

The Big Goon gave her a ten this time along with the *Vogue,* which she seemed to appreciate. She asked if he wanted anything else and he said, "Oh you bet I do." Nodding like a bobble-head doll, his eyes fixed on her two big prizes. "But right now, I'm working on a little something that's gonna make me big and rich." He winked at her and said, "Just gimme a few minutes."

"I'll give you anything you want," Carmelita said, touching his arm. "Anything." Then she turned and went back to the bar, leaving the Big Goon to imagine the possibilities.

It took a minute for the Big Goon to stop imagining his face planted squarely between her *tetas*. When he did, he returned to the task at hand. It didn't take long to find what he was looking for. It was on page twenty-nine. A perfect shot of Peyton Manning, number eighteen, throwing another touchdown pass. The Big Goon pulled his buck knife and stabbed Peyton in the back with the blade, then proceeded to cut the number 1 from his jersey.

Using a paper napkin as a glove, he reached into his pocket and pulled out the envelope from the Posada Rosa Hotel. He shook the note onto the table, unfolding it with care, weighing the corners with an ashtray, two empty shot glasses, and a salt shaker. Using the buck knife, the Goon carefully pried the dollar sign off the page. He rubbed the glue stick on the back of Peyton Manning's 1 and stuck it to the left of the 5, then put the dollar sign back, deftly raising the ransom from $50,000 to $150,000.

The Big Goon chuckled and finished his beer and another shot as he admired his handiwork. Sometimes he surprised himself at how smart he was. In fact, he was so caught up in his genius that he failed to notice Carmelita had returned. Though when he did, he was quick enough to notice that she had two more shots on her tray and another button popped on her blouse.

The Goon looked up, halfway hoping she'd seen the note and was impressed by the idea. Hoped she'd get turned on by his outlaw side. Carmelita demurred as if she hadn't seen a thing. She leaned over again, lingering as she put the Jim Beam on the table next to the note. "I admire ambition in a man," she said. "Without it?" She just shrugged.

"Man's gotta have *cajones*," the Big Goon said, reaching under the table to grab his package.

Carmelita, still leaning over the table, smiled provocatively and whispered, "*Muy grande cajones.*" Now she gestured at the note. "It looks very exciting."

The Big Goon moved over, inviting her to sit. Then he said, "Tell me this, *mamacita,* can you keep a secret?"

42

SLIM AND HOWDY WERE QUICK TO AGREE WITH UNCLE ROY
that kidnapping and ransom seemed the most likely explanation for
Jodie's disappearance. Not only did it make more sense, given the
evidence, but they found it much easier to think in those terms than
to contemplate the violent alternatives.

Even as the words went unspoken, Slim and Howdy could see
the dark thoughts crossing Uncle Roy's mind. A grim look would
flash across his weathered face like he'd seen the crime-scene photos
or had been called to the morgue to identify the body. He wouldn't
hold the expression long, couldn't stand to keep the images in his
mind beyond the moment. The old man would defend himself by
taking a hard draw on his cigarette, throwing a steely gaze at his visitors, and making tough guarantees about the hard things that were
going to befall whoever had done this. "Mark my words," he said. "I
have resources, and I will use them all if necessary."

"Yes, sir," Howdy said, not doubting the old man for a minute.

Uncle Roy couldn't stay seated any longer. The idea of not doing
something when something needed to be done was more than he
could tolerate. He saw himself as a man of action, even if the action
he engaged in was pointless. He stood and made his way to a window, pain in each step, then turned and walked back. Pacing would
have to suffice for now, offering the temporary illusion that he was
doing something.

He stopped at a table covered with framed photos and yellowed
newspaper articles. Roy Hobbs as a young cowboy in the 1930s,

working a cattle drive with guys with names like Buster and Boots. Another, dated 1946, showed ten roughnecks standing in the shadow of an old wooden oil rig, the whites of their eyes standing out against the grease, mud, and grime that covered their faces and overalls.

As Slim watched Uncle Roy fuss with one frame, then another, pausing now and then to allow for a fond grunt or a smile, Slim figured the old man was going to avoid the present by telling them about his past. But, to Slim's surprise, Uncle Roy turned around and said, "You talked to her brother yet?"

"Called him," Slim said. "Left a message."

"He came by the Lost and Found the other night," Howdy added. "Said he was going to be up in Abilene all week taking depositions in some big class-action suit he's involved in."

"Is that what he said, a big class-action suit?" Uncle Roy turned his back on the table of memories and continued pacing.

"Yeah," Slim said. "Suing a pharmaceutical manufacturer, I think."

Uncle Roy let out a derisive snort and shook his head. "You could fertilize a hundred fifty acres with all the bullshit comes out of that boy's mouth."

"Well, he *is* a lawyer," Howdy said, trying to give him the benefit of the doubt.

Uncle Roy smiled and looked as if he might take another shot at Grady's character, but he stopped and thought better of it. Whatever he felt about his nephew was immaterial to the present discussion. "I'm sure he'll call," Uncle Roy said. "Just don't expect much when he does."

Slim nodded, glanced at Howdy, who shrugged with his eyes.

Uncle Roy lit another cigarette and said, "What about Jake? You talked to him?"

"Jake?"

"Rattlesnake Jake," Roy said. "Jodie's ex-husband."

Rattlesnake Jake sounded familiar, but Howdy couldn't think why. And he didn't think to ask because he was too surprised at the news Uncle Roy had just delivered. Howdy said, "She was married to somebody before Frank?"

"She didn't tell you?" Uncle Roy looked at his boots and shook his head. "Don't blame her I guess. Nobody likes talking about their mistakes. But yeah, she was a kid when she fell for Jake, maybe seventeen. He was a charmer and not much else of any use. Everybody tried to talk her out of it, but you know how that story ends. Divorced after about eight months and moved up to Oklahoma to avoid being looked at like cheap used goods. Anyway, Jake Heller, that's his last name, shed his charm like a snake sloughing off its skin as he got older and, tell you the truth," Uncle Roy said with a finger to his head, "I think he's not right, mentally. I see him now and then and he's got this look in his eyes like some hermit gone crazy living in the desert, talking to lizards and such." Roy turned to look at Slim and Howdy. "Now that I hear myself talking about it, he's as good a candidate for this as anybody. You oughta pay him a visit."

"You know where he stays?"

Roy shook his head. "Not sure he's got a fixed address 'cept for his business. You've probably seen it, driving through town. Rattlesnake Jake's Exotic Pets." He shook his head like trading in serpents and spiders was a less-than-respectable way for a man to make a living.

"Oh yeah," Howdy said. "That green-and-orange building on the main drag. Noticed that the day we drove into town. And that's Jodie's ex, huh? I'll be damned."

Slim said, "What about the Lost and Found? I mean until Jodie gets back?" He figured it was best to keep ringing the bell of optimism.

"We'll keep it open," Roy said as he crossed the room to a large display case filled with sidearms. "Duke knows how to run the place. You two just keep doing whatever you agreed to at night. During the day, I'll pay you to check on that fella you called Link, and Jake too."

"Fair enough," Slim said.

Uncle Roy opened one of the panels in the case and pulled a single-action army .45. It had elephant ivory grips with a buffalo head carved in the handle. He pointed the seven-inch barrel across the room at the .22 he'd set on the table earlier. "That .22 all the gun you got?"

"Yes, sir," Howdy said.

Uncle Roy slid the .45 into its holster and tossed it to Howdy.

Then he pulled an engraved Colt single-action with a smooth ivory grip and a nickel finish and tossed it to Slim along with the holster it rode in on. "There," he said. "Now you're properly armed."

While Slim and Howdy admired the guns, Uncle Roy said, "Listen, I never had children of my own, so Jodie's as close to it as I'll ever have. Her parents are both gone and I'm what she's got left. Well, me and Grady. But I'm her godfather and I take that seriously."

"Yes, sir," Howdy said. "I can see that."

"I don't care if I have to hare-lip every cow in Texas," Uncle Roy said. "I will find out what happened. And somebody's gonna pay."

43

LINK MADE HIS HOME ON A PICKED-SCAB OF LAND A FEW miles east of Del Rio. There, perched at a slight angle, in the middle of this dusty little piece of heaven, was a stolen FEMA trailer Link had dragged out here from Mobile, Alabama, in the wake of Hurricane Katrina. He'd gone there to check on family and friends after the storm and, while there, ran into a buddy who showed him how to con the taxpayers out of a trailer.

Said it was a piece of cake, and it was.

He brought it to Texas, no questions asked, and planted it in one of the less densely populated square miles of Val Verde County. A real estate broker might have said it offered exquisite solitude. Another way of saying it was the only structure as far as the eye could see.

Slim and Howdy got out there around ten that morning. Link's truck wasn't there, just an ATV up on blocks off to the side of the trailer. There were no signs of life as Slim parked the truck and the two of them sat there, waiting for the dust cloud to blow by.

"Doesn't appear to be home," Howdy said, like that was an engraved invitation to break in and look around.

Slim stroked his goatee a couple of times before turning his sunglasses toward Howdy. He said, "If you'll recall, Black Tony didn't appear to be at home when we first broke into his house either. Remember how that ended?"

Howdy thought of Crystal and smiled. "Yeah, that was some fun, wuddn't it?"

"Barrel of monkeys," Slim said as he opened the door. "Let's take a quick look."

"That's all I'm sayin'."

They got out of the truck, headed for the trailer, both wearing the sidearm Roy Hobbs had given them. Howdy's was hidden under his long black duster. Slim's toreador jacket left his .45 showing. And quite smartly.

No one answered the door, which was locked, so they started trying windows.

Slim reached the back door first. Also locked. He peeked through the glass and thought he saw some legs, but in a place that didn't make sense to him. He paused, did a double take. Looked again. He cupped his hands around his eyes, pressed against the glass. A sick feeling on the horizon, approaching fast. It took a moment before his brain could accept what he was seeing. When it registered—when it really hit—Slim almost got sick.

He shouted for Howdy as he kicked the door open and rushed inside. He got too close for comfort and took a quick step back from it. It was too late to help and he knew it. He muttered, "Jesus." He stared, not knowing what else to do.

Howdy raced in a second later, running into Slim before he looked up too. "Oh, no."

She was hanging from a beam. Her hands and feet were bound. She was lifeless.

Always had been.

She was a mannequin.

It took a fraction of a second for them both to realize this, but that fraction was sickening. That single instant of thinking it was Jodie left them gut-punched and sick on adrenaline. Oddly, coming to the realization that it *wasn't* her—in fact, that it wasn't a person at all—was a secondary shock to a system that was doing all it could to come to terms with the first one.

After a moment, Howdy reached out, grabbed its leg, pulling it toward him. Kind of stunned, he said, "It's a dummy." He let go, sent it swaying.

The two men gazed slowly around the trailer and soon realized they'd stepped into someone else's world. A dark place, rendered even darker by the creaking sound of the hangman's rope swinging back and forth under the weight of the dead.

After a minute Slim reached out and stopped it. "Enough of that."

Howdy gestured at the kitchen counter. "Check it out." Magazines on sadism, masochism, and bondage. Howdy flipped a few pages, looked at some of the pictures, and found himself wondering what made some people tick.

Slim wandered into the living room where he found more magazines, these on extreme piercing and body modification. A disturbing gallery of split tongues, bolts, and ball bearings sewn under the skin, and necks with three-inch surgical staples inserted along the vertebrae for show. He used the eraser end of a pencil to turn the pages of a quarterly publication called *SubIncision*.

Howdy, over by the stereo, perused Link's CD collection. A library of industrial-gothic-bondage rock. Death Rattle. Carcass. Skulls of Doom. "Not a big fan of Perry Como," he mumbled.

Slim, meanwhile, still flipping through the magazine, came to some photos that stopped him cold. He stared in disbelief for a moment before saying, "Holy mother of that's-got-to-hurt."

Howdy looked up from the CDs, said, "Whatcha got?"

"You ever heard of trepanation?"

"Trepidation? I'm having some right now."

"No," Slim said. "Trep-AN-ation."

"Nope," Howdy said. "Do I want to?"

"It's the practice of opening a hole in the skull, exposing the brain."

"Ewwww."

"Apparently you can do it with your own drill," Slim said. "Though they suggest having a friend do it for you."

"Safety first," Howdy said.

"Yeah, says here trepanation allows the brain to breathe properly and release toxins that are otherwise trapped." Slim pointed at the page. "They got pictures."

"I bet they do," Howdy said. "But I'll pass." He looked at a few more CDs before curiosity got the better of him. He pushed the stereo's power button without checking the volume, and a second later there was an explosion of pure, jaw-dropping sonic aggression that knocked Howdy two feet backwards. Seven hundred watts shoving the Lords of Agony through multiple subwoofers, roaring with tortured squalls, shrieking feedback, and lyrics of whiskey-black hatred.

Howdy stabbed his finger repeatedly toward the power button until he killed the thing, returning the trailer to a sudden, creepy silence. He looked over at Slim, a bit chagrined. "Sorry."

Slim pulled his fingers from his ears, checked for blood. "Don't do that."

Howdy moved away from the stereo. Next to the CDs were stacks of 8mm video cassettes. "Looks like a home movie buff," he said. The videos were labeled with dates only, no subject matter. "You see a playback deck anywhere?" He held up óne of the cassettes. "This one might be worth watching."

"What makes you say that?"

"It's dated yesterday."

Slim looked around then shook his head. "DVD player's all I see."

Howdy looked down at the coffee table, pointed at the cigar box. "Ten bucks says our boy's a dope smoker."

Slim shook his head at the sucker's bet. "I'll keep my money, thanks."

Howdy opened it. There were a couple of dozen Polaroids. Different angles of a windowless room with an empty cage in it. A bare bulb dangling from a frayed wire. What might have been a black leather hood hanging on a hook. Shadows made it hard to see. In the background what looked like a rack of flogs and whips and a stool. "Looks like a . . . dungeon."

Even though he found it hard to believe, Howdy said, "You know, there are a lot of people who do this kind of thing for . . . fun."

"A lot?"

"Okay, some, a few, I have no idea." He gestured around the trailer. "But look how many different magazines there are. Somebody's keeping them in business."

Slim seemed skeptical. "You think Jodie's into this? With Link?"

Howdy shrugged. "Who knows? People have secrets, right? She didn't tell us about Jake, the ex-husband. Hard to imagine she'd confide in us about her taste for humiliation and torture if she's too private to mention a bad marriage."

"There's a difference between the two?"

Howdy gave an understanding nod.

They thought it over for a minute before they both shook their heads. "No way," Slim said. "Not Jodie."

"I agree," said Howdy, picking up the handcuffs that were next to the cigar box. "At least not voluntarily."

"So where does that leave us?"

"We need to find this dungeon."

"Yeah." They looked around some more, hoping to find a clue.

Howdy came across something familiar made of leather. He picked them up, admired the craftsmanship, and said, "Hey, these chaps are nice." He held them to his waist. They were too long for him.

A second later, Slim found a shipping box. "Got something," he said. The address label was for "Mr. Link" but at a different location.

"Where?" Howdy asked.

"Some box number on a farm-to-market road," Slim replied. "No idea where, though. We can stop at the post office on the way back through town. Ask them."

Howdy put the chaps down and said, "What's in the box?"

"It's empty," Slim replied after a look. "Except for this receipt." He unfolded the piece of paper, read it, then looked up at Howdy. "It was a five-piece hog-tie set."

44

SLIM AND HOWDY WERE HALF A MILE SHY OF THE DEL RIO
post office when Howdy announced that he'd figured out a way to
kill two birds with one stone. "We really just need somebody who
can tell us where this address is," Howdy said. "Doesn't have to be a
postal worker."

"No, but it's right up there," Slim said, pointing ahead. "Just on
the other side of the tracks. It's not too far from..." It dawned on
him and he said, "Oh, yeah. Good idea."

So, they pulled into the parking lot at Rattlesnake Jake's Exotic
Pets.

Not exactly Pets-R-Us. Rats and mice were the cuddliest critters
available for purchase. And *them* you'd have to thaw out and blow-
dry if you really wanted to cuddle. Jake sold them frozen, by the
sack, food for the snakes that were his main stock in trade, and not
just rattlers and copperheads either. As Jake liked to say, he didn't
put "Exotic" on the sign 'cause he liked the way it looked.

So, thanks to the Internet and a flexible sense of what constituted
"legal," Jake was selling Russian saw-scaled vipers, East African
Gaboons, anacondas and boas to customers around the world, all
from his brightly colored little hut in Del Rio, Texas.

As Slim and Howdy approached the door, they thought they
heard something, like a man in pain, moaning and cursing. They
paused for a moment, listening. It was coming from inside.

Like a delayed soundtrack, the noise took Slim back to Link's
trailer and his recent education in alternative lifestyles. Some of the

stranger photos came to mind. He cast a leery glance Howdy's way and said, "After you."

The place was a maze of metal shelving stacked with terrariums and aquariums covered with screen mesh. The store buzzed with heat lamps and had a smell that was harder to put your finger on than your nose. Jake's desk was centered at the back of the room, up on a riser like a judge's bench, allowing him to survey his whole slithering kingdom simply by looking up from the computer.

But right now there could have been two dozen northern blue-tongued skinks doing the Charleston in the aisles and Jake wouldn't have noticed. He was hunched over his desk, a hundred-watt bulb in a gooseneck lamp bent to shed harsh light on the onerous task that had Jake grunting, panting, and cursing like he was in the throes of delivering twins.

This led Slim and Howdy to exchange another, slightly more troubled, glance before they approached further.

The words, "Sonuvabitch, that hurts," escaped from between Jake's clenched teeth, but just barely. He took a series of short breaths, puffing his cheeks like a Russian weight-lifter psyching up for a two-hundred-kilo snatch.

Slim and Howdy stopped just a few feet away. They still couldn't see what Jake was working on, and Jake remained so focused that he didn't realize they were standing there until Slim cleared his throat and said, "Excuse me."

Without a flinch, without looking up, Jake replied, "Be right with you."

"Take your time," Howdy said.

Curiosity drew them closer still. After a couple more steps they could see an open tackle box at Jake's elbow. The top tray was filled with Hula Poppers, GatorTails, a bottle of pain pills, and a stun gun. Next to that was a metal canister, the kind used for camping-stove fuel, its screw cap dangling by a string looped around the neck. There was a strip of masking tape slapped on the front of the canister with "Isoflurane" scrawled in blue ink.

One more step before Slim and Howdy could see that Jake had a filet knife in his right hand with which he was digging at the index finger on his left.

The finger was swollen to twice normal size, like a rotten sausage in the sun, primed to pop. They could see where blood clots had formed under the skin, along with rancid black patches of dead and dying tissue covered with hideous gray blisters filled with, well, who the hell knows what fills a gray blister, but there they were. At least six of them.

Was that gangrene?

"That looks like it might hurt a little," Howdy said, peering over the top and catching a whiff of something ripe.

Jake shrugged, then leaned to the side, putting his nose over the opening of the metal canister. He took a long sniff, held it in, wobbled a little, blinked a few times, then exhaled. "Ahhhhh, s'not too bad," he slurred. Sweat beading on his upper lip, he put the blade on the stretched-tight skin and, after the briefest hesitation, Jake ran the filet knife along the side the finger. "Eye, yi, yiiii," he said.

The cut flesh split like a boxer's lip. Jake held the sliced finger over some paper towels, applied some pressure, grunting and wincing as he coaxed a yellowish-pink fluid from the wound. "Whew boy," he said, panting and sucking air between his teeth.

While this dripped onto the paper towels, Jake leaned over and took another long whiff from the canister. Then, in a predictably haphazard fashion, he wrapped the finger with a large roll of sterile gauze. Finally, after a deep breath, he looked up at Slim and Howdy with red-rimmed eyes, bloodshot and teary. "Sorry 'bout that," he said, dabbing his eyes with a shirt sleeve. "Now, what can I do for you?" Like he'd just put a Band-Aid on a paper cut.

Slim and Howdy, who had watched the entire spectacle unfold with a mix of wonder and revulsion, continued to stare at Jake for a moment. Howdy's eyes drifted over to the tackle box and he found himself thinking those must be some damn good pain pills.

But what's with the stun gun?

Jake just kept grinning, like this was precisely the sort of thing that went on here all the time.

Slim and Howdy both seemed a little put off. It was hard to say if this was a reaction to the gangrenous finger or the idea that Jodie actually married this guy. First of all, he seemed to be a barking lunatic. Secondly, and there really was no nice way to say it, Jake was ugly as a mud fence. It was hard to believe that Jodie, even steeped in the ignorance and hormones of youth, had fallen for either of these qualities.

But the way Uncle Roy told it, Jake, in his youth, had what was considered interesting looks. Some said exotic. A lean face with wide-set cheek bones and dark eyes gave him a look that girls thought was sexy and dangerous at the time. Unfortunately, twenty-five years and forty-some pounds later, he just looked like a bad mug shot. Crimes of a sordid nature, perhaps a senator, if you had to venture a guess.

As for the crazy, that always plays sexier when you're young.

And while it seemed unlikely that Jake's looks could have any bearing on Jodie's disappearance, the fact that Jake appeared non compos mentis made him, in their minds, if not a likely suspect, then at least someone worth talking to.

"Uhhh." Slim pointed at Jake's finger. "You sure you don't wanna go to the emergency room for that?"

"What, this?" Jake held it up. "Are you crazy? You have any idea what they charge to drain a snake-bit finger over there? It's a damn crime what they get away with." He shook his head. "No, sir, I got better things to do with my money." He chuckled in a manly fashion and said, "Besides, I do this all the time." He pointed with the filet knife. "Looks worse than it is."

"If you say so," was Slim's response.

Howdy couldn't help but notice that Jake had some scratches on his arms and face. Wondered how he got those.

"Yeah, it's uh occupational hazard," Jake said. "Usually just have to drain it a few times, keep that ointment on it, gets better." The swagger in Jake's voice gave way all of a sudden to some doubt as he said, "Though I gotta tell ya, this one's lasted a little longer than usual." He gave a reluctant shrug like he knew the truth. "Much as I hate to say it, I might lose this one." He wagged the putrid finger at them as he said, "But that don't mean I'm gonna let the hospital win." He shook his head some more. "See, that's what they want."

Howdy had to squint at him and say, "I don't think I follow."

"See, that's why they charge so much for draining the thing," Jake said. "So you won't come in and get it done, right? Then it gets like *this* and they figure you'll get all scared and be happy to come in and pay 'em ten times as much to cut the damn thing off. And that's just plain crazy."

"That's crazy all right," Slim said.

"That's what I'm sayin'." Jake winked at him. "How stupid do they take us for?" He nodded at the computer, said, "Shit, I got online, did a little research. Found just what the doctor ordered, so to speak." He opened one of the desk drawers and pulled out a box. "Got one of those do-it-yourself amputation kits they sell. Got all the instructions, diagrams, everything." He admired the box for a moment, then shook his head in awe. "I tell you what, the stuff you can get on the Internet these days, it's unbelievable."

"Unbelievable," Howdy said. "That's just one of the words that comes to mind right now."

"Yeah, so, anyway," Jake said, looking back and forth at the two men. "Could I interest one of you boys in a Mexican red-kneed tarantula? On special, today only."

"No thanks," Slim said. "We're—"

"No? How 'bout a reticulated python? She's a beauty," Jake said. "Lemme show you." He stood up.

And that's when Jake saw their guns. His expression soured, as though betrayed, and he pointed the fat, gauzy finger their way. "What's this shit? You two with Parks and Wildlife? This about those damn lizards?"

"Nope, nothing like that."

"Well, what then?"

"We're, uh, private investigators," Howdy said, thinking it sounded pretty good.

"Oh, hell." Jake sat back down. "You working for that woman's lawyer, aren't you?" He shook his head. "Look, I told the cops already. That sumbitch came in, paid cash for three broad-banded copperheads. Nothing illegal about it. He didn't tell me what he was going to do with 'em. And I'm not obliged to ask."

"I wouldn't know about that," Slim said, looking past Jake, taking inventory of the items on the table behind him. He took note of a new coil of rope, half of it used already.

"Besides," Jake said. "The woman lived, right? Probably learned a good lesson about being more careful who she sleeps with." Jake chuckled when he recalled the facts of the case as he understood them. "In fact, I bet she never gets in a bed again for the rest of her life without looking under the sheets reeeeeel careful to see who or what's there."

"That's not why we're here," Slim said. "We're looking for your ex-wife."

Jake's head tipped backwards and he smiled. He said, "Yeah? Which one?"

"Jodie."

"Williams or Hobbs? I married two of 'em." He winked. "Top that."

"Hobbs."

Jake nodded, then aimed the wad of bloody gauze westward. "Well, you just keep down this road a piece and you'll get to a honky-tonk called the Lost and Found. She runs the place, or so I'm told. I stay away from there. But if you see her, tell her I said send me some money."

"Have you seen her lately?"

"Have I seen...No, see, that's one of the reasons people get divorced," Jake explained. "So they don't never have to see each other again. Ever, ever, ever. At least that's what Jodie said when we were leaving the courthouse that day. Seemed kinda bitter, if you ask me."

"Jake, lemme just cut to the chase," Howdy said. "Jodie disappeared last night. We think somebody kidnapped her."

Jake looked at the two men as if they'd just proposed marriage. A sort of stupefied disbelief. "And you think it was *me*?"

"Well, let me ask you something." Slim reached across the desk, grabbing the stun gun. "What do you need this for?" He triggered it and the electricity spit and crackled between the two electrodes.

Jake dropped his head and shook it like he'd been caught red-handed. Then he looked up smirking, and said, "I'm gonna go out on a limb here and guess that neither one of you's ever been grabbed by a twelve-foot Burmese python." He waited until they both shook their heads before he said, "Well, for future reference, let me tell you there's two good ways to make it let go. You can either kill it or you can hit it with a few volts. As a reptile retailer, I find it's easier to sell snakes that are still alive, so I opt for the volts. But that's just me."

"Uh-huh." Howdy gestured at Jake's face and arms. "I suppose a Burmese python gave you all those scratches?"

"Are you kidding?" He glanced at his scarred forearms. "I spend half my life in the desert looking under rocks for snakes and spiders. Plus I been married five times. Of course I'm all scratched up."

Slim was behind the desk now, picking up the coil of rope. "Lemme guess, you use this for roping the really big spiders, or maybe an ex-wife now and then?"

"I got a horse," Jake said. "I camp a lot. Rope is useful."

Howdy picked up the canister of isoflurane and gave it a sniff. He looked a little woozy when he said, "And what about this?" He took another, longer sniff. Then he smiled as a warm, happy sensation washed over him. "Hey, that's nice." He sniffed some more.

Jake suddenly threw up his hands. "Oh hell, you got me," he said. "I might as well confess." He aimed the gauzy finger at a door behind him. "Jodie's in the back, tied up with the rope, just like you're thinking. These scratches? Got 'em during the struggle." He snatched the canister of isoflurane from under Howdy's nose. "Finally knocked her out with this." He took another sniff for himself, a long one, then set the canister back on the desk.

Whereupon Howdy picked it up and took one more hit. High as a kite and imagining himself in a detective story, he said, "You got an answer for everything, don't you, Jake?"

Howdy went to take another hit, but Slim snatched the canister away from him. He took a good whiff, just to see, then screwed the cap back on. "That's enough of that," Slim said. Then it hit him. "Whewwwww." A goofy smile all over his face, he said, "Lead me not into temptation."

"Oh, shit!" Jake slapped his good hand on the desk, startling the two anesthetized detectives. "I'm such an idiot!"

Slim regained some of his senses and said, "What're you talking about?"

"I forgot to send a damn ransom note," Jake said. "You think it's too late?" He covered his eyes with his hand. "Man, that's embarrassing."

Slim and Howdy looked at one another like maybe Jake wasn't their best suspect after all.

"I believe you two boys have a problem with premature accusation," Jake said with a smirk. "Now I appreciate you thinking of me for a part in your big kidnap case and your chance at being heroes and all, but you got at least one major problem with your theory." Jake held up his lanced and weeping finger. "Diamondback bit me six days ago. Somebody grabbed Jodie last night, it wasn't me. I can't pick up a garter snake with this hand, let alone grab a struggling wildcat. And I know from personal experience that Jodie will put up one helluva fight if you try to get her to do something she don't want to." He shook his head, thinking back to that night all those years ago. "Damn shame to find that out on the honeymoon, but what're ya gonna do?"

Howdy gestured for the canister behind Slim's back.

Slim shook his head, kept it out of reach.

"I wish I could help," Jake said. "I really do. But except to pass her on the road, I haven't seen Jodie in years. If she's got enemies, I don't know who they are. If I did, I'd tell you. Hell, if I knew someone was holding her against her will, I'd go over there myself with something poisonous, I swear. Of all my ex-wives, she's the one I wished was still around, every now and then."

"Jake, you seem sincere and all," Slim said. "But there's one thing you haven't explained." Slim held up the canister. "What about this?"

"Oh, that's for anesthetizing snakes," he said, pointing forked fingers at Slim and Howdy. "Now, are you sure I can't interest you in that Mexican red-kneed tarantula?"

45

"JAKE, WE GOT NO USE FOR A TARANTULA," HOWDY SAID. "No matter what color its knees are. But if you've got a map, we could use some help finding this place." He showed Jake the address taken from the box at Link's trailer.

Jake pulled out a map and found the location of Link's presumed dungeon. It was over in Kinney County, just south of Brackettville, about forty-five miles from Del Rio. "Spofford Junction," Jake called it.

As soon as they were in the truck, Howdy said, "Jake may be crazy as a soup sandwich, but I think we can scratch him off the list of suspects."

"What?" Slim shot Howdy a look of surprise and said, "Why?"

"C'mon," Howdy said. "It's obvious."

"Not to everybody."

"Even with two good hands, I doubt that boy could wrestle Jodie into submission, let alone get her into the trunk of a car." Like that's the way you're supposed to do it.

Slim shook his head like he was the best detective in the truck. He said, "See, that's why they came up with that word 'accomplice.' Jake doesn't have to be the one who did the actual abduction. In fact, given his former—presumably tumultuous—relationship with Jodie, it's the dumbest thing he could do. The prime suspect is always the ex. Husband, wife, girlfriend, whatever. Jake may be crazy, but he knows that much. He'd want an alibi. And that's why he'd get an accomplice." Slim paused before he said, "And what makes you think they'd stick her in the trunk of a car?"

Howdy shrugged. "Where else you gonna put a kidnap victim? Riding shotgun?"

"I've never done it," Slim said. "But my point is: Rattlesnake Jake's a good suspect."

"Better than our boy with the whips and chains?"

Slim's head rocked side to side as he said, "Yeah, well, I'm not saying we don't track Link down. But, you know, he almost seems too obvious, don't you think? Be foolish to eliminate Jake just because Link *looks* like a home run."

"Are you kidding?" Howdy looked back over his shoulder and gestured with his thumb. "Did you forget the thing hanging by the noose in Link's kitchen? And those magazines?"

"Listen, I got friends subscribe to *Guns & Ammo,* doesn't make them killers," Slim said. "Besides, what about the rope and the scratches and all that?"

Howdy held out his hands. "He had innocent explanations for everything."

"Yeah, a little too innocent for my taste," Slim said. "Sounded almost rehearsed. And did you notice how quick he was to pull that map and point us toward Link?"

Howdy shook his head. "You may be crazier than Jake." He touched a finger to the brim of his hat, then pointed down the road. "My money's on Link the kink."

Slim shook his head. "You prefer a simple disgruntled former employee over a bitter, mentally unstable, drug-addled, paranoid ex-husband who sees his ex-wife getting ahead without him? His old flame leaving him in the dust, humiliating him for all of Del Rio to see? Probably been eatin' at him ever since she came back to town. Sees her success. Knows his own failures." Slim snapped his fingers. "The boy finally snapped."

"I think you sniffed too much of that juice," Howdy said. "It's clouding your judgment."

"Or cleared my head."

"Right," Howdy said. "Let's get back to your accomplice theory. If somebody's in cahoots with Jake, who is it?"

"No idea," Slim said. "Maybe Duke."

"Duke?"

"Why not? I'm just saying anything's possible."

They carried on like this for another ten minutes as they sped east on U.S. 90, across the Val Verde County line. Neither one of them wanted to say, "Do you think she's still alive?" They were both thinking these words, had been for a while, but there was something about saying them that seemed wrong, like bad luck, so neither one did.

After a while, Slim said, "You know, I read this article one time that said something like ninety-five percent of kidnap victims—now I'm talking about adult kidnappings, not children. That's a whole different ball of wax. Let's not go there. But something like ninety-five percent of kidnapped adults are abducted by someone they know," he said. "Except for, like, U.S. corporate executives in foreign countries." Slim seemed pretty sure about this.

"This article say anything about the percentage that live to tell the tale?"

"Most of 'em, actually," Slim lied. In truth, there was no article, just some vague memory of an FBI statistic on the news a year ago mixed with some wishful thinking. Slim figured they'd both feel better if they talked and acted as if Jodie would be all right as long as they kept looking for her.

Howdy pointed at the upcoming intersection. "Here's your turn."

Slim took the right onto the 131, heading south now, toward FM 1572.

Ten minutes later they rolled past the past in the form of the old Spofford Hotel, what remained of it anyway, and the depot for the Southern Pacific Railroad. A mile after that they reached the address they were looking for.

It was a crumbling mansion built by a Randolph P. Crawford in the early 1900s after the Kinney County irrigation canal turned the area into a thriving farming and ranch community. Mr. Crawford, who had inherited substantial acreage in the area, subdivided his land, made the proverbial killing, and built his Xanadu. Fifteen years later, somebody farther to the north with the money to buy better political connections got control of the water rights to the west fork of the Nueces River and that was all she wrote for Spofford. Within a few years, the population had all but blown away with the dust.

But the Crawford house remained, slouching a little more with each passing decade. It sat two hundred yards back from the road, an ominous silhouette looming on the horizon. According to legend, after the Spofford bubble burst, old man Crawford hung himself in the house. Locals said the place was haunted, and it looked like there might be some truth to it.

Slim pulled up the dirt driveway, stopped about halfway to the house. They could see Link's truck and a late-model blue sedan parked up there.

Howdy turned his head sideways, said, "You hear that?"

"Yep." The sound of a stereo, muffled, but obviously blasting somewhere inside the house. "Doesn't sound like Perry Como either."

Figuring no one would hear their approach, Slim drove straight to the front and parked between Link's truck and the blue sedan.

Standing in front of the crumbling old manse, tilting his head back to look up at the onion-shaped dome atop the turret, Howdy said, "Bet this was quite a place back in its day."

Slim nodded. "It's an Eastlake," he said. "Queen Anne–style Victorian." He pointed at the fancy spindles and lacy, ornamental details. "See all that wedding cake stuff? Designer named Eastlake made that popular."

"Just goes to show you," Howdy said.

"Yeah."

A couple of one-by-six boards formed a prohibitive X across the front door, so Slim and Howdy moved around the side. There was more noise, this time from the generator that was providing the power for the stereo that kept blasting the furious noise. They peeped in the windows, there was no one on the first floor. Howdy elbowed Slim and pointed at the door to the storm cellar. "Down there."

They opened the door to a blast of industrial-strength death metal and the smell of sweat and leather. There was a sturdy flight of stairs going down to a landing, then a ninety-degree turn before the stairs continued to the dungeon.

They drew their guns and started down. No one would hear them coming, but they could still be seen, so they were careful how they approached.

From the landing they could see everything. It was the room from the Polaroids. The stool and the frayed wire with the lone bulb. The rack of flogs and whips. An empty body harness hung from the ceiling, like all that was left was the victim's skin. Off to one side, a heavy table displayed an array of power tools and a branding iron.

After circling the room, as if trying to avoid the thing, their eyes finally came to rest on the cage in the middle of the floor. Inside, someone bound with latex, chains, and a full black leather hood. No way to tell if it was Jodie, the local Sweet Potato Queen, or the mayor of Houston, but it sent a shiver up Slim's and Howdy's spines that would have bucked a rider.

Link was standing next to the cage, cracking a whip, head back and howling. He looked like Lord Humungus from *The Road Warrior,* powerful and debased. His leather neck collar flaring at the shoulders. The shiny metal face mask with holes punched for air brought to mind a psychopathic hockey goalie from the Dark Ages. He bent down, shouting something at the person in the cage, but Slim and Howdy couldn't hear it over the noise coming from the six speakers arrayed around the chamber.

It sounded like the Orcs of Mordor had formed a band and were still trying to get their shit together. The group was actually called Death by Infection, four terminally bored and musically inept kids from the suburbs of Denver who found their grinding, violent, ugly noise was the best way to annoy their parents and get chicks. Their mostly unintelligible lyrics hit the ears like a bludgeon. Something about political degradation and tendons between their teeth, but it was hard to say for sure.

Slim couldn't take the noise any longer. He drew a bead on the stereo.

Howdy shook his head, pointed at Link.

Slim shrugged, turned, aimed at Link.

Howdy shook his head again and gestured for Slim to lower the .45 and just follow.

Because of the hood and all the noise, the woman in the cage—who they both hoped was Jodie—had no way to know they were crossing the room, heading for Link. The captive continued to struggle against the five-piece hog-tie set, to the point of testing its one-year limited warranty.

Slim and Howdy had to cross twenty feet of open floor to get to

Link. They walked fast, just in case he turned around. As Slim passed the rack of cudgels and flogs, he holstered his gun and grabbed a Louisville Slugger that didn't seem to get much use here in the dungeon. He choked up on it, one-handed, as he approached Link. He took one last step, bringing the target within reach, then he sapped the big son of a bitch on the back of the head.

46

LINK PITCHED FORWARD, LANDING LIKE A LEATHER SAND-
bag draped over the cage.

The woman inside reacted like a blind mole rat, head tipped up as
if sniffing for clues, aware that something had happened but having
no idea what it was. The only thing missing was a set of whiskers.

Then the gunshot.

It scared everybody except Slim, who had fired it, killing the
sound system and Death by Infection with a single shot. "There." He
holstered the .45 and said, "Enough of that."

In the quiet that followed, the captive in the cage stiffened visibly,
suddenly aware that others were here and something was going on.

Slim nudged Howdy, said, "Give me a hand." They grabbed Link's
arms. Slim nodded at something nearby. "Over there."

On hearing their voices, the woman began struggling and screaming, trying to say urgent things. But coming from under the mask, it
all pretty much came out as "Mmmrrpphh!"

"Jodie! It's me and Slim," Howdy said, as he struggled with his
half of Link. "Just give us a second."

Squirming from the hog-tie position, she looked like an X-rated
rocking horse, grunting all the while as Slim and Howdy—also
grunting—wrestled Link into a kneeling position with his head and
arms through the holes of some Medieval stocks, his legs in an ankle
hobbler.

The captive kept struggling and screaming to the point that
Howdy got nervous, started glancing over his shoulder. Was it a

warning? Did Link have a nasty little apprentice lurking in the shadows with a hatchet?

After they secured Link, they found the keys to the cage, popped the lock, and swung open the rusty hinges. Howdy grabbed the legs and pulled. When he could reach it, he unzipped the hood and pulled it off. "There you go."

Much to their surprise, it was a man. And the first thing he said was, "What the *hell* are you doing?!" He was furious. "You ruined the scene!"

Slim looked at him and said, "You ain't Jodie."

He had sunken cheeks and a pencil-thin mustache that gave him the appearance of a Depression-era carnival barker. Bowed up in the hog-tie position, the man wiggled back and forth. He was all red-faced as he shouted, "You have any idea how long we've been trying to get this shot?" The man looked over and saw Link, unconscious, in the stockade. "Oh, great." He turned, looked up at Howdy. "Undo this thing, would ya?"

Howdy set the guy free and said, "What's going on here?"

"What's it look like?" The guy went to a space under the stairway landing and turned off the three-thousand-dollar Sony digital unit. "We're making a film," he said. "I'm the producer. Morgan Bryson. Bryson Entertainment." He offered his hand but nobody took it.

Slim said, "You're producing *and* you're in the movie?" Like he knew that was a bad combination.

"I also wrote it," he said. "Welcome to low-budget hell." Bryson went over to get a closer look at Link. "You didn't kill him, did you?" Link moaned, answering the question. "Good, my Brando lives." Bryson unlocked the stockades and ankle hobbler, then stepped aside as Link flopped backwards onto the floor with a thud. He saw the bullet hole in the sound system, rubbed his hand across his face. "You idiots! There goes my soundtrack."

Howdy grabbed Bryson by the arm. "Look, Mr. Speilberg, we're not particularly concerned about your shooting schedule."

Bryson jerked free of Howdy's grip. "You're killing me, you know that?" He gestured at all the equipment. "I'm renting this stuff by the day. Have any idea what that costs? No, of course not. What do you care? You're not in the business. And what do you want, any-way? A part? You want to be in the movie? Jesus, everybody wants to be in show business but nobody wants to pay the dues."

"We're looking for a woman named Jodie Lee," Howdy said. "I don't suppose you know anything about her disappearance."

Bryson wasn't listening. He had pulled a BlackBerry from his pocket and was thumbing away at the tiny keyboard. "You have any idea how close we are to the deadline for Slamfest? If we miss it"—he set the BlackBerry down and crossed the room, disappearing into a shadowy corner—"we'll have to premiere on YouTube."

Howdy was running out of patience. You could hear it when he said, "Look, Mr. Scorsese, I asked you about Jodie Lee. You wanna hold still for a second and give us some answers?"

"My answer's simple," Bryson said as he stepped out of the dark-ness with a snub-nosed .38. "This is a closed set. You've assaulted my lead talent. If you don't leave, I'll assume you mean to assault me as well and I'll be forced to shoot." He thumbed the hammer back and wagged the gun at them. "Now let's see the hands."

"Great," Slim said, as his went up. "All the producers in the world and we get the Phil Spector of the indie film set."

Howdy's hands remained by his side. Bryson wagged the gun again. "I said, put 'em up."

Howdy tilted his head slightly toward Slim and mumbled, "On three."

Slim cut his eyes sideways and said, "On three what?"

"One..."

"Wait a second. I don't know the plan."

"Don't do anything stupid," Bryson said, unsure where to aim. "Two..."

"At least give me a clue," Slim said.

"Three!"

Bryson fired a shot just as Slim dove to his right and rolled to cover behind a thick crate. Howdy jumped left and grabbed the tri-pod in a full nelson, holding his gun to the digital camera like a hostage's head. He looked at Bryson, dead serious, and said, "Drop the gun or the Sony gets it."

After a dramatic pause, the producer said, "You wouldn't."

"Try me," Howdy said. "And while you hesitate to do so, let's get back to the whereabouts of Jodie Lee."

"I don't even know *who* she is," Bryson said. "Let alone where."

"No? What about your big playmate?" Howdy said. "Jodie caught him stealing from her. She fired him. He was pissed off. And come to find out he's keen on bondage and sadism. I'm thinking he knows something."

"Speaking of pissed off," Slim said as he came from behind the crate. "Next time you start countin' to three without giving me more information—"

"You get hit?"

"No, but—"

"All right, then, let's just focus on finding Jodie."

Bryson kept his gun on Howdy. "I tell you what. Back away from the camera and maybe we can work something out where nobody gets hurt."

"You don't get the camera until we get Jodie."

Out of the corner of his eye, Slim noticed Link's hulking figure rising from the floor with the Louisville Slugger. He let out a roar as he charged Howdy from behind. Slim drew his .45 and squeezed off a shot that was meant to get Link's attention, which it did, seeing as how it hit him in the hand. The bat tumbled to the ground as did Link, who was now howling like a coyote.

Howdy kept his gun on the camera as he turned to see Link curled up on the floor like a bear holding a wounded paw. Then he looked at Slim. "Nice shot."

Slim gave a casual shrug like he'd hit what he was aiming at. Then he turned his aim on Bryson.

"One more time," Howdy said. "Where's Jodie?" He cocked his pistol.

"Okay, okay." Bryson set the .38 on the floor and raised his hands. "Search the house, do whatever, just don't shoot the camera."

They grabbed the .38 and stuffed Bryson and Link into the little cage. Getting the door closed was like sitting on an overpacked suitcase. The two men were pressed inside like sardines in a can.

Slim and Howdy went through the old house from basement to attic. There was evidence of squatting and sordid behavior in most of the rooms. Sterno cans, cigarette wrappers, empty bottles, a broken crack pipe. One room had an old metal bed frame with burlap bags as a thin mattress and some rope tied to the headboard. But no obvious signs of Jodie.

After their fruitless search, they returned to the dungeon. Howdy seemed to be in a sour mood. Link was cursing and making threats while Bryson was bitching about cost overruns and distribution problems.

Howdy went over to the table where the power tools were laid out. He picked up the drill and squeezed the trigger. *Whrizzzzz.* He walked over to the cage where Link's head was pressed to the bars, unable to move. Howdy said, "Link, I saw that magazine of yours." *Whrizzzzz.* "The article on trepanation was damn interesting." *Whrizzzzz.* "Now, I'm just going to ask one more time." He touched the drill to Link's shiny head.

47

AFTER FINISHING WITH THE BUDDING FILMMAKERS, SLIM and Howdy made the drive back to Del Rio. They walked into the Lost and Found around halftime of the Sunday night game, Titans and Texans tied at 14. As per Uncle Roy's instructions, Duke had been sitting on the door, checking IDs, waiting for Slim and Howdy to return. The three of them were comparing notes when Howdy casually mentioned his use of power tools on Link's head.

"That's not the kind of drilling we usually do in Texas," Duke said, apparently unfazed by Howdy's methods. "You hit oil?" By which he meant, did Link talk?

"Didn't go deep enough," Howdy said. "Sumbitch seemed genuinely excited at the prospect, so I didn't want to give him the satisfaction."

This seemed to startle Duke a bit. "Excited about getting a hole drilled in his head?"

"He's from Alabama," Slim said, like that explained a lot.

"What about her ex-husband? You talk to him?"

Slim and Howdy recounted their visit to Rattlesnake Jake's, up to and including the sale price of the Mexican red-kneed tarantula. "I still think he's got a lot to account for," Slim said. "Something's seriously off about that boy."

"He's a sick puppy, all right," Duke said. "Wouldn't surprise me if he's involved. Might wanna put one of my guys on him. See if he leads us anywhere."

"Good idea," Slim said. "I was thinking he might have an accomplice."

Howdy shook his head. He still didn't think it was Jake, but he didn't feel like arguing the point. Link still struck him as the better suspect. He looked at Duke. "What'd you find out?"

"Me and the boys rattled a lot of cages," Duke said. "Talked to everybody we know. Put feelers out to those we don't. Only thing that popped was word from this smuggler we know down around Piedras Negras, said he heard something secondhand about some big gringo bragging on this kidnap-for-ransom scheme he was running."

"Oh yeah?" Howdy was starting to wonder if Link and Bryson had pulled one over on them. "Any details?"

Duke shook his head. "Nah, it was one of those guy-who-heard-it-from-some-other-guy sort of things, no specifics."

"Nothing about this big gringo having a bunch of studs in his scalp?"

"No, I think that would've come up," Duke said. "Our man said it was just some asshole at a bar, talking big, trying to impress some girl."

Slim nodded, said, "So that narrows it down to, what...half the men on earth?"

"Roughly," Duke said. Then, a second later, "Oh, by the way, Jodie's brother called. Said he got your message and canceled the rest of his depositions up in Abilene. He's on his way back first thing tomorrow. He'll be in his office."

"We'll pay him a visit," Howdy said. "See if he's got any ideas on suspects."

The rest of the night was business as usual. The Titans scored two quick touchdowns early in the fourth to put the game out of reach. After that Howdy did a couple of sets before they gave last call and started running everybody out.

It was a little after midnight. Slim was locking the cash box when the door creaked open. Without looking up, he said, "Sorry, partner, we're closing up."

Roy Hobbs hobbled through the door and said, "Good. We don't need interruptions." He moved past Slim, pulling an envelope from his pocket. "I just got the ransom note."

48

THE RANSOM NOTE WAS PINNED TO THE BAR WITH FOUR shot glasses. Slim, Howdy, Duke, and Roy were hovering around it.

We have the woman.
unharmed.
$150,000 u.S.
You have thirTy-Six Hours.
Los Zetas.

Howdy said, "*Los Zetas?*"

"It's a gang," Duke replied. "Mercenaries, really. Mexican police trained by U.S. Special Forces is how the story goes. They were going to be the secret weapon in the War on Drugs until they realized the other army had more money. So they work for the Guerrero cartel now."

"Wait a second," Slim said. "These the guys who rolled the five severed heads onto the dance floor at that nightclub a while back?"

"In Mexico City," Duke said. "That's them."

Roy scoffed at all this. "It's not *Los Zetas*." He sounded certain. "We do business. We have an understanding." He tapped one of his unfiltered cigarettes from the pack, lit up.

"Maybe they have a new understanding," Howdy suggested.

"I doubt it," Roy said, blowing a blue cloud. "But I'll make a call. My bet is, that's a red herring. Kidnapper just wants us too scared to think about doing anything other than handing over the money and running."

Slim thought about that for a second before he said, "I could see how that might work."

"What about the money?" Howdy asked. "Thirty-six hours isn't a lot of time."

"The money's not a problem," Roy said. "Problem is getting the money to the kidnapper. With the possible exception of Duke here, I wouldn't trust any of my employees with a hundred fifty grand in a suitcase." He looked at Duke. "No offense."

"None taken," he said.

Roy turned his weathered face toward Slim and Howdy. "I want you two involved."

"Involved?"

"In the exchange."

"You'd trust *us* with the money?"

"Jodie trusts you," Roy said. "That's good enough for me."

"What about calling the cops?"

"No!" Roy slammed a fist on the bar. "Absolutely not. Out of the question! I got enough problems. First thing they'd do is call the feds and that's the last thing I need. No police. Period! We'll handle this ourselves."

"Okay," Howdy said. "What do we do first?"

"We wait," Roy said. "Wait until we find out how it's supposed to go down."

49

AROUND TEN THE NEXT MORNING SLIM AND HOWDY WERE walking down a sidewalk on their way to see Grady. They were a block off Main Street, directly behind the old Roach's Clothing Store. What once had been a tidy and thriving little downtown had devolved into a depressed mixed-use area of pawnshops, gun stores, and decrepit office buildings.

"It was dangerous as hell," Howdy said.

Slim shrugged. "Paid off, didn't it?"

"That was dumb luck and you know it," Howdy said. "And the man ain't gettin' paid to test his luck."

They were discussing a play call from the third quarter of last night's game: A double-reverse with a pass back to a tackle eligible on fourth and long. "They were up by seven," Howdy said. "And on their own thirty-five."

"Probably why they caught the defense off guard," Slim said.

Howdy was shaking his head and working on a retort when something across the street caught his attention. The next thing Slim knew, Howdy had grabbed his arm and pulled him into a recessed doorway.

Slim yanked free of Howdy's grip, said, "The hell are you doing?"

"Shut up!" Howdy used his hat to hide his face as he peered out from the shadow of the doorway. He gestured across the street and said, "Tell me that's not Boone Tate coming out of that gun shop."

Slim took a peek and said, "I think you're right. And who's that big sumbitch with him?"

"And what's in that package he's carrying?"

After watching Boone and Brickman get into a Ford Taurus and drive away, Howdy stepped back onto the sidewalk, looked at Slim, and said, "You think it's a coincidence?"

"That we happened to see him?" Slim nodded. "I'd say by definition it's a coincidence."

"Okay, but is it a coincidence that he's shopping at Guns Galore in downtown Del Rio."

"Well," Slim said, "you did take his gun."

"And he's going to drive all the way to Del Rio to get a new one?"

"Maybe he's got a coupon."

Howdy glared at him as they stopped, waiting for the light to change before crossing the street.

Slim brushed something from the lens of his sunglasses and said, "You know, I think this points out there are a few suspects we haven't really considered up to now."

Howdy started to nod. "Now that you mention it," he said, "Black Tony comes to mind."

Slim joined in the nodding. "You gotta figure he'd like to get back at us for parking that Trans Am in his living room."

Howdy mulled that over for a second before he said, "Yeah, though I'm not sure how he'd track us to Del Rio."

"Don't think it would matter much *how* he did it, *if* he did it. Same's true of Dempsey Kimble and the other fella at the Piggin' String, that Buddy Cooper. I mean it's not like we've made a lot of friends along the way."

"I see your point," Howdy said. "But the fact we just saw Boone Tate and we ain't seen the others, kinda points in his direction."

"I guess, but why kidnap Jodie? Why not just ambush us one night, coming out of the club? Something like that makes more sense."

They walked half a block before Howdy said, "Unless he's trying to . . . frame us for the kidnapping."

Slim shook his head. "Boone Tate's a lot of things, but clever ain't one of 'em."

When the light changed, they crossed the street and Howdy said, "Did you ever see that movie, *The Big Lebowski?*"

"Yeah." Slim nodded and laughed as he remembered a line of dialogue. "Hey, careful, dude, there's a beverage involved!"

Howdy said, "And didn't the old man fake his wife's kidnapping in the first place? Something to do with laundering money or something."

"You think Uncle Roy's trying to clean some of his dirty money?"

Howdy thought it over, then shrugged. "No, doesn't really make sense, does it?"

"Not that I can figure," Slim said.

Howdy stopped and looked at the street address on the door. "This is it."

It was a dismal little office building with a Space for Lease sign in the window.

They walked into the lobby behind a group of three men, looked like day laborers with the day off, who kept walking straight up the stairs.

Slim and Howdy went to the building directory. Howdy scanned it while Slim faced the other direction, looking at the dispiriting, almost Soviet, design of the place and wondering what the hell they were thinking when they built it.

"Little bit of everything in here," Howdy said after inspecting the directory. "Insurance, a couple of Realtors, a chiropractor, a temp agency, and a few lawyers."

Slim was still passing judgment on the interior design of the dim lobby. He paused long enough to say, "Where's Grady's office?"

"Second floor."

They took the stairs, then down the hall to suite 220-223, which turned out to house not only Grady's office but also the insurance agent and the chiropractor. The three of them shared a willing receptionist who smiled at the sight of the two handsome cowboys and said, "Can I help you?"

"Yes, ma'am." Howdy tipped his hat and said, "We're here to see Grady Hobbs."

A perfunctory glance at the appointment book before she said, "He's in a conference with clients at the moment." Like it was IBM. "It shouldn't be long if you'd like to wait." Gesturing at the seventeen-year-old furniture.

"That's fine." They took their seats and flipped through some old magazines, looked around. No brass and walnut paneling here. It was all drywall and dropped-ceiling, big panels of acoustic tile. Looked like originals from the 1970s.

Slim stared at a large water stain in one of the panels. He would have sworn it was in the shape of the Louisiana Purchase. Howdy, who was suddenly trying to remember when they stopped using asbestos in building materials, was looking at the same stained panel but was more impressed by the forty-five-degree angle from which it was dangling. It looked like it should have dropped by now, he thought.

They'd been looking at the stained tile for about five minutes when the door opened and three men walked out of Grady's office. They were the same three men who had entered the building in front of Slim and Howdy. The only difference was that all three of them were now wearing foam-rubber cervical collars, and one of them was limping.

Slim and Howdy exchanged a look. Neither one of them said anything, but it made both of them wonder about the area of law in which Grady specialized. This didn't look like class-action tort material so much as something else.

"He'll see you now," the receptionist said.

"Thanks." They went in, pausing to look around as they entered. It was like a small bomb had gone off in a second-rate stationery store. Yellowed boxes overflowed with accordion files. Coffee-stained depositions, demand letters, and delinquent motions scattered and stacked and strewn among Styrofoam cups, half-eaten doughnuts, and the first impression was of someone you wouldn't even let represent you in imaginary kangaroo court.

"Hey, guys, c'mon in." Grady stood and waved his hands around. He was wearing the same suit as the last time they saw him. "Forgive the mess," he said. "Just move that stuff anywhere you can, grab a seat."

Slim took a stack of files off a chair and moved them to a spot on the floor near a small closet that was partially open. Inside he could see a box of cervical collars and some crutches.

"Looks like you're a busy man," Howdy said.

Grady snorted a laugh. "What they say about this being a liti-
gious society? It's true," he said. "And, as you can plainly see, it's also
messy." He sat down and tipped one and then another of the Styrofoam cups to see if there was anything left, but there wasn't.

Except for the suit, Grady didn't look like the same good-time
Charlie who had showed up at the Lost and Found a few nights
ago. Probably hadn't slept much since hearing about his sister. His
jittery movements and twitchy eyes belonged to a man burning the
candle at both ends, eating poorly, drinking too much coffee, scurrying from one fire to the next, trying to keep his life from erupting
in flames.

At least that was the impression Howdy got.

Slim noticed something similar. That sort of Willie Loman aspect
of a guy struggling to maintain the happy face even as he knew that
his window of opportunity in life was fast closing, if indeed it had
ever been open. Grady was desperation wearing a smile.

But he was ready to get down to business. He squared a legal pad
and a pen in front of himself. "I got back as soon as I could," he said.
"What exactly happened?" He leaned forward, projecting concern.

Grady made an occasional note on the legal pad as Slim and
Howdy delivered the play-by-play from Saturday night up to the
point when they found Jodie's phone in the century plant.

"Jesus." Grady began massaging his temples with his fingertips.
"And of course the cops won't help because there's no evidence that a
crime's been committed, right?"

"Their words exactly," Howdy said.

"Naturally." Grady nodded, affirmation that his lawyerly mind
knew how these things worked. He made a note about the cops and
said, "And at this point we don't even know if we're looking at kidnapping or an abduction?"

"What's the difference?"

"Kidnapping involves a demand of some sort, ransom money, cus-
tody of a child, something like that," Grady said. "Abduction is…"
He paused as if he didn't want to finish the thought. "Well, serial killers tend to abduct, make their demands on the person they grab."

"It's kidnapping," Howdy said. "A ransom note showed up last
night."

Slim nodded. "A hundred fifty thousand dollars."

Grady seemed genuinely shocked. "A hundred and fifty thousand?!" Like he might fall out of his chair. He wrote "150,000" on the pad and underlined it three times. "That's a lot of money."

"Yeah."

"It's also proof that a crime's been committed," Grady said. "Do the cops know?"

"Uncle Roy wants to keep them out of it."

Grady nodded. "I bet he does."

"The note was signed by *Los Zetas,*" Howdy said. "That's this Mexican—"

"I know what it is," Grady said. "They're some evil *hombres,* too, essentially narco-terrorists. They send the note straight to Uncle Roy?"

"Yeah."

After a moment, Grady began to nod slowly as if that made all the sense in the world. "Well," he said. "There you go." He held his hands out as if they contained the obvious.

"What do you mean?"

Grady didn't seem real keen on airing dirty laundry but, at the same time, he felt a need to explain himself. "How do I put this?" He looked off at the far corner of the room, then back at Slim and Howdy. "Uncle Roy's not exactly a pillar of the community."

"Your point being?"

"Point is, Roy Hobbs is a criminal." Grady flashed a grim smile, one that said he wasn't proud to say the words but that Slim and Howdy had just forced him to. "You seen where he lives?" Grady made a distasteful face and said, "You don't buy a place like that doing honest work, not around here anyway. What did you think, he won the lottery?"

Howdy shrugged, said, "Jodie told us he had several business interests, including the Lost and Found."

"That's it?"

"Well," Slim said. "She hinted that he might treat tax law as more of a suggestion than an actual requirement."

"Yeah, well, that's true as far as it goes," Grady said. "He also owns the Truck 'n' Go Quicky Stop, out past the city limits." He gestured in the general direction. "You know about that?"

"Yeah, we've been there," Howdy said. "Looked like a real moneymaker."

"Hell yes it's a moneymaker," Grady said with a scowl. "Damn thing's a whorehouse as well as an outlet for stolen goods and illegal gambling." He started counting on his fingers. "They also sell coke, crystal meth, heroin. Pot by the pound. Those rows of CDs and DVDs are all pirated. I suspect they smuggle illegals too. Got cops in one pocket, judges in the other. Sumbitch is bulletproof." Grady waved his hands like he was shooing all that stuff away. "Not that I'm pure as the driven snow or anything," he said. "But my point is, Roy Hobbs deals with the very bottom of the barrel. The kind of folks who'll seize an opportunity when they see one. No matter who gets hurt."

"Folks like *Los Zetas,*" Slim said.

"Exactly," Grady replied. "But not exclusively. There's no shortage of disreputable types in Roy's universe. Hell, it's a virtual requirement if you want to work for him. Like that Duke character." He wrote the name on the pad under the "150,000." "I think we have to look at him as a suspect. He knows Jodie's routines. Knows Roy can put his hands on lots of cash. He also knows Roy wouldn't want the cops involved."

"Okaaaay," Howdy said skeptically. "But how does that make sense if the cops are in Roy's pocket?"

"He's not worried about the locals," Grady said. "This is a federal crime. He's worried they'll call in the big boys. And the feds *aren't* in Roy's pocket. Listen, I'm not saying it *is* Duke. It could just as easily be one of the goons who works under him. Somebody tired of working for peanuts, gets a bright idea, grabs the boss's niece, lives happily ever. Like I said, there's no shortage of miscreants in Roy's world."

"Roy thinks the whole *Los Zetas* thing is a ruse," Slim said.

"Might be," Grady said. "It's possible. But at the same time, I think you treat it that way at substantial risk."

Howdy nodded, thinking about those heads rolling onto the dance floor in Mexico City. "Can you think of anybody else who might try something like this?"

Grady folded his hands on top of the legal pad and thought about it. "Only other person comes to mind is her ex-husband Jake Heller." He shook his head and wrote Jake's name on the pad, drew a snake next to it. "He might be crazy enough to try. Though I have serious doubts about whether he's smart enough to think of it in the first place."

"We talked to him," Howdy said. "Also a disgruntled former employee named Link. Slim thinks Jake might have done it with an accomplice. But I'm leaning toward Link."

"Then there's this guy name of Black Tony," Slim said. He told Grady about all the people they'd antagonized from Beaumont to Fort Worth, including their recent citing of Boone Tate outside the gun shop.

Grady dutifully wrote "Link" and "Brushfire" and the other names on the pad. Then he said, "What did the ransom note say other than the amount?"

"Said Jodie was unharmed and they'd be in touch," Slim said. "Mr. Hobbs asked us to be involved in the exchange, however it goes down."

"Well, be careful," Grady said. "I wouldn't trust Roy Hobbs farther than I could comfortably spit a rat."

50

THE SECOND NOTE CAME IN THAT DAY'S MAIL. A PLAIN white envelope, postmarked Eagle Pass, Texas, just across the Rio Grande from Piedras Negras.

Another cut-and-paste job. It said,

WWW dot JODIESAFE DOT COM

Roy gimped over to his computer and typed in the URL. The browser linked to a page, somewhere out there in the World Wide Web. The page was black except for a white rectangle in the middle of the screen.

Inside the rectangle it said, "Click here."

The moment Roy clicked the button, his printer began spooling up and the Web page blinked out, replaced a moment later by a standard error message. "Page Not Found. Permanent Fatal Error." He tried it again but the page had disappeared.

By now, the printer had spit out a page of instructions.

"Horseback only," it read. "No vehicles. Have GPS."

There were two sets of numbers that Roy recognized as longitude and latitude, right down to the minutes and seconds. Somewhere in Mexico.

According to the instructions, he had two days to reach the location.

He was to leave the money at the site, in a shack. There he would find directions to Jodie's location.

If the money wasn't right, the kidnapper would move Jodie before Roy reached her. The price would go up and they would start over.

If the money was right, the deal was complete, hostage would be waiting, unharmed.

Clock starts at sunrise tomorrow.

Roy went to his safe and removed $150,000. It was a lot of money but he didn't mind. He stuffed it into an old saddle bag, then he called Slim and Howdy. Told them to meet him at a ranch outside Ciudad Acuna at dawn the next day.

51

SLIM AND HOWDY CROSSED THE BORDER BEFORE FIRST LIGHT
and found their way to the ranch, which turned out to be one of the
many properties Roy Hobbs owned on both sides of the river. This
was ten acres with a barn, corral, and a caretaker's house.

They found Roy cinching the girth on a buckskin mustang, about
fifteen hands high, its mane, tail, and lower legs black as molasses.
Roy looked up, squinting as the cigarette smoke curled into his eyes.
"All right, boys," he said. "Let's get this show on the road." He ges-
tured at three other horses, tied up nearby, saddled and outfitted
with everything they'd need for two days and nights in the desert.
Sleeping bags, cook gear, food, water, two-way radios, maps, and
GPS receivers all around, in case they got separated.

There were two quarter horses, one was a bay, the other a buckskin. Slim turned to Howdy and said, "If it's all the same to you, I'll
take that bay." As if it reminded him of something or someone.

"Fine by me." Howdy liked the looks of the buckskin anyway.

Neither Slim nor Howdy recognized the other breed. "That's a
Cayuse Indian pony," Roy said. "Comes out of a strain of Spanish
mustang. Helluva horse. That one's Jodie's favorite. Named him
Chulo. Figured she'd like to ride him back after we get her."

"Yes, sir," Slim said, as he adjusted the stirrups to accommodate
his long legs. "I bet you're right."

Howdy went over to the buckskin, rubbed his muzzle, let his hand
glide down his strong neck, then he started taking off the saddle.

"What're you doin'?" Roy asked.

"Got my own saddle," Howdy said. "All broke in." Which he soon pulled from the bed of the truck. "Might as well use it."

When they were all ready, Roy swung himself up on that mustang like a man half his age. Slim and Howdy followed suit and somebody asked where they were going.

Roy pointed southwest. "Serranias del Burro," he said. "An old mining area out in the desert." He glanced over his shoulder and said, "You boys ready?"

They nodded, so Roy gave that mustang a little leg, went "Tch," and off they rode into the Mexican wilderness.

The plan was: ride till noon, give the horses a break, eat lunch, then get in a couple more hours before they stopped to camp. In the morning, they'd zero in on this shack, where—assuming the kidnapper was being straight with them—they were to leave the money and find directions to Jodie's location.

It was a fine day with skies bright as diamonds. Riding into a quarter million square miles of mountainous desert colored by the morning light was enough to make Slim and Howdy forget, however briefly, the circumstances that brought them there. It had been too long since either one of them had been on top of a horse without a fence or a power line or a phone pole in sight, and there was something powerful about that for both of them.

At first they rode in silence, as if they were in the world's largest chapel, a place where talk seemed sacrilegious. Believers simply soaked in the unflinching beauty of it all. Creosote bush and tobosa grass, tall spiky ocotillos and candy barrel cactus. The ubiquitous shades of gray, green, and brown interrupted now and then by a slash of yellow from the blooms of tarbush and zinnias, or the red throat of a whiptail lizard, or the dark end of a black tailed jackrabbit. All you needed was to keep your eyes open and your mouth shut.

And for a while that's what they did.

But then, out of nowhere, Roy Hobbs just started talking. "Thing I hate most about this," he said, "is that I brought it on myself." He paused before continuing, "And what's worse, I brought it on Jodie." He shook his head like a man guilty of too many things. "I swear, anything happens to her, I'll never forgive myself." He wasn't saying this directly to Slim or Howdy, he was just saying it to get it off his chest.

"Mr. Hobbs, I think you're mad at the wrong person," Slim said. "The one you ought not be in a forgiving mood toward is whoever kidnapped Jodie."

Roy didn't seem to buy it, like that was just something to make him feel better, not something that absolved him of his culpability. He shook his head some more and said, "It's all because of who I am, what I do."

"No, sir," Howdy said, "I don't think so."

"No? Then why?" Like you think you're so smart.

"'Cause you've got the money to pay," Howdy said. "That's all. Doesn't matter how you got it, you could've struck a well. I doubt a kidnapper cares one way or the other how clean or dirty somebody's pile of money is, long as it's a pile. They just want the dough."

Roy Hobbs thought about that for a second, figured there was at least some truth to it. "Maybe you're right," he said. "I just can't help but think that if I wasn't who I am, or if I wasn't afraid of what might happen if I called the FBI, we'd be in a better position to get Jodie back."

"*If* this, *if* that," Howdy said. "It's like my dad used to say, Mr. Hobbs. If my aunt had balls, she'd be my uncle."

Roy smiled at that. "Mine always said, if wishes were horses, beggars would ride."

"There you go," Slim said. "Things are what they are and talking about 'em doesn't change 'em."

Howdy threw some extra optimism in his voice when he said, "I got a good feeling about this, Mr. Hobbs, I do. Don't ask me why, I think they just want the money. I think Jodie's fine and all we have to do is follow the instructions and we'll get her back."

"Yeah," Roy said. "You may be right. They probably just want my money. And they can have it. Trouble for them." They rode on for another moment before he said, "Course if you're wrong, they'll probably kill us all and leave our bones bleaching in the desert."

Slim turned slowly, aiming his dark glasses at Roy Hobbs. "You're just little Miss Sunshine, aren't you?"

52

AROUND NOON, THEY CAME ACROSS A SMALL LAKE, DECIDED it was a good place for lunch, let the horses get some water, rest a minute. Roy pulled out his map and his GPS receiver. Every now and then he looked around as if to get his bearings, then he'd return his attention to the map's coordinates. "We're making good time," he said, holding a wary glance over his shoulder.

Howdy passed out some sandwiches and pulled his canteen from his saddle. They made small talk as they ate, a conscious effort all around not to think too much about Jodie. Where you from? How's the horse riding? That sort of thing, until Howdy asked about what Roy did before he got into the saloon and truck stop business.

"Oh hell, I did my share of running cattle and mending fences," Roy said. "Like everybody in Texas, I guess. Then I heard there was a better way to make a living, so I went to work in the midcontinent oil fields."

This struck a chord with Slim, who said, "No kiddin'? Doin' what?"

"You name it," Roy replied with a casual shrug. "Roustabout, roughneck, mud logger, whatever kind of job I could get."

Slim smiled and pointed at the older man, feeling a bond. He said, "You know, before my dad went in the air force, he was a pipeliner all around those fields."

Now Howdy got a surprised look on his face. He turned to Slim all the sudden and said, "Get outta here! My dad was a pipeline engineer for a bunch of operators in that part of the country." He shook his head and smiled at the coincidence. He tipped his sandwich toward Roy. "Dad used to say a man had to be crazy to work on those rigs back then."

"Crazy or unemployed," Roy said with a laugh. "But it's true. It was some kind of dangerous." Roy tapped a cigarette from his pack and lit it. "Like this one thing we did called 'spuddin' the pipe,' where the driller'd lift it to the top of the derrick, drop it, and then jam the winch brakes on to shake that mud loose. Problem was sometimes those big steel mounts in the crown block would break and fall on the men below."

Roy took a deep draw on the cigarette before continuing. "I saw this one kid, eighteen years old, got killed his first *hour* on the job." Roy paused to exhale, and during that time he seemed to see the boy's face. "That was tough to watch," he said. "But things like that were more common then, I guess. We were all a little harder." He shook his head, thinking about it. "Lucky to get out alive, I guess."

"And with all your parts," Howdy said.

"Yeah, that too," Roy agreed. "But I tell ya, working the range and those rigs taught me something. Taught me that cowboys and oil-rig workers and truckers and farmers and most everybody else spends a fair cut of their paychecks just trying to enjoy themselves when their work's done. And it seemed to me that providing the supply for that demand was a better way to make a living than getting kicked by a cow or having crown blocks dropped on your head." Roy took another drag on his cigarette and said, "So that's how I ended up doin' what I do."

Looking at old Roy Hobbs, listening to him tell stories out in the middle of the Chihuahuan Desert made Slim and Howdy feel like they were in the company of the last of a dying breed at the tail end of a period of history. Roy was an authentic Texas archetype who, in *his* youth, had ridden with genuine old cowboys, men who had been part of the real Wild West back in *their* day. They told their stories to Roy, passing on whatever truth might be in them. And now, sitting here, Slim and Howdy felt like they were getting a little of that before it was lost to the world.

Then it was time to go. They got back on their horses and kept riding toward the mountains in the distance. Roy, pleased at the chance to tell his stories, talked for a while about his cowboy days before he turned to Slim and said, "Son, I'm curious why you wanted that bay so bad instead of the buckskin." Like he'd seen something in the choosing and wanted to know what it was.

Slim sliced off a little grin and nodded as if he'd been caught. "Just reminded me of a horse I had when I was a kid," he said.

Howdy figured that was all the answer Roy was going to get for his question, but Slim surprised him by saying, "My dad was still in the air force there at Laughlin and he had this runnin' buddy name of Spooner Pruet, this Texas Ranger–looking sheriff out of Port Isabel, Texas. Mom never liked him but, well, anyway, Dad and Spooner used to go down to Zaragoza, Mexico, to these illegal quarter-horse races. I was always buggin' 'em to take me along, and this one time they did. And I swear I'll never forget it.

"People came from out of nowhere for these races," Slim said with a sweeping gesture. "Line these makeshift quarter-mile outlaw dirt road racetracks with flatbed Mexicali, melon farmer–style trucks. They had these beat-up metal speakers on the tops blaring mariachi music like something out of a Speedy Gonzales cartoon. Everybody walkin' around eating churros and making bets and side bets on the next race. And then, somebody'd shoot a pistol and two horses would tear down the road with everybody hollerin' and whistlin' and jumpin' up and down for the next thirty seconds. And then it started all over again. I swear, it was the most fun I can remember in a single day."

As they loped along through the desert, Roy listened with a fond smile and a slow nod, as if he'd been to those very races and was just making sure Slim got his facts straight.

As for Howdy, he could see so clearly the picture Slim was painting that he stopped thinking about how he'd never heard Slim talk so much except when he was onstage or trying to worm his way into a woman's loving embrace, or at least her panties.

Slim aimed his hand out in front of them and said, "There was a tall cornfield at the end of the track, barely past the finish line. And these horses with these crazy 'weekend jockeys' hanging on for dear life would make a mad dash down that quarter-mile track and disappear off into the cornstalks at a dead run." Slim laughed a little thinking about it.

"So," Slim said, "this one time, Dad and Spooner bought this broke-down old bay named Pitchfork." He paused as if he felt the characterization wasn't fair to the horse. "I guess he wasn't really that broke-down," Slim said, on second thought. "But you definitely weren't going to see him in the Preakness, you know? Anyway, they must've been drunk or something, convinced they were going to get rich racing old Pitchfork at Zaragoza Downs, as they called it. So Dad's job was to train him, which he didn't have a clue about, but, anyway, come the big day, we all went down to Zaragoza to run Pitchfork. They agreed that Dad should be the jockey since he'd been the trainer, right?

"So, while Dad was getting ready for the race, Spooner was running up one side of that dirt track and down the other making bets. Back at the starting line Dad had a couple of shots of this hundred-and-fifty-proof liquor they make out of sugarcane, then he got in the saddle, and *bang!* Somebody fired the pistol and Pitchfork took off like he thought somebody was shooting at him. Dad's eyes got wide as a belt buckle and I've never laughed so hard in my entire life watching him try to keep one leg on each side of that horse." Slim did an imitation of his dad heading down the track, all loosey-goosey like a rag doll on a wild animal.

Howdy was laughing, too, but he managed to ask, "Did he win?"

"Oh hell no," Slim replied. "About three-fourths down the track, Pitchfork just slowed to a natural trot, didn't matter how much leg or spur he got. Dad dog-cussed that horse all the way across the finish line, going so slow they didn't even make it to the cornfield. I think if Dad had a gun, he'da shot Pitchfork right there," Slim said. "He was kind of competitive. So afterwards, me and Dad were loading Pitchfork back into the trailer and Spooner showed up with the look of a man who'd lost an awful lot of money. Dad asked him how much he had bet, and Spooner said, 'Five hundred dollars.' Like it was the end of the world.

"Dad looked at the sky like he wanted the Lord to take him right then and there and the horse too as long as he was at it. Then he looked at Spooner and said, 'I told you not to bet that kind of money on this nag.'

"Spooner jerked his head back in surprise and said, 'Are you nuts? I was betting *against* you.' Then he pulled out a wad of dollars and pesos and shook it at us, and we laughed about it the whole way back to Del Rio."

Roy, glancing over his shoulder but not at Slim, said, "What happened to old Pitchfork?"

Slim nodded, like he was getting to that part of the story. "Dad and Spooner joked about putting him out to stud," Slim said. "But they decided the fact he was a gelding was too much of a hurdle to overcome, so they gave him to me. And I kept him 'til we moved to New Mexico."

Howdy thought of the air force base up in Albuquerque. "Your dad get transferred up to Kirtland?"

Slim's smile sort of slipped away at the question, and after a moment, he said, "No. It was something else."

53

THE DESERT WAS COLD THAT NIGHT. HOWDY GOT A FIRE
going with the dried grass and kindling he gathered while clearing
their campsite. He poked at it until it was burning to his satisfaction.

A minute later Slim came walking out of the dusk with an armload of firewood, dropped it nearby, said, "That oughta get us
through the night."

"You see Roy out there?" Howdy asked as he grabbed a piece of
wood from the pile.

Slim brushed off his sleeves and aimed his goatee to the north.
"Yeah, he's out that way, circling the camp like he thinks we're fixin'
to get attacked by Indians or something." Slim pulled Roy's saddle
and sleeping bag a little closer to the fire, then did the same with his
own. He sat down and warmed his hands, letting the flames hypnotize his eyes for a moment.

Howdy did the same.

Every now and then they heard the *fwoop* of a pallid bat dodging
in for one of the big moths or whatever insect had been drawn to the
light of the fire. They'd look up just in time to see the odd blonde fur
and black face winging back into the darkness.

"Hope Jodie's keepin' warm," Slim said. "Wherever she is."

"Yeah, gets cold out here all right." Howdy flipped up the collar
on his duster, pulled it tighter around his neck.

Fwoop! They looked up again. Slim reached back and grabbed his
saddle blanket, pulled it over his shoulders. They sat there thinking

about Jodie, but not speaking. A few quiet minutes passed before Slim said, "So your dad was a pipeline engineer, huh?"

Howdy looked up from poking the fire, surprised that Slim had asked a personal question. "What? Oh. Yeah, he was."

Slim gave a nod. "Still at it?"

"No," Howdy said. "Lost him to cancer a couple of years ago."

"Oh." The way you do when you hear that sort of thing. "I'm sorry." Slim bowed his head slightly, eyes closed. A moment of respect before he said, "What was he like?"

Howdy stared at the fire and repeated the question while he tried to think of the best way to respond. The short answer was "hard-drinking, cigar-smoking engineer," but that didn't really capture him. Didn't do him justice. After a moment he looked up at Slim, squinting slightly. "He was smart," Howdy said. "Had an absolutely brilliant mind. And I'll tell you what else. He was the most prin-cipled, decent man I've ever known." Howdy turned his eyes back to the fire, a melancholy smile pushing at his bristly black mustache as he thought about the times he'd hunted and camped with his dad, sitting around fires just like this, talking, telling good stories and bad jokes. Something he missed.

Howdy tossed another hunk of wood on the fire and said, "When I was about sixteen, we were living in Shreveport. Dad got me this sixty-four Fairlane and spent a couple of weeks showing me how to take out the stock six and drop in a 390 with a big Holley on it."

"I bet the puppy could fly," Slim said.

"Oh yeah." Howdy nodded for a second or two. "First Friday night after we tightened the last bolt, I'm downtown, cruising. There was this one stretch of Congress Street, starting at Third, where all the lights turned green one after the other about two seconds apart. Just bink, bink, bink, bink, bink, bink, like approach lights for a runway or something. Just beggin' gearheads to come test their cars.

"So I pulled up to the light at Third Street and this guy, I guessed he was a few years older than me, pulled up in this red Cutlass, started revving his engine. I looked over and he gave me that look and I revved my engine a couple of times before the light turned green, and tore outta there like Big Daddy Don Garlits. Smoked him off the start line," Howdy said with a clap of the hands. "Left him flat in the dust." He flashed a smile at Slim. "And I felt about ten feet tall...until I looked in my rearview mirror and saw him behind me, coming up pretty fast. In my lane, with a blue light up on his dash."

"Oh, that ain't right," Slim said.

"Pulled my ass over for drag racing."

"In fact, that's just plain wrong."

"That's what I thought," Howdy said. "But the cop disagreed and took me down to the station, made me call my dad, which I damn sure didn't want to do since I'd told him I was going to show the car to a friend of mine in Bossier City, which is pretty much in the opposite direction of downtown Shreveport. So I figured I was in deep shit not only because I'd lied but because I got arrested on top of that. But I called, told him where I was, and asked could he come and get me. There was a long pause before he said, yeah, he'd be down.

"So he showed up, talked to the cops. They gave me my ticket and we got the car outta impound. Then I followed Dad home, dreading every mile. I tell you, that was the longest drive of my life."

"Your dad pretty good with a belt?"

"Worse," Howdy said. "He'd talk to you until you felt so bad about letting him down and how disappointed Mom would have been if she was still alive, and that kind of thing until you would've gladly taken a beating instead of all the guilt and shame."

Slim chuckled his understanding.

"We got back home," Howdy said. "He sat me down at the kitchen table, poured himself a drink, and sat there with me. And for the longest time he didn't say a word. Just let me sit there, makin' me imagine what he was going to say and how he was going to punish me. I figured for sure he'd take the car away. Finally, he said, 'That officer told me you were doing sixty-five in a thirty.'

"I said, 'Yes, sir, I'm real sorry. I know I was supposed to—'"

"'In what, six blocks?' Dad shook his head, looking all disappointed and said, 'You should've been doing at least eighty.' He rapped his knuckles on the table, then stood up and said, 'Get your timing light, son, something ain't right.'"

Howdy had a big smile now. "I couldn't believe it," he said. "I jumped up, headin' for the garage when he stopped me and said, 'In the future, be more careful about who and where you race. But, son, more importantly, don't lie to me. Because where we gonna be if I can't trust you?' Dad just shook his head and we were done with it. Headed out to the garage and got to work."

Slim thought about saying something along the lines of "He sounds like a helluva guy," but instead he said, "Did y'all ever get the timing right?" He looked at Howdy and winked, and then they both smiled.

"Sure did," Howdy said. He could still hear the burble of the idling engine and smell his dad's cigar and his drink as it mingled with the gas fumes, grease, and exhaust. After a second, Howdy tossed another hunk of wood on the fire and realized he'd been talking about himself the whole time. So he said, "How about *your* dad? He stay in the air force?"

"No," Slim replied. "They let him...He got discharged."

It was clear enough Slim didn't want to talk about it and Howdy wasn't going to push him. But then, out of nowhere, Slim said, "My dad got in a fight, at a bar, over some girl. Unfortunately the guy he punched was an air force captain. So they tossed Dad in the brig for the night. He broke out with a couple other guys, roughed up some MPs who got between them and the door. Next day they all got caught trying to hop a freight train. And for that, my dad got seven years in Leavenworth," Slim said. "Seven years."

Howdy, in disbelief, said, "Are you serious?"

Slim gave a disconsolate nod. "I was about ten, I guess, when all that happened. Mom didn't tell me any of it. Said the air force had sent Dad on a secret mission and he wouldn't be back for a long time."

"Seven years?" Howdy shook his head. "Man, that's tough."

Slim stared at the fire as he said, "We moved around a lot after that. Lived with Mom's sister down in Corpus for a while, then moved up to Oklahoma City, then out to an oil lease on a reservation near Blanco, New Mexico."

"All that time your mom stuck to her story?"

"Yeah, in fact every now and then she'd tell me the air force had given her a report on the progress of the mission and it was going good," Slim said. "But the older I got the more I figured he'd either died on this mission or they'd gotten a divorce and she didn't want to tell me. It wasn't until I was in college that she told me the truth. She said Dad didn't want me to see him in prison." He shook his head like he still found it hard to believe. "By the time she told me all this, he'd gotten out."

"What happened?"

"He disappeared," Slim said. "Don't know if he just felt too disconnected from us or if he was too proud to come back as an ex-con or if he just came out a different man than he went in. But I've never seen him again." Slim looked over at Howdy and something passed between them. A shared loss that connected the two men. Howdy wasn't sure what to say. So he just tossed another hunk of wood on the fire.

Fwoop. They both looked up. Then Slim said, "You know, I'm not the superstitious type, but I'm starting to think there's something wrong with Del Rio."

"Wrong...how?"

"Doesn't seem like I can be there without something—or some*one*—disappearing on me. Started with Dad." He gave a slight shrug. "Next time I lived there it was my guitar, and then Caroline. And now it's Jodie," Slim said. "I'm starting to think Del Rio is Spanish for 'the place where things go missing.'"

The words seemed to strike Howdy as an interesting notion. He said, "The place where things go missing. Kinda mysterious. I like it." Howdy frisked himself for his songwriting pad, which he'd failed to bring. He pointed at Slim. "Remind me of that later, because that might be a good song."

Slim smiled and said, "Sure, no problem."

"Okay," Howdy said. "I can see your point about Del Rio. But look at it this way." He started counting on his fingers. "First, we got your guitar back. Second, you seem to be doing okay in the girl department without Caroline. And third, we figure to get Jodie back tomorrow. After that maybe we can track down your dad, take him back to Zaragoza, see if they're still running those races."

Slim smiled at the thought of it. He said, "Wouldn't that be something?"

There was a rustling in the creosote bush behind them. Their hands went to their guns as they both turned around. They relaxed when they saw it was Roy, cigarette dangling from his lips, returning with more firewood. "Boys," he said, "I think we're being followed." He dropped the wood on the pile.

Slim and Howdy stood up, looked around. "You think it's the kidnappers?"

"Could be," Roy said, scratching his neck. "Also could be bandits. Or could be I'm just a crazy old coot."

Slim and Howdy didn't see anything, but they got the sense Roy knew what he was talking about. "What do we do?"

"Just stay ready," Roy said.

"For what?"

"Anything."

54

JODIE WOKE UP GROGGY AND SORE. IT WAS BARELY LIGHT.
She was lying on a cot. Still dressed for work. Wondering where she
was and how she got there. Why her shoulder hurt so bad. Her hands
were tied in front of her but not so tight she couldn't wiggle free. She
sat up, rubbing her wrists, trying to remember anything that would
explain her circumstance. It had been a long time since she'd woken
up, bound, in a strange bed. In fact, the last time it had happened,
she had participated and there had been a handsome man nearby
with an eager look on his face. But not this time. This time she was
alone in a small room, a shack of some sort.

Her mind was foggy, but not from a hangover. It was like someone had erased part of her hard drive. Had somebody slipped her
a ruffie? She'd heard those things make you forget the last twelve
hours but, no, if someone had slipped her the date-rape drug, they'd
forgotten about the rape part as far as she could tell.

Small favors.

She took a deep breath and thought back. Last thing she remembered was leaving work. She had a headache and designs on a hot bath.
Stopped at the night deposit, then drove home. Called Howdy on the
way about locking the office. She was walking to the front door of her
house, and then... then she woke up here. Not much help.

Jodie noticed the quiet and stillness of wherever she was. And the
smell. A nice smell, but not the smell of Del Rio, that was for sure.
More like way out in the country. The desert. Wisps of sage, flower-
ing cactus, creosote.

Sitting on the edge of the cot, waiting for her head to clear, Jodie moved her arms and legs, twisted her torso this way and that. She tried to stretch the sore out of her shoulder. She felt okay otherwise. So that was good. She hadn't been raped or beaten. Just kidnapped. *Lucky me,* she thought, in that weird way people think about luck. It wasn't winning-the-lottery lucky, but given a choice of picking one thing from the list of three, she'd take kidnapping over beaten and raped.

Yeah, Jodie thought, this was her lucky day, all right.

After a minute, her eyes adjusted to the dim light. She stood and felt her way around the room. No furniture other than the cot and a small table on which she found a few bottles of water, and a bucket she took to be her privy. There was even a roll of toilet paper. And good toilet paper at that. Quilted even. Which struck her as very weird.

She wondered why someone rude enough to kidnap her would be considerate enough to provide quality toilet paper? Or toilet paper at all for that matter? Sure it was a gift horse but, after being abducted, Jodie figured its mouth was worth looking into. Still, she didn't see anything useful when she did.

The walls and floor of the room were rough-hewn planks. Old. There was a window and a door but both were nailed shut. No amount of kicking helped. She could tell the door led to another room but there didn't seem to be anything beyond that, other than outside.

It wasn't long before Jodie could see light coming though the space between some of the planks. She pressed her face to the wall to see what she could in the pre-dawn light. Small hills. Mesquite, fourwing saltbush, acacia. A mule deer in the distance. That narrowed her location down to four states in the southwestern U.S. and most of northern Mexico. *Great,* she thought. She was in a shack in a desert. She felt her pockets and wondered what had happened to her cell phone.

She called out, "Hello? Anybody there?" *Nada.* Silence. "Guess not." She picked up a bottle of water and took a drink. Figured if she was going to bust out of jail and cross a desert, she better get hydrated.

55

THEY BROKE CAMP AN HOUR AFTER SUNRISE. THEY DIDN'T talk much as they saddled up. Everybody moved with a sort of grim determination like they all knew there was the possibility today could be a bad one but nobody was gonna dare say it.

Roy swung up onto his mustang, checked his weapon, then holstered it with a leathery slap. He snugged his hat on tight, looked at Slim and Howdy and said, "Let's go."

They rode to the southwest for a couple of hours, Roy checking his GPS against the coordinates in the kidnapper's instructions. It was another hour before they came to a low ridge overlooking a long valley with the Serranías del Burro bordering the far side. Roy scanned the basin with his binoculars, then handed them to Howdy. "Down there somewhere," he said, pointing generally toward the middle of the valley.

Howdy could see large rock outcroppings and a couple dozen small wooden structures here and there on the valley floor and a few more on the slopes of the foothills. All of them stood alone, half a mile or more from the next. "What are those?"

"Dog houses," Roy said. "Old miners' shacks. A hundred years ago, this area was mined for silver, copper, gold, and turquoise. Lots of one- and two-man operations working these claims that were too small for open-pit mining, so they'd dig straight down until they hit a vein of something, then they'd burrow horizontal to follow it, sometimes for three, four hundred yards or more. They built the shacks next to, or on top of, the mine shafts so they could guard their claims. Smugglers use 'em now for storage or a place to rest or hide or whatever."

"So," Howdy said, "how're we gonna work this?"

They talked it over and agreed that somebody was probably watching the shack, so they didn't want to go riding down there as a trio, revealing their numbers. Slim volunteered to ride down and deliver the ransom. If it turned out to be a trap, Roy and Howdy would be close enough to get there quick to help. If the directions to Jodie's location were there, Slim would leave the money and head for Jodie while Howdy and Roy watched for whoever was collecting the dough. Roy and Howdy would then follow whoever collected the money until Slim radioed to say that he had Jodie, at which point Roy and Howdy would swoop in and try to catch the bad guy and retrieve the cash.

Roy handed radios and GPS receivers to Slim and Howdy so they could stay in contact and, if they all got separated, they'd have a way to get back together. "Be careful," Roy said, as Slim spurred his bay. "Son of a bitch might just be sitting in there waiting to shoot whoever shows up with the money."

"Thanks," Slim said. "I'll keep that in mind."

It took him fifteen minutes to ride down into the valley. Following the GPS and the coordinates he zeroed in on one of the shacks. Stopping about fifty feet away, Slim tied his horse off on a scrubby little hackberry. He took the saddlebag, pulled his gun, and approached the door at an angle that cast his shadow behind him. As he got closer, he crouched and shouted, "Don't shoot! I've got the money." Not that he expected any cooperation from someone planning an ambush, but he would have felt stupid not saying something.

In a minute he was close enough to peek inside, didn't see anybody. So he opened the door and went in. The shack was empty except for a couple of old crates and some rusted tin cans. On top of one of the crates was a sheet of paper held down by a chunk of copper ore.

The directions said to ride west to another set of coordinates. Slim pulled his map and found, roughly, the location. He raised Howdy on the radio and said it looked like about a half hour's ride. "It says to look for the shack with a longhorn skull over the door."

"Call us when you find it," Howdy said. "We'll be waiting on the bad guys."

"Roger that," Slim replied. He got back on his horse and headed west.

Howdy and Roy watched the shack from a quarter mile away, hidden in some Texas mountain laurel. About ten minutes later, Howdy noticed a cloud of dust approaching from the south. He pointed and said, "Here we go."

It was an old El Camino, bouncing through the desert, heading straight for the shack.

56

THE BIG GOON WAS AT THE WHEEL, WIDE-EYED AND GIDDY at the prospect of his impending wealth. This was it, he thought. His chance to break the cycle of poverty and crime that had been his entire life. His chance to escape the shackles of privation. His chance—finally—to get ahead.

The Big Goon, as it turned out, was born poor and had a bad setback. In his entire life, he'd never had more than four hundred dollars to his name. Even his best armed robbery had netted only two hundred and seventy bucks. Sure, he'd tried car jacking and burglary in fancy neighborhoods, stealing jewels and rare coins. But fences—at least the ones he found—never offered more than a dime on the dollar, and usually less. And, after paying off security guards and partners and so forth, the Big Goon was always right back in the same hole where he started.

About the only thing he found less profitable than the crimes he committed was getting arrested for committing them. Of course the Big Goon knew that legal council was one of the costs of doing business, but the price seemed to be going up with each incarceration. All the hearings and motions and trials added up to a lot of billable hours. And the Big Goon had learned early in life never to go with the public defender. If his mama had said it once, she'd said it a thousand times, "Court-appointed lawyers are for suckers."

And so it was that the Big Goon had his very own attorney. And he seemed to be a pretty good one. He got the Goon off scot-free now and then, and got his sentences reduced on other occasions, but no matter what the verdict, he *always* sent a bill. And after five years of this the Big Goon was so deep in debt to his legal representative that he had no realistic expectations of being able to pay him off.

Until now.

When all was said and done, the Big Goon figured to take care of the Boss Man and walk away with a hundred grand in his pocket and Carmelita in his arms. Livin' *la vida loca*.

He parked the El Camino right next to the shack. When the dust settled he got out, looked around, then lumbered inside. It took a moment for his eyes to adjust to the darkness. And when they did, it took his brain another moment to process what they saw.

It was his morally flexible attorney sitting on one of the crates with a saddlebag in his lap.

Grady smiled and said, "Surprise!"

The Big Goon blinked a couple of times, slow and dim like a spadefoot toad trying to reason. Then he said, "What the hell're you doin' here?"

"Waitin' on you," Grady said, like it was part of the plan.

"You're supposed to be in court." He pointed toward Texas. "For your alibi."

"I know," Grady said. "But things change."

The Goon didn't like the setup. If the Boss Man was deviating so wildly from his carefully devised plan, maybe there was a whole different plan to worry about, one that didn't involve the Big Goon breaking even, let alone coming out a hundred thousand ahead and riding off into the sunset with a big-breasted Mexican girl. This eventuality led the Big Goon to think about the gun stuck in his pants.

Grady said, "The strangest thing happened." He hefted the saddlebag. "We asked for fifty thousand, right? But there's a hundred and fifty grand in here." He dropped his jaw in mock surprise. "Can you believe it? I mean, what do you think *happened*? You think they can't count? Or maybe they just like us." Grady tilted his head like the RCA dog.

The Big Goon stammered for a second, before he said, "Shit, I don't know, uh—"

Grady held up his free hand to silence his partner. "No, I'm impressed," he said. "I mean if we were following the original plan, this would be brilliant."

"What do you mean, if we were following the original plan?"

Grady gave an apologetic shrug. "Like I said, things change." He flashed a barracuda smile and continued, "But the good news is that when we're done here, you won't owe me a thing." His smile turned to a frown. "The bad news, however, is that the cops will get an anonymous phone tip that leads them to your apartment where they're going to find some incriminating evidence. Magazines with the letters cut out, some of Jodie's personal effects, that kind of thing. Odds are against them ever finding your body out here, of course, so they'll figure you escaped, and they'll issue a warrant for your arrest. Hell, you'll be considered an international fugitive. Won't your mama be proud?"

"That ain't right."

"So little is these days," Grady said as he pulled the gun from under the saddlebag and shot the Big Goon. Sent him staggering backwards into the wall with a thud and a surprised expression. Or maybe it was disappointment. Either way, he slid down the wall, looking at the blood spreading on his shirt. He ended up a big heap on the floor, his head lolled to one side.

Grady kicked the crate he'd been sitting on, revealing the trap door beneath. He bent over and opened it. He dropped the saddlebag down the shaft and prepared to step onto the ladder, turning his back to do so.

That's when the Big Goon pulled his gun and shot Grady.

"Son of a bitch!" It shattered a rib under Grady's right arm, spun him around, and hurt like the aforementioned son of a bitch. He barely kept his feet on the ladder. Struggling against the pain, Grady managed to squeeze off a couple more shots in the Goon's general direction. The Goon tipped himself sideways and stayed down, giving Grady enough time to drop into the mine shaft, closing the door after himself.

57

WHEN HE HEARD THE FIRST SHOT, HOWDY LOOKED AT ROY and said, "The hell was that?"

"Sounded like a gun."

"Well I know *that*," Howdy said. "What did he do, go in there and commit suicide?"

After the second shot, Roy said, "If so, he ain't very good at it."

When they heard the number of shots that followed, they took off for the shack, riding like they'd been struck by lightning. They brought their horses in behind the El Camino, then ducked behind it for cover, waiting to see what would happen next. But nothing did. Everything was still and quiet until Roy called out, "*Policia!*" There was no response. Roy raised up over the El Camino and fired a shot high at the shack, figuring if someone was in there, they'd shoot back. But there was no response.

They waited a moment before making their move. Then, guns drawn, they came from behind the El Camino, Roy in front, Howdy around the tailgate. They reached the shack, opened the door, and eased inside. Beams of sunlight cut through the smoke and dust, the air thick with the smell of gunpowder. The Big Goon was slumped to one side, the bloody patch on his shirt still spreading, and a gun in his limp hand. Roy kicked it away.

Howdy said, "Recognize him?"

Roy shook his head and lit a cigarette.

Howdy looked around, trying to make sense of the scene. "Where's the saddlebag?"

"Don't see it." Roy checked the back wall for another way out, but there was none.

"So"—Howdy pointed at the Big Goon—"the one guy we saw come in here is dead. The saddlebag is gone, even though nobody came back out." He looked at Roy. "It's a regular magic trick."

"It's a trick, all right," Roy said. "But ain't magic." He walked to the middle of the shack and thumped his heel on the floor a couple of times. Sounded hollow underneath. He bent over and found the notch in the wood that served as a handle. He threw it open and they stood back, ready for more bullets. But none came.

The two of them leaned over and looked down the black hole. An old wooden ladder dropped into the darkness. With a flick of his boot, Roy knocked a rock into the mine shaft. It landed a second later. "Not too deep," Roy said. "Must've been mining turquoise."

Howdy went out to the horses and came back with a flashlight, started down the ladder. He reached the bottom where the shaft turned ninety degrees. He called up to Roy, "I'll go this way. You take the horses and head west. Meet me at the other end."

58

SLIM LET THE GPS GUIDE HIM UNTIL HE NOTICED SOMETHING about ten yards off to his right, merging with the path he was taking. He rode over and looked down. Tire tracks. Other than mule deer, these were the only tracks of any kind that Slim had seen in the last two days. You didn't need to be an Eagle Scout to figure who had laid these down or where they went.

"Yah!" He spurred the bay to a gallop. Chulo charging along behind them, tethered by his reins.

It wasn't long before Slim could see the shack in the distance, the sun-bleached longhorn skull hanging over the door. As he approached, Slim figured there were only three possibilities. One, the shack was empty and he'd been on a wild goose chase. Two, booby trap or an ambush. Or three, Jodie was inside.

Maybe alive, maybe not.

Hoping for the best, Slim yelled, "Jodie!" to let her know help was on the way, but he was riding so hard he couldn't hear if she responded.

In fact, Jodie had replied by muttering, "Oh, damn," after which she had fallen over sideways, dropping the last of the quilted toilet paper before she began struggling to pull up her jeans, her underwear now slightly wet thanks to Slim's brilliant display of bad timing. That, plus she was woozy from the ether.

Slim brought the bay up just short of the shack, using the energy of the sudden stop to dismount in one fluid motion, essentially launching him forward. "Jodie! It's Slim!"

Jodie scrambled to her feet, careful not to kick the bucket she'd been straddling a moment earlier. She shouted, "Slim! In here!" Tucking her shirt in with one hand and banging on the wall with the other.

The moment he heard Jodie's voice, Slim realized he was two-out-of-four in finding things that had gone missing from Del Rio. He was on a roll. Maybe he'd take Howdy up on his offer to go searching for his dad after this was all over.

Slim crashed through the outer door and into the first room of the shack. Ahead was a second door, padlocked. There was a table by that door, on top was a crumpled white cloth and a bottle of ether. But no key to the lock. Slim put his hand on the door and said, "You okay?"

"Yeah," Jodie replied. "Sure glad you're here."

"Sorry it took so long," Slim said. "How much room you got in there?"

"Not much. Why?"

"I've got to shoot the lock off. Stand back and cover your ears."

The padlock was no match for the .45. Slim kicked the door open and before he knew what happened, he was enveloped by Jodie's arms. Tightly. He hugged her back. "It's okay," he said. "You're all right."

"Thanks to you." Jodie reached up all the sudden, put her hands on Slim's cheeks and pulled him to her. She gave him a big, wet lingering kiss, which took him by surprise.

When it was over, Slim stood there, pleasantly stupefied and gently smacking his lips, as if tasting the kiss.

Still in his arms, Jodie swayed as her knees grew weak.

Slim congratulated himself, figuring the swoon had resulted from his mad smooching skills. Wouldn't be the first time. He tilted his head back, smiling as he looked down at her. "You okay?"

Jodie closed her eyes and shook her head while saying, "I think I'm going to throw up."

Took the air right out of Slim's balloon. "What?"

Jodie pushed away from him, holding her hands out for balance. "It's not you," she said. "Whatever they've been drugging me with, makes me nauseous and kinda woozy. I'll be all right." She took a couple of deep breaths.

Slim looked around the shack, taking some comfort in the fact that he wasn't the cause of the nausea. He saw the culprit on the table and, thinking *you just never know how something might come in handy,* he grabbed the ether and the cloth and said, "Whaddya say we get out of here?"

Jodie gathered herself and headed for the sunlight. Outside, she stopped cold in her tracks, looking at the horses. She did a double take. Then she threw open her arms. "*Chulo!*" He began to whinny and throw his head up and down. She went over and hugged his neck, then looked back at Slim as if it had just dawned on her. "Is Uncle Roy with you?"

"He's with Howdy, lookin' for the kidnapper," Slim said as he put the ether in his saddlebag and pulled out a sandwich. "You hungry?" He tossed it to her and said, "There's a pistol in your saddlebag." While Jodie ate, Slim went back to the shack and pulled the long-horn skull off the wall.

Jodie said, "What're you doing?"

"Getting a souvenir," Slim replied. "For the bar." He held the skull in the air. "It's symbolic."

"Of what?"

"Of being Lost... and Found," Slim said with a wink.

She laughed. "I'll hang it over the stage and think of you and Howdy every time I see it."

"I'll be hurt if you don't." He tied the skull onto the back of his saddle, then grabbed the radio and called Roy. "I got her," Slim said. "Safe and sound."

They could hear the relief in Roy's voice when he said, "Good job, son. Now bring her on over here. And hurry! We're on this sumbitch's trail."

"On our way," Slim said. "We'll be there in a minute."

And they would have been, too, except for the man who was drawing a bead on Slim at that very moment.

59

AS HOWDY APPROACHED THE FAR END OF THE TUNNEL, A sudden metal banging noise made him jump and cock his pistol. A second later when something dropped from out of nowhere, landing a few feet in front of him, Howdy nearly shot it before realizing it was an aluminum ladder and Roy was up above, lowering it down to him.

As Howdy climbed to the surface and dusted himself off, Roy told him that Slim had Jodie and they were on their way.

"I told you I had a good feelin' about this," Howdy said.

"That you did," Roy said. "But we ain't done yet." He kicked at the fresh pile of dirt next to the mine shaft. "We need to get after the one what dug this hole and double-crossed his buddy back at the shack." Roy squatted on his haunches, looking at something dark in the dirt. "Blood," he said. "Whoever he is, got a hole in him."

Howdy followed the footprints and the blood. They led a few feet away, just where the tracks from a four-wheel ATV started. Howdy got his binoculars to see if he could spot the wounded man. It took a moment to locate the ATV scurrying through the miles of scrub. Then he pointed and said, "There he is. Looks like he's heading for those rocks." He turned to Roy and said, "Whaddya wanna do?"

Roy pointed a gnarled finger toward the fugitive and said, "I wanna get that sumbitch." He turned and looked the other way. "But I gotta see Jodie first."

Howdy put the binoculars to his eyes, following the kidnapper. "The longer we wait, the harder it'll be."

Roy knew it was true. He looked back and forth like a nervous bird. "Let's give 'em a minute. Slim said they'd be here quick." Roy looked around again, but this time in a different direction. A strange looked settled on his face.

Howdy said, "What is it?"

Roy squinted, gazing at the horizon, said, "We ain't being followed anymore."

60

"THEY'RE WAITIN' ON US," SLIM SAID AS HE SLIPPED THE radio back into the saddlebag. "You ready?"

Jodie walked over with Chulo, handed the reins to Slim. "Give me a second," she said, slinging her holster over her shoulder. "Have to visit the powder room." She smiled and headed for the shack. "Back in a flash."

Slim walked the horses a respectable distance away to give Jodie some privacy. But in doing so he made himself a better target for those lurking in the crevices of the outcropping fifty yards to the east.

As soon as the man in the rocks had a clean look, he fired.

The first shot caught Slim in the shoulder. The second one missed. The report of the gun followed by Slim's string of obscenities spooked the horses, but he managed to keep control as they reared and bucked and danced in dangerous half circles.

Jodie jumped when she heard the commotion, but managed not to tumble over sideways. She yelled, "Slim! You all right?" She came racing outside, buckling her holster in a hurry.

Slim was running toward her, blood on his shirt, leading the horses. "C'mon!" Another bullet whizzed by his ear. Slim ducked as he pointed at a boulder not too far away. "Over there!" Just before diving for cover, he slapped the horses' rumps, sending them out of the line of fire. Slim and Jodie landed in a heap behind the big rock.

When they gathered themselves and caught their breath, Jodie gestured at her shoulder, while looking at Slim's and said, "What happened?"

"A shot came from those rocks," Slim said. "Grazed me."

"Let me look." She already had his shirt unbuttoned and pulled open. "It's a pretty good gash," she said. "You have any first-aid stuff?"

"Yeah." Slim gestured off in the direction of the horses. "In the saddlebag."

"Naturally."

A couple of shots ricocheted off the rock.

"I think we're safe here," he said.

"We're also trapped," Jodie replied as she loaded her pistol. "We can't go either way without giving them a shot." She peeked around the rock but couldn't see anything useful. "Who the hell's shooting at us, anyway?"

"They didn't say."

Then a man shouted, "Throw out the money!"

He sounded Mexican and suddenly Slim was thinking of *Los Zetas* and the heads rolling across the dance floor.

Jodie nudged Slim. "What money?"

"The ransom," he said.

"Ohhh." Jodie had been so focused on trying to figure out where she was, how she might escape, and why she had quilted toilet paper, that she hadn't thought much about the possibility she was being held for money. Hoping it wasn't tacky, she said, "How much?"

Slim raised up and fired a few shots in the direction of the bad guys. Then he said, "How much what?"

"What was the asking price?"

"Oh, a hundred fifty," Slim said.

"What?" Never been so insulted in her entire life. "A hundred fifty bucks?" She couldn't believe it.

"A hundred fifty *thousand*," Slim said.

"Oh. That's more like it."

A few more shots whistled over their heads.

Slim and Jodie looked at one another and nodded. They popped up and squeezed off a half-dozen rounds, just to let the bad guys know they could. Ducking back behind the boulder, Jodie mimed using the radio as she said, "I think we better call Uncle Roy and Howdy. See if they can help us out."

"Yeah, well..." Slim gestured at the horses again. "We can get the radio when we're grabbing the first aid."

"Ahh."

The man yelled again, "I said throw out the money!"

"We don't have the money," Slim yelled. "I left it in the other shack, as instructed."

61

THE MAN YELLING AT SLIM WAS THE BARTENDER FROM *¡Camaron Que Baila!* Went by the name of Ignacio. Nice enough guy, but with a weakness for large breasts, like many good men, especially after a few drinks.

Ignacio had been trying to get his hands on Carmelita's fun bags for quite some time. So, when she came to him asking for help on this deal, promising whatever he wanted in return, well, he fell for it, like many good men, especially after a few drinks.

On the other hand, when he was sober, as he was now, Ignacio was more practical, a man who took a dim view of screwups, especially when he was on the humiliating end of them. He turned slowly, fixed Carmelita with disquieting eyes, and said, "The *other* shack?" He looked to the sky and muttered something along the lines of "*Vos puta pendeja.*"

Carmelita, proud and somewhat short-tempered, slapped Ignacio but good and launched into a vigorous and lengthy attack on his manhood accompanied by a finger poking his chest. It was a verbal onslaught so withering it made Ignacio wonder what he'd ever seen in her and why was he was out in the middle of the desert shooting at strangers who, apparently, had no money.

The answer was simple enough. Five days ago, toward the end of happy hour at *¡Camaron Que Baila!* the Big Goon had told Carmelita the entire plan. However, owing to the fact that he was spectacularly drunk and that his Spanish was as rudimentary as her English, several crucial details about the money-for-hostage exchange were miscommunicated. Which explained why Carmelita and Ignacio had followed Slim from the ransom shack to where they were now.

Carmelita couldn't believe how this whole thing was shaking out. Story of her damn life. First the Big Gringo tells her to follow the guy to the wrong shack, and now, when she's really in need of a little help, Ignacio shows *his* true colors.

Men, she thought. *Screw 'em all!* Though she probably cast these thoughts in a colorful Spanish idiom.

Carmelita had had it up to here being treated as nothing more than a set of big chi-chis that delivered drinks. This deal was her ticket out and she'd be damned if she was going to leave empty-handed.

She snatched the gun from Ignacio and reloaded, figuring the next best thing to having the ransom money was having the thing to trade for it. She cupped a hand to her mouth and yelled, "We'll take the *señora!* Send her over!" She fired a shot over their heads like an upside down exclamation mark.

Jodie couldn't believe it. She said, "What is this, a game of Red Rover?" She turned and yelled, "You come and get it!" Then she fired a couple of shots in their direction.

Carmelita made an obscene gesture and shouted, "*¡Vete a la chingada, puta baracha!* I will count to three. *Uno...Dos...*"

At about *dos* and a half something landed on Carmelita's cowboy hat—one of those straw jobs with the rim curled up taco style— knocking it to the ground. The thing wasn't small either, whatever it was, but it disappeared after the hat landed. It was a weird moment.

Carmelita and Ignacio lifted their eyes slowly, looking at the rocks above them. They saw nothing.

Until a moment later, when Carmelita picked up her hat.

And they both jumped.

It was a western diamondback rattlesnake, thick and angry. Ten buttons rattling as he coiled. Agitated and ready to strike.

Invoking the names of various saints, Carmelita and Ignacio backed away as far and as fast as they could, but they were trapped in their confined space, still within striking distance of the big snake. Like most people, Carmelita and Ignacio had an abiding fear of deadly reptiles so, a moment later, when two big black-tailed rattlesnakes came raining down from above, crowding and further agitating the diamondback, Carmelita and Ignacio lapsed into a black panic. They pressed themselves to the rock and tried to climb, but it was useless. Ignacio slipped and screamed like a schoolgirl when one of the black-tails struck his boot.

The fangs and the white inside the mouth was too much for Carmelita. She was pie-eyed and hyperventilating when she opened fire, cursing and praying and weeping as she squeezed off one wild shot after another, eventually wounding Ignacio in the foot, leading him to say, "*¡Hijo de la gran puta! ¡No sirves para nada! ¡Hijo de mil putas!*" All while hopping on his other foot.

Slim and Jodie had to look. Had to see what all the shouting and shooting was about, since it no longer seemed to be about them. What they saw was a heavy-breasted woman in a straw cowboy hat high-stepping into the scrub followed by a man who was cursing and limping as fast as he could. "*¡Eres el imbecil mas grande en el mundo!*"

They appeared to be heading for a Jeep parked a quarter mile away.

Carmelita turned suddenly to fire toward Slim and Jodie, out of frustration more than anything. As she paused to take aim, the cactus paddle next to her exploded. Twice. Two shots, large caliber, an inch apart. Carmelita stared at the holes, then turned toward the outcropping.

At the top, a man with rifle and good aim. Still aiming in fact.

Carmelita yelled, "*¡Afeminado! ¡Chupaverga!*" Then she turned and headed for her Jeep.

Jodie and Slim fired several more shots over their heads, as if to say, "*Adios, malparidas.*"

As the Jeep disappeared in a cloud of dust, heading for Piedras Negras, Slim and Jodie stepped out from behind the bolder to look for their benefactor. "There he is," Slim said, pointing at the top of the outcropping.

Jodie shaded her eyes and said, "Kind of a pudgy guy? Waving a bandaged hand?"

"Yeah," Slim said. "That's him."

"Ohmigod." Jodie squinted and said, "Is that Jake?"

"Hey, baby!" He waved his big gauzy paw.

Slim smirked and said, "Isn't that your first husband? The one you didn't tell anybody about?"

She said, *"¿Vas a callate?"*

So he shut up.

While Jake climbed down from his perch and recaptured his snakes, Slim got the horses and let Jodie patch his wound. Then they called Roy, found out where to meet up.

Later, when Jake came back with his horse, Jodie asked what he was doing out here.

"After I heard you'd been snatched, I got worried about you," Jake said. "So I started following your boys. When I saw 'em heading into the desert, I figured I might be of some help. Plus I needed some new inventory." He held up his sack. "Came in handy too."

"Well, thanks," Jodie said, thinking he really needed to lose a few pounds. "You saved our bacon."

"Yeah," Slim said. "Owe you one."

They swung up on their horses and headed in Roy's direction. Jodie rode up alongside of Jake, asking about the bulky bandage. "What happened? You get bit?"

Jake held up the four-fingered hand with great pride. "What happened is I saved about ten...thousand...dollars." He nodded like he understood how she might find it hard to believe how smart he was. "See, they sell these do-it-yourself kits on the Internet..."

62

GRADY COULDN'T DRIVE THE ATV TO SAVE HIS LIFE. WHICH is to say that even if there was a hospital within fifty miles, he'd never make it there. Wasn't his fault, though. The rough terrain was crowded with sharp and jagged plants, and dodging them only sent you into ruts, rocks, and treacherous sandy pits.

Grady's legs were scratched to hell and he'd almost tipped over twice already. He was weak and woozy from blood loss and losing control of his muscles.

Why'd the big son of a bitch have to go and shoot him?

Grady was light-headed and thirsty. His mouth had gone to cotton and his breathing was rapid and shallow. Pulse was up, blood pressure was down. A bad combo. His skin was soft and clammy.

This wasn't part of the plan. He hadn't prepared for this. Not for being shot.

He knew someone was after him, too, saw the horses in the distance. Apparently the threat of *Los Zetas* wasn't enough. Now, Grady figured if he didn't die in the desert from his wounds, he'd be going to prison for a long, unpleasant time. He couldn't decide which fate was worse.

Ow! Ow! Now he had bugs in his teeth. Big ones too. Bitter and caustic on his gums. Stinging, like the dust in his eyes. Some sort of Mexican blister beetle that left him spitting and puckered and wondering how and why everything had gone so terribly wrong.

Not just now, but in his entire life.

But there was no point thinking about that, was there? Not now.

The fates had it in for Grady Hobbs. They were bound and deter-mined to crush him under their boot heels. Been that way all his life. Wasn't fair. Never had been. No point acting surprised.

But what was worse—the thing that really chapped his ass—was that the people most responsible for Grady being in this circum-stance would never be held accountable.

Like Mr. Noxby. That's who came to mind first. High school chemistry. Gave him the D that killed his GPA and any chance he had to get into a decent college, which in turn would have given him a shot at Ivy League law schools, and a big career.

I mean, who the hell cares about the atomic weight of cesium? In all of Grady's years in the real world, in courts of law, that tidbit of information had proved to be important exactly zero times.

But that D *was* important. It was the first nail in the coffin that would bear Grady's career to the grave. It was the first thing that led to the next thing that made the third thing happen and so on. Hell, Grady Hobbs's legal career was dead on arrival after the damn D. No Harvard or Yale for Grady Hobbs. No, sir, not after that.

But would Mr. Noxby suffer any consequences? Don't ask. Hurts just to think about it. Or maybe that was the bullet wound.

Grady was growing weaker. It was getting harder to control the ATV. But he knew he had to hang on, tough it out. It was his only hope. Just get somewhere he could hide, rest, get his strength back. Delusional thinking at its best.

Grady had squeaked into the lowest-ranked law school in the nation, where he graduated in the bottom ten percent of his class. Took three tries to pass the bar, and that was *with* cheating. So he was doomed right out of the gate. His résumé wouldn't get him past the receptionist at a second-rate law firm.

Which explained why Grady Hobbs was in Del Rio, Texas, hand-ing out foam-rubber cervical collars.

And Grady blamed Mr. Lloyd Noxby. Not the gambling.

It couldn't have been the gambling that brought him here. This was just a rough patch Grady was going through, that's all. Every-body had 'em. A few early-season college losses. Some unforeseen injuries, a couple of bad calls. Hell, things had gone the other way, Grady would be in tall cotton right now and Jodie would be at work, ordering kegs of beer. But, as it was, Grady was rubbing up against a thirty-thousand-dollar debt and the vig it rode in on.

Grady placed his bets out at the Truck 'n' Go Quicky Stop. Del Rio's one-stop shopping spot for all your vices. He bet football, basketball, and baseball. College and pro. Insisted he didn't have a problem. Insisted what he had was a system. Usually a winner, too. But sometimes it turned on him.

And when it did, he was screwed. He didn't have the money and he knew what happened if he didn't pay. So he embezzled funds from a client account to settle the gambling debt. Of course then he had to find a way to get the money back into the client account before he got caught and disbarred.

The swoop-and-stop scams brought in decent money, but in a town of just thirty thousand he couldn't run enough of them to solve his problems, not without calling attention to himself. Last thing he needed.

Then he had the idea. The ransom would repay the client account and put Grady a little ahead. It was a beautiful plan, elegant, verging on the poetic. Grady would be getting his own money back from the man who took it in the first place.

But then the Big Goon had to go and shoot him. Spoiled everything.

Grady's vision was going snowy, which explained why he didn't see the rock. When he hit it, the ATV went airborne and sent Grady flying. He was lucky to land on hard-packed dirt instead of a prickly pear. It knocked his breath out, and some more blood too.

The man on horseback was getting closer, could see him in the distance.

Grady struggled over to where the ATV landed, upside down. He was too weak to flip it upright. Wouldn't have mattered anyway, it was busted.

He managed to pull the saddlebag from underneath, then he struck out on foot. For where, he had no idea.

63

HOWDY AND ROY WERE SURPRISED TO SEE THREE RIDERS approaching instead of two. When he pulled his binoculars and saw the big gauze bandage, he chuckled and muttered, "I'll be damned."

As they rode up, Slim broke into a grin and said, "Howdy, you remember Jodie's first husband, don't you?"

Howdy pointed at him. "The one she never told us about?"

"That's him."

"Sure," Howdy said. "Hey, Jake."

Roy aimed his thumb at the reptile retailer. "I told you somebody was following us."

Howdy said, "So how's that finger doin'?"

Jake uncorked his canister and took a whiff. "What finger?" He gave a loopy smile and saluted with his gauzy hand.

"Ohhh." Howdy sort of tipped his head sideways in thoughtful fashion, said, "Well, it was probably the right thing to do."

"Hell yes," Jake said. "Like havin' an extra ten grand in the pocket."

Howdy turned to look at Jodie. "And just think, half of that could've been yours."

Jodie twisted up an acrid smile and said, "When you boys are done, maybe we could get back on the trail of the nice man who kidnapped me."

"Plenty of time for that," Howdy said. "He flipped his ATV right over there. Set out on foot. Took off that way." He pointed toward a large rock outcropping.

"That's Lujan's Hill," Jake said. "He's probably up in that big cave."

"It's got a name?"

"Does if you're a local." Jake sniffed the canister again. "Famous old smuggler named Eliodoro Lujan used it for drops, pickups, storage, whatever. Smugglers probably still usin' it," Jake said. "It's at the end of a shallow box canyon, about ten feet up a steep path. Real easy to defend, but you're trapped."

Slim said, "Howdy, did you get a look at the guy?"

"Only from a distance, from behind," Howdy said. "But he's got to be in pretty bad shape. He was already shot and bleeding before he flipped his ATV."

"We better hurry then," Roy said darkly, cigarette dangling from his lips. "Don't want him to die before I get a chance to kill him."

They rode to the mouth of the canyon and made plans. It was suicide to charge straight up the trail if the cave had a strategic advantage, so they opted for diplomacy. They figured the first thing to do was try to talk him into surrendering in exchange for getting to a doctor. If he refused, they knew they could just wait him out.

"It'll take one tough hombre to choose to die like that," Roy said.

They elected Howdy ambassador. The canyon was narrow, wide enough for a man or a horse but too narrow for much else. As Howdy worked his way in, he could see the kidnapper's tracks leading straight for the cave. Howdy got close enough to be heard. He yelled, "You're bleeding pretty bad, friend! Your best bet's to come on out and let us get you to a doctor!"

In response, Grady fired a couple of shots and yelled back in a loony south-of-the-border accent. "*¡Vaya al infierno!* We are *Los Zetas*! My associates are coming. Leave now or die!"

Howdy thought the man sounded a lot more Cuban than Mexican, in fact more like Al Pacino playing Tony Montana than anything else.

The reason for this was twofold: One, Grady was a big fan of *Scarface* and, two, at the moment, he was high as a weather balloon. The reason for this was simple. It turned out that smugglers *were* still using the cave, as Jake suggested. The place was stacked to the roof with bales of seedy Mexican pot, cartons of Ecstasy, and bricks of methamphetamine and cocaine just waiting to be picked up and carried across the border.

By the time Slim, Howdy, and their posse showed up, Grady had been in the cave for nearly an hour, self-medicating. He started with the cocaine, using it as a topical where he'd been shot and on all the strawberries he got wrecking the ATV, and some on the gums. Then he popped some X and snorted just enough meth to help keep him awake and thinking clearly. He was feeling much better now. Much bolder too. In fact, he dared anybody to come in after him. He fired a few more shots out toward the desert and yelled, "*¡Metete el pito por los oidos!*"

Instead of that, Howdy stuck his *finger* in his ear, scratched it, and said, "Hold that thought." He went back to where the others were waiting. "He ain't interested in surrender," Howdy said. "Should we just wait him out?"

"Let him bleed to death?"

"That's up to him." Howdy shrugged.

"I've got a better idea," Slim said, his impatience showing. He went to his saddlebag and pulled out the ether. He stuffed the rag in the mouth of the bottle like a Molotov cocktail.

Jake leaned in for a look. "Whatcha got there?"

"Ether," Slim said.

"Are you crazy?" Jake backed up. "That shit's explosive!"

"That's the point," Slim said. "What if we throw this over there? When the dust settles, we'll tell him the next one goes in the cave if he doesn't surrender."

"But we don't have a next one," Jodie said.

"Yeah," Slim said. "But he doesn't know that."

Nobody could think of a good reason not to give it a try, so Slim turned to Roy with his hand outstretched and said, "Borrow your lighter?" Roy tossed it to him.

Slim was about to put the flame to the rag when Jake's good hand stopped him. "Hang on," he said, pointing toward something on the horizon. They all looked. Two black Hummers driving hard in their direction. "Looks like we got company."

"The guy said his partners were coming." Howdy seemed surprised. "I figured it was a bluff."

"Looks real to me," Jake said. "We better take cover."

Roy told everybody to spread out and hide while he got the horses out of sight. Slim, Jodie, and Jake hid in the rocks to the left of the canyon, Howdy and Roy to the right.

A couple of minutes later the two Hummers pulled to a stop, one behind the other. Eight armed men got out, stretching and casually milling around the vehicles. One guy stepped aside to take a piss.

Based on how casually the smugglers were acting, Roy figured the men hadn't seen them as they approached. He further assumed they had come to pick up or deliver contraband. Either way, Roy thought, if they went in the cave he could kiss his $150,000 good-bye, not to mention the satisfaction of killing the kidnapper. And he couldn't let that happen.

So he took careful aim and shot the man just as he zipped his fly.

And then all hell broke loose.

The other smugglers dove behind the Hummers, yelling in Spanish, racking their weapons. One of them shouted where he'd seen the shot come from and all seven men stood and opened fire on Roy's position.

Roy pressed himself so hard to the ground he was getting dirt in his ear. The shrapnel of rock and lead was flying like a hailstorm coming from all directions.

Slim and the others knew they had to do something fast or Roy's goose was cooked. They reacted instinctively. Slim and Howdy opened fire on the Hummers, Jake and Jodie joined a second later. Howdy got one smuggler. Slim wounded another. Air hissed out of the big tires and the windows exploded.

The smugglers didn't know whether to shit or go fishing. All they knew was that a lot of people were shooting at them from five or six hidden positions while they were stuck behind their Hummers. There was no way to sneak up on or flank their enemy without crossing a hundred yards of open space like a target in a shooting gallery. So they stayed put, taking whatever shots they could get.

Roy didn't like his angle, couldn't get a good shot, decided he needed a better position. He figured if this was his last great day, he couldn't be timid about it. He was going for higher ground. He'd gone ten feet when he took one in the shoulder, knocking him off balance. He slipped on some loose rocks, slid down the incline, wrenching a knee before landing in the open, exposed to the smugglers' fire and unable to move.

Jodie jumped and yelled, "Uncle Roy!"

They all knew he'd be dead soon if somebody didn't get there quick. "I got him," Howdy said. "Cover me!"

Slim and Jake laid a blanket of fire as Howdy made a mad dash for Roy's position, scrambling over rocks, ducking and dodging as he went. He hit the desert floor, running like hell as the smugglers emerged when they could to spray the air with automatic lead. Then he saw Jodie, ahead of him. She was hell-bent for leather as she hurtled through the scrub, solely focused on saving her uncle.

Howdy saw one of the smugglers step out from behind the Hummer to pick her off. Shooting across his body on a dead run, Howdy got the guy's attention long enough for Slim to draw a bead and finish the job.

Jake, meanwhile, was using his rifle to keep the smugglers jumpy. He wasn't aiming to kill, just to let them know he could if he wanted.

Jodie reached Uncle Roy and tried to drag him to safety but it was too much for her to do alone. "Get to cover!" Roy said. But she wasn't leaving him. She got between him and the smugglers and used her last three bullets. Like she was *his* godfather.

Howdy was almost there. He could feel the lead rocketing past him and he said a little prayer, though he used some words that weren't usually heard in church. He dove, like sliding headfirst into second, all the while shouting, "Get him! Go! Go! Go!" He never stopped moving, rolled up to his feet, grabbed Roy's arms, and muled him over to a spot behind a boulder, lucky to be alive, and they all knew it.

Everything was adrenaline and chaos. They were huffing like race horses as they checked Roy's wound. It wasn't good. Jodie said he'd be all right, not because she knew he would but because that seemed like the best thing to say. She wiped his forehead with her sleeve and wondered what was going to happen next.

There was a momentary lull as everyone reloaded, a brief season of quiet, except for the hungry breathing and the slide of cartridges and magazines into metal slots.

After a minute, Howdy raised Slim on the radio. "We're holed up behind a rock," he said. "Roy's bleeding some, but Jodie says he'll make it. How 'bout y'all?"

"We're good up here," Slim said. "Looks like four of these guys are still in the game, maybe five." He paused. "Hang on a second." Paused again. "I hear something."

It was the unexpected roar of a V8 engine, suddenly amplified when a large rock peeled off the muffler and the rest of the pipes from the undercarriage of the El Camino.

The smugglers spun around just as it roared over a dune and came crashing onto the desert floor. It fishtailed a few times before straightening out, plowing straight toward them.

The Big Goon was at the wheel, one bloody hand out the window, gripping a gun, taking potshots because that was all he had left.

There was nothing between the smugglers and the El Camino. All they could do was shoot back as the thing bore down on them, hope to kill the driver or the engine or something.

Slim saw his opportunity. It was now or never, and he had to be fast. He grabbed the jar of ether and Roy's lighter. The Hummers were too far to hit from where he was. Had to get closer. The smugglers turned their backs to deal with the oncoming El Camino and Slim made a break for it, racing into wide-open space, nothing to protect him. He got as close as he needed, stopped, and pulled out the lighter. Flick.

But the desert wind blew it out.

The El Camino bore down on the Hummers as the smugglers unloaded on it.

Slim flicked the lighter again. Wind blew it out. And again. No luck. *Flick, flick.* "C'mon!"

The smugglers were between a rock and a hard place. If they stayed, they'd get crushed in the collision. If they ran, the snipers in the rocks could pick them off.

Slim had his thumb going like a piston now. *Flick, flick, flick, flick, flick.* "C'mon!" The wind kept blowing it out. *Flick, flick, flick, flick, flick.* He hunched over to shield the wind. Finally, it caught.

One of the smugglers turned back around, considering his options. When he did this, he saw a tall man in dark glasses standing just twenty yards away, something flaming in his hands.

The smuggler figured whatever it was couldn't be good. He squeezed off a few shots but Slim held his ground, didn't flinch, couldn't afford to. He made the heave, the flaming cloth trailing from the bottle as it arched gracefully toward the Hummers.

The El Camino got there first, doing about seventy. It was a stunning collision. An enormous sum of energy, noise, and destruction. Tons of steel and gasoline, mass and velocity, meeting in a single violent moment, splitting gas tanks and launching the Big Goon through the windshield like a three-hundred-pound rag doll.

The ether explosion a moment later was an astonishing second act. The bottle shattered in the midst of all the fumes and gasoline, triggering a hellish, roiling fireball.

Jake, who happened to be taking a whiff off his canister at the moment, looked at the expanding orange-and-black bubble rising toward the blue desert sky and said, "Whooaaa."

When the dust finally settled and there was nothing left but the smoldering carcasses of the vehicles, they could see the three surviving smugglers retreating into the desert on foot.

Jake came down from the rocks to retrieve the horses and the first-aid kit. Roy let Jodie patch his shoulder, but not without manly complaint. "Oh, hell, I'm all right," he said. "No need to treat me like I'm a little baby. Ow!" He jerked away when she hit it with the alcohol.

Jodie smirked, said, "You're a tough old bird, all right." She gave him a kiss on the head, which also required him to feign objection.

Slim, Howdy, and Jake just kind of stood there, quietly watching Jodie tend to her uncle. As she reached for some tape, she noticed something and gestured at Howdy's left leg. "What happened to you?"

Howdy looked down and saw the bloody hole in his jeans. Didn't even realize he'd been hit during his mad dash to Roy's side. He ripped the hole a little wider to take a look. "Yeah, you know, now that I see it, it hurts a little." He cleaned it out and slapped a bandage on it. Wasn't terrible, he said. He'd live. As he was doing this, he thought, *Bullets, like love, always leave a scar. Or should it be, Love, like a bullet, always leaves a scar?* Seemed like that might be worth exploring. He wished he had his notepad.

As Jodie finished taping the patch of gauze over Roy's wound, he looked up at Jake and said, "You did some good shooting back there, son. I may have underestimated you by a bit." He gave a respectful nod. "I'd say you're all right."

Jake tipped his hat to the old man, whom he'd always liked, despite everything. "Glad I could be of help, Mr. Hobbs."

"And you two," Roy said, wagging a finger at Slim and Howdy. "Thank you."

Slim accepted it with a gracious nod. Howdy touched a finger to the brim of his hat and said, "Still one thing left to do."

"Yep." Roy buttoned his shirt and got to his feet. "Let's go do it."

They talked strategy and reloaded before returning to the canyon. Once again, Howdy approached the cave and called out to the kidnapper, suggesting that surrender and medical treatment was still his best bet.

But there was no response.

"Maybe he's dead," Jake said as he bent down to see if there were any tarantulas under a rock.

"Or maybe he's playing possum," Roy countered. "Trying to lure us in."

After a moment of hesitation that might also be viewed as time to think, Howdy moved a little closer to the cave, cutting across the path, purposely leaving himself exposed to the gunman to see if he was paying attention.

But no shots were fired.

Slim moved closer, same as Howdy, pausing to tempt the kidnapper into taking a shot.

But nothing happened.

A moment later, Jake and Jodie moved up behind Slim and Howdy and they all started to think the kidnapper had bled to death. Howdy yelled again but there was still no reply. Slim threw a rock into the cave. Nothing.

So they started up the steep path to the entrance, quiet as they could. Slim and Howdy in front, Roy bringing up the rear, a bit behind the rest of them, thanks to his bum knee. Jake and Jodie were in between. As they got closer they heard something coming from inside. They all crouched, knowing it would do them little good if the kidnapper came out shooting now. But no such thing happened.

They listened for a moment before Slim said, "Is that...singing?"

They looked at one another with curious, squinting expressions before Howdy said, "Sounds like that Youngbloods song, 'Get Together.'"

"I love that song," Jake said. And he started to sing, "C'monnnn people now..."

Jodie gave him a cross look and held up a finger. "Shhhhhh."

Jake dropped to a whisper. "Smile on your brother..."

Slim and Howdy crept into the cave, saw the bales of pot stacked to form a short wall ahead of them. The kidnapper was apparently on the other side, sitting on the ground, leaning against the bales.

They could hear him singing quietly to himself, "Try to lovvvve one anotherrrr..."

Slim and Howdy, guns drawn, came around the bales of dope and saw him sitting there, with the saddlebag in his lap, rocking gently back and forth as he sang. They looked closer as if hoping there was some chance it was just a guy who looked like Grady, but they knew better.

It was him.

He was bruised and bleeding. Not that he seemed to mind. His pupils were dilated, his mouth was dry, and he was clenching his jaw from all the Ecstasy he'd taken, which explained why he didn't mind the bruises and bleeding.

Jake saw him next. Despite the fact that it made him feel better about himself, he knew it was going to hurt Jodie and *that* he regret-ted. But what could he do?

Slim and Howdy looked at one another like they'd both lost a bet. It hurt knowing that Jodie was about to find out. They wished there was something they could do to protect her, but there was nothing to be done but deal with the aftermath.

Jodie came around the bales. When she saw her brother, it didn't make sense to her. But there he was. Her mouth opened slightly, like a tiny mail slot, but nothing came out. If there was a right thing to say, she couldn't think of it.

Jodie had never felt so heartsick. She was crushed. Gut-punched.

Betrayed. Used. And not by some stranger. This wasn't some random crime, which somehow would be easier to accept. She'd been targeted. Her life endangered. For money. By her brother. It hurt in her heart, her soul. It hurt down to the bone. Then a thought crossed her mind, and she almost laughed. *At least now the quilted toilet paper makes sense.*

Jodie looked at Slim and Howdy, disbelief in her eyes. They sort of shrugged and shook their heads like maybe there was a good explanation they just hadn't thought of yet. But they all knew better.

Grady was so high he didn't realize they were standing there. He'd taken more Ecstasy while they were fighting the smugglers. Now, deep in the throes of entactogenic intoxication, he was gently stroking the saddlebag, marveling at the tactile sensations he was experiencing. Not only that, but wishing he could share the feeling with the entire world.

Despite his wounds, Grady was enveloped in a caress of positive emotions and a rich, creamy sense of well-being. He had abandoned all defense mechanisms and was positively awash in comforting insight and introspection. And he felt like sharing.

"Grady?" The word escaped like a prisoner from Jodie's mouth.

When he finally looked up and saw them all standing there—all but Roy, who was still gimping his way up the steep path—Grady knew he was in trouble. But he was so high, all he could muster was, "Uh-ohhh." And feebly at that.

Then, like a dinner host suddenly realizing he'd forgotten to offer appetizers, Grady grabbed the open box of Ecstasy and offered it to his guests. He shook it. The pills rattled. "These are great," he said, speaking slowly. "And I know if you all felt the way I do right now, we could move past this." He nodded as he stretched his arms out wide. "I really would like a hug," he said.

After a pause, when no one else made a move, Jake started toward Grady, arms spreading.

Slim stopped him with a glare. "No hugging."

"Oh, c'mon," Grady said, his eyes closed in rapture. "A big group hug? Everybody? That would be so great. We can have a good cry and start the healing. What do you say?"

They'd never seen a dopier smile. He was damn near sympathetic.

That's when Roy limped in behind the rest of them. He pushed through to get a look at this man who had tried to use his goddaughter to steal his money. It was bad enough when he saw Grady sitting there, grinning like the village idiot with the saddlebag in his lap. But when Grady failed to show the slightest concern that his mark had just walked in, that he exhibited no shame, that he showed no fear or respect whatsoever, that pushed Roy over the edge. He said, "You are one sorry son of a bitch."

Then he drew his pistol and raised it to shoot.

But Jodie stopped him. "Uncle Roy!" She shook her head. "Don't." She tried to wrestle the gun from him, repeating, firmly, "Don't." She looked him in the eye and said, "Please."

The gun slid from his hand to hers. And Jodie said, "Allow me."

EPILOGUE

GRADY'S WOUND WAS SUPERFICIAL. STILL, JODIE FELT A LOT better getting that out of her system.

Howdy took the gun from her before she could try again, though he was pretty sure she'd done exactly what she'd intended the first time and had made her point.

Slim kept Uncle Roy away from all the guns, as he remained in a sour mood, belligerent, and disinclined toward forgiveness and letting the healing begin.

They patched Grady up the best they could, enough to stop the bleeding.

Jake rigged a travois behind his horse to carry Grady, even left him with the bottle of isoflurane, sympathetic to the man's pain. Then the six of them made the long ride back to Del Rio.

It gave Jodie and Uncle Roy a lot of time to talk. They realized it was up to them whether or not to throw the matter into the judicial system. They weighed the pros and cons of having a lawfully convicted kidnapper in the family versus keeping the matter in-house. But short of imprisoning Grady themselves, they couldn't think of an acceptable solution.

In the end they called the cops. As Jodie herself said in open court when asked about the decision, "Just because blood's thick, doesn't mean it's stupid."

In a bit of what the Big Goon might have considered justice (had he lived to consider anything), Grady was forced by his finances to settle for a court-appointed attorney who was one of the few lawyers in Texas to have a less impressive résumé than Grady.

At Grady's suggestion, the attorney called a press conference to announce that his client was going into rehab for a gambling addiction.

"It'll incline the jury pool toward sympathy," Grady said. "Get the message out that that's what forced me to such desperate measures in the first place. We want to convince 'em that Grady Hobbs didn't kidnap his sister," he said. "His addiction did."

Unfortunately for Grady, the good citizens of Val Verde County weren't buying it. Turned out the abdication of personal responsibility was a nonstarter in this part of Texas. They'd seen variations of this defense trotted out in other parts of the country, from Hollywood to Washington, D.C.—and to great effect—but it didn't fly in Del Rio.

Grady got seven to ten. With good behavior, he'd be out in five. After that, awkward family gatherings.

The day that the jury handed down Grady's verdict, another jury handed down a decision of its own, naming Link as Best Male Lead in a Live Action Short for his role in *Submission Impossible,* which also won Best Live Action Short. In his acceptance speech, Morgan Bryson thanked a long list of people including his mama, the Lord, Link, and these two unnamed cowboys who had inspired the controversial trepanation scenes at the film's climax, which everyone agreed was the thing that put them over the top in their category.

Link, standing at the podium with gauze wrapped around his wounded skull, was so overcome by emotion as he accepted his statue that he was nearly speechless. Finally, as he dabbed tears from his eyes, he said, "Uh, I just wanna thank the folks at FEMA. Without them, none of this would have been possible."

The next day the two of them left for Los Angeles. They had meetings.

After they had met, Boone Tate and Lloyd "Bricks" Brickman stayed drunk for several days working out an elaborately flawed plan

to rob the Lost and Found, killing Slim in the process while fram-
ing Howdy for the crime: However, when their cash started running
low, they went to the gun shop to sell Brushfire's pistol so they could
buy more hooch. The owner wasn't interested, however, so they were
forced to use the gun to rob a convenience store where they made off
with thirty-four dollars and some malt liquor.

Meanwhile, Bricks, with his keen understanding that simpler is
better, decided that instead of following the complicated plan to get
back at two guys he didn't know, he'd simply kill Boone Tate and
take his car and his wallet.

They were in the fleabag motel where they'd stayed the last two
nights, drinking and scheming when Bricks came up from behind
Boone Tate and wrapped his huge hands around Tate's throat.
That's when the door caved in followed by a man carrying the largest handgun anyone had ever seen. The man had Bricks dead in his
sight.

With his big mitts still tight around Boone Tate's neck, Bricks
looked at the man and said, "Who the hell're you?"

"Drake Dobson, skip tracer," the man said. "Your buddy's bail bondsman hired me. Put him down, would you? He's no good to me dead."

"What about me?" Bricks asked.

"I'll let the cops sort that out."

"Damn."

Slim and Howdy played out the week at the Lost and Found underneath the longhorn skull they hung over the stage. After closing,
they sat around with Jodie trying to perfect that margarita recipe.
No luck, but lots of laughs.

They refused Roy's offer of a reward, though they accepted the
generous bonus Jodie slipped into their paycheck.

And then it was time to hit the road.

"Can't you stay another week?"

"You said you'd booked old J. Fred Hawkins through the end of
the month," Howdy said.

"I can unbook him." She was only half-kidding.

Slim shook his head. "Wouldn't be right."

She understood, asked where they were heading.

"New Mexico," Howdy said. "Talked to a friend who runs a joint outside Albuquerque."

"Well, you better come back soon," Jodie said. "I'm already starting to miss you."

She hugged them both and walked out to the parking lot to see them off. Jodie had to laugh when she heard them arguing about whose turn it was to drive.

"No it's not."

"Gimme the keys."

Jodie stayed on the porch to wave good-bye.

When they got in the truck, Slim sat there for a few moments, shaking his head. It looked like he might start laughing.

Howdy cranked the truck and was about to put it in gear when he noticed Slim's smirk. "What?"

Slim gave a little snicker, then looked over at Howdy and said, "You know, I had my doubts about you... about us."

"You ain't the only one," Howdy said. "But you gotta admit, these last two weeks have been some kind of fun."

Slim peered over the top of his dark glasses, casting a dubious look at Howdy.

"Okay... how 'bout interesting?"

Slim smiled and gave a nod. "Interesting's a good word." He looked at Howdy and held out his hand.

Howdy smiled and shook it. Then he gestured toward the windshield and said, "Whaddya say we get this show on the road?"

"Hang on a second." Slim popped the glove box, pulled out the radar detector that had been there all along, and said, "Here, knock yourself out."

Howdy dipped his head and glared at Slim from under the brim of his hat. "You rascal." He set the Viper on the dashboard and plugged it in. Then he put the truck in gear, honked the horn, and held his hat out the window in a gesture of farewell.

Slim waved good-bye from his side.

Jodie smiled and blew a kiss as Howdy drove out of the parking lot and into the sunset.

Slim consulted a map and said, "Looks like your best bet's the 90 west to the 285 then up to l-10 at Fort Stockton."

Howdy turned slowly, looking at Slim as if he'd suggested taking a goat path all the way to New Mexico. He shook his head and said, "We're shootin' straight up the 277 toward Sonora."

"What?" Slim stabbed a finger at the map. "Might as well go through Atlanta we're gonna backtrack that far."

"Hey, I'm driving."

Slim grunted sullen disapproval and turned his attention back to the map.

"You'll get your turn," Howdy said.

There followed five miles of awkward silence as Slim calculated the inferiority of Howdy's route versus his own, down to the tenth of a mile.

As they came around a bend, something appeared on the horizon. Howdy saw it first. He squinted and said, "What's your policy on hitchhikers?"

Slim was still looking at the map, admiring his superior geometry and sense of direction. He said, "Depends how far *backwards* you gotta drive to pick 'em up. Why?"

"Just curious," Howdy said with a shrug.

A moment later Slim felt the truck slowing down, so he looked up.

She had silver tips on her boots, raven hair, and gypsy cowgirl eyes. She was standing there with all sorts of curves and angles and, somewhere on her body, a tattoo of a butterfly landing on a rattlesnake, though they didn't know that yet. She had her thumb in the air, a guitar case at her feet, and what felt like a magnet drawing them in.

A hint of unease crept into Howdy's voice as he pulled to the side of the road. "Hitchhikers can be trouble."

Slim nodded. He could feel it too. "Still," he said, "she looks like the kind of trouble I don't mind."

ABOUT THE AUTHORS

KIX BROOKS began performing at age twelve in his hometown of Shreveport, LA. He performed in clubs and other venues throughout high school and college, eventually landing in Nashville. He wrote songs for a living throughout the '80s and in 1990 Brooks teamed up with Ronnie Dunn to form Brooks & Dunn, the highest-selling duo in the history of country music. Brooks served as President, in 2004, and Chairman, in 2005, of the Country Music Association (CMA). He is also on the boards of Vanderbilt Children's Hospital and the Nashville Convention and Visitors Bureau, and is the local spokesperson for Monroe Harding Children's Home. Brooks has been married to his wife Barbara for twenty-six years and they have two children, Molly and Eric.

RONNIE DUNN, the son of a truck-driving father and church-going mother, raced from those humble beginnings in Tulsa to a performing partnership with Kix Brooks that catapulted them into the heart and soul of country music fans everywhere. Since their initial pairing in 1990, Brooks & Dunn have been at the top of the country music singles charts numerous times with songs like "Brand New Man," "Boot Scootin' Boogie," "You're Gonna Miss Me When I'm Gone," "My Maria," "Only In America," and "Red Dirt Road." They are the industry's most award-winning duo, and continue to dominate the music industry with over thirty million records sold.

BILL FITZHUGH is the award-winning author of eight novels, including *Pest Control, Highway 61 Resurfaced,* and *Fender Benders* which received the Lefty Award for Best Humorous Novel at the Left Coast Crime Convention. His work has been sold to major Hollywood studios, and has been published in the US, UK, Japan, and Germany. A native of Jackson, Mississippi, he currently lives in Los Angeles where he hosts a show on XM Satellite radio called *Fitzhugh's All Hand Mixed Vinyl.*